WICKED FUN

Jane Hawkins: Unretired Serial Killer
Book 1

DAVE PASQUANTONIO

STERLING & STONE

WICKED FUN

Prologue

JIMMY WHITESIDE GRABBED the bulging trash bag and stormed out of the kitchen. "And that's how you clean up, Amanda!"

He threw open the door to their cheap third-floor apartment and tromped dramatically down the stairs, not bothering to throw on a coat despite the frigid night temperature outside, because Jimmy Whiteside was a man's man, and a man's man didn't let a Massachusetts winter keep him from doing what needed to get done.

Fucking Amanda, he thought as he lugged the bag outside to the dumpster. He shook his free right hand. His dominant hand. The knuckles were a little raw, but much less so than Amanda's nose. Stay home sitting on your fat ass all day instead of keeping the place clean? You get what you deserve.

Jimmy stepped through the slush and the sleet to the edge of the parking lot outside the building, then lobbed the bag up and over into the dumpster with a satisfying thwack. Working over Amanda always made him a little phlegmy, so he spit a big wad at the dumpster, then made to turn.

"Hey, Jimmy," purred a woman's voice from behind him.

He whirled. "What are you doing here? Amanda can't come out and play tonight."

The woman, bundled up and wearing gloves, laughed. "Who says I'm here for Amanda?"

Jimmy's small mind raced as best it could, but it got stuck on confusion. "Why you acting all flirty?"

"Who says I'm acting?" The woman stuck an unlit cigarette between her lips. "Say, you got a light?"

Jimmy slapped at his pockets. "Nah, it's upstairs."

"Oh. Then I'll ask him." She pointed behind Jimmy.

Jimmy turned, but all he could see was the building. He squinted. "Who you mean?"

Then he felt something cold puncture the back of his neck, and within seconds, his body started grinding to a halt. He slapped ineffectually at the back of his neck, and between the slapping and whatever had been injected into his body, he slipped, landing hard face up next to the dumpster.

"The fuck you do to me?" he asked, but it came out more like a baby mewling, since his mouth and tongue weren't working. He tried again, but now his lungs felt like blocks of ice. He tried scrabbling to get up, but that didn't work either. So he lay there, forgetting who he was, where he was, or who this woman was.

"Fucking Jimmy Whiteside." The woman pulled out a lighter and lit her cigarette. "Huh. Guess I had a light after all."

She bent down, examining him in the poor light, then reached to his neck and yanked off his necklace, a Harley-

Davidson pendant, Jimmy's favorite keepsake, with her gloved hand.

That's mine, he thought, but he couldn't figure out how to get it back or why she'd want it. Or why he couldn't feel anything in his body.

The light from the building's spotlights dimmed and kept getting dimmer, until Jimmy's world was reduced to one thing: the shining face staring down at him.

The woman took a deep drag of her cigarette, got close to Jimmy's face, and blew a stream of smoke at his unresponsive eyes. "Live to ride, ride to live," she said, dangling the necklace over him. "Enjoy your ride to hell, Jimmy."

Day 1 (Sunday)

"LET's go over the night of the murder again," Detective Ramsford said.

Jane Hawkins nodded, then took in her shabby surroundings as Ramsford flipped back a few pages in his notebook. The station's interview room was windowless; the concrete walls were the color of bile, the same color as Ramsford's tie, and were peeling due to Port Fletcher's ocean air. The ceiling had new LED lights, or at least new since Jane had last been in here, so the bile color was crisper, but one bulb had already failed and blinked randomly, like someone didn't know Morse code but kept trying anyway. Maybe it was on purpose, a new interrogation technique to keep the innocent scared and the guilty annoyed.

Jane blew a stray gray hair out of her face and shifted in her chair, an uncomfortable plastic seat, decades old, on which someone had carved a penis, which pointed at her crotch. An hour into the interview and her ass was killing her, but she kept a neutral face as Detective Ramsford continued flipping pages. She leaned to peek at herself in the scratched mirrored viewing window behind the detective. She wasn't guilty of this murder, so if anyone was watching, they'd get no show from her.

Ramsford gave her a stern look, his eyes hard. "From the top. You said that Bobby Ellings called you on the afternoon of the 16th."

"Yes."

"And this was about what again?"

Keep the answers short and simple. "He had borrowed money from me. A month ago. He called out of the blue and said he was ready to pay up."

"And this was how much again?"

"Six thousand dollars."

"Six thousand dollars," Ramsford echoed, scribbling away. "And then what happened?"

The stray hair fell in her face again. She blew it back again. "I told him I'd be free later. He suggested nine o'clock, so I was there at nine."

"Nine." He raised his eyebrows in that I-don't-believe-you way. "Very prompt of you."

"I didn't like Ellings. That's no secret. I didn't want to spend any more time with him than needed. I had no reason to get there early."

"And you left straight from your place to go to his place."

"Yes."

"No stops in between, no errands."

"That's right."

"And from Port Fletcher to his place in Hingham, at that time of night, it's a what, a ninety-minute drive?"

"A bit less, maybe an hour and fifteen minutes." Ramsford knew that. He was hunting for a time discrepancy. She'd played this game before.

"And when you got to the building, his apartment door was wide open."

She returned his hard look, using her gray eyes to her advantage as she bored into him. "I definitely didn't say *that*. I *did* say that I knocked, then the door creaked open."

"Jane, that glare of yours," Ramsford said, grinning. "It always throws me off."

She laughed. "I'm the one in the hot seat, Bill. I mean, *Detective Ramsford*. Do you mean to tell me that when you interview a real suspect who stares at you, you start babbling?"

"It's different with you here, Jane. I interview people all the time," he said, leaning back on his penis-free chair. "But usually not celebrities."

Jane waved the celebrity comment away. "Come on, you've known me for years. I'm just a regular person. And you've helped me out a lot."

She glanced down at her own notebook. She'd been taking notes too, just not about the pretend interview. She'd been writing down possible book plots, along with some things she needed at the grocery store.

Jane liked to write accurately about small-town police interviews for her cozy mystery novels. She'd mock-interviewed with everyone on the small Port Fletcher force over the years, including several times with Bill Ramsford, but she'd run into him a few weeks ago, mentioning that she was thinking about her new book, and he invited her to the station to brush up. He clearly didn't like being alone. She was alone, too, but she wasn't lonely. She had no desire to keep anyone close to her, except for her daughter, but her daughter had no desire to keep close to Jane.

Although Jane had been a law-abiding citizen for twenty years, it was smart to stay on the good side of the local police. You never knew when you'll need the law on your side.

They chatted for a few minutes about some new interrogation techniques that Bill had picked up in an online course, then he started paging through the note-book, as if to start the mock interrogation over. Jane cut that short for the benefit of her sore ass. "Oh, my good-ness, look at the time." There was no clock in the room, and she wasn't wearing a watch. "You've been so helpful, Bill."

She stressed the last word and added a small smile for his benefit. Bill had asked Jane out a few times over the years, both before and after his divorce, and she'd always passed, as she had no interest in another relationship after Donald, but they'd remained friendly.

Ramsford straightened, running a hand down his bile tie. He really should find a lover, and one with good taste. He clearly needed wardrobe advice. "My pleasure, Jane. Can't wait to read the new book."

"Then I do hope I'll see you at my book launch tomorrow night."

He beamed. "I traded shifts to be there."

They stood, and Jane extended a hand across the table. "Then I will see you tomorrow, Detective Bill Ramsford. And again, thank you. You've been such a help."

JANE DROVE BACK HOME, her car windows rolled down to usher in the first warm air of the year. April on Cape Cod could mean 70 degrees or snow, and in the first few weeks of this month, Port Fletcher, nestled mid-Cape and facing Cape Cod Bay, had seen both already. Maybe spring had finally arrived. More likely, this was a typical Massachusetts false spring. Massachusetts weather could be an asshole.

After arriving home, Jane changed into jeans and a hoodie, then went outside to putter in the yard. It had been a bitter, windy winter, unsurprising when you live on a peninsula jutting into the north Atlantic, and the yard of her Cape-style home was littered with cast-off branches and the leaves from the next-door neighbor who never raked.

Hands on her hips, she surveyed the cleanup. She'd pile the branches next to her fire pit, then rake up the leaves and dump them over the fence and into her neighbor's yard.

Your leaves, your mess.

As she puttered, a few couples and singles from the block strolled by, soaking in the Sunday sun. They gave Jane genuine waves hello, and she mimicked them back.

"Can't wait for tomorrow night!" they said. Or "Congratulations on the new book!" Or "Port Fletcher is so lucky to have you!"

If only Port Fletcher knew what they *really* had in her. Who she was to them and who she *really* was were so, so different.

After an hour of picking up limbs and raking, she'd had enough. Back inside, she opened a can of Sprite, took a big swig to create some room, dumped in some rum, and plopped onto her couch.

A picture of her late husband Donald, displayed only for infrequent guests who expected a widow of twenty years to honor the memory of her murdered spouse, graced the mantelpiece, although it was hidden by two thick candles she'd never light. Her eyes never settled on Donald's picture, instead always brushing passed it. Donald had made her who she was today, or at least he'd set this version of her in motion. He wasn't worth a glance, dead or alive.

All the other pictures on display featured people she'd never met and places she'd never been. She had no other family except for Kate, she never vacationed, and the mantel looked too empty without pictures. Jane was, to Port Fletcher, the type of person who should have friends everywhere and plenty of pictures on display, so she did what she could to keep up appearances.

Jane got up from the couch, swiping the cold Sprite can across her forehead. She made sure the doors were locked, then tramped upstairs, shed her clothes, and showered, washing away the cleanup sweat and grime, letting the hot water work into her neck and shoulders. If this were a TV commercial, the shower would release all of her tension, a "Calgon, take me away!" moment of bliss.

If only real life worked like that.

Her writing office was in the second of the home's two bedrooms. She put on a robe, then went to her office and sat at her desk, fired up her too-ancient computer, which served well for writing but not for much more, and checked her email. A note from her agent, Margo — she'd overnighted a box of a dozen books, and would Jane sign them and use the enclosed label to send them back in the same box? A few gifts, a few copies for Margo, and so sorry she couldn't make it to the Cape for the book launch. Jane wasn't expecting her to make it — they had a business relationship and weren't friends, although sometimes Jane suspected that she and her agent had different views about their relationship. No problem. She replied that she'd look for the books and get them back right away.

This was the only room in the house in which Jane felt truly comfortable. A single copy of each of her books took up the top shelf of a pine bookcase. She never read her books after finishing them, but they served as accountability. Keep writing if you want your work out in the world. Above the bookcase hung a few framed newspaper articles featuring a younger and smiling Jane — gifts from Margo, so Jane hung them up in case Margo ever visited, which she never had. Next to the articles hung a plaque announcing that Jane had been nominated for an Agatha, an industry award for cozy mystery writers. She'd lost to author Louise Penny that year, but it was fine — the winning plaque would probably have been too big for her wall anyway, and Louise Penny probably had a bigger office.

Sunday was typically Jane's errand day, and today's errands were walkable, so she changed back into her prim and proper interview clothes for the stroll to town, finishing the outfit with sneakers. Port Fletcher always expected Jane Hawkins to be prim and proper.

Ritual time. She checked every closed window to make sure it was locked, making sure that the first-floor windows had tape on them from the sash to the casing. She bolted the back door twice, checked her purse for her keys three times, and tucked a piece of red thread into the jamb as she shut and locked the front door. Old habits truly are the hardest to give up.

Jane's off-the-beaten-path neighborhood lacked both sidewalks and traffic, so she walked along the side of the road until she hit the main drag leading to town. Since it was the first nice day of the year, plenty of people were out and about, including several people walking their dogs.

Dogs. She'd drop off her weekly food donation at the local shelter tomorrow and say hi to Rigsby, a collie mix she'd been thinking about adopting. Rigsby was a very good girl and would make for a great companion. Jane wasn't sure she was ready for a companion, or even if she needed one, but she'd fallen for Rigsby as soon as she'd seen her.

Are collies good guard dogs? Or just good dogs? She'd have to decide if she was looking more for protection or companionship. Not sure one dog could excel at both. It would have to be a pretty special dog.

Jane jaywalked across Main Street to Knead, Port Fletcher's best bakery in her opinion, though that was a competition between only two. This bakery was walkable, which made it Jane's winner. Inside, the six tables were taken up with townies, all regulars. Port Fletcher caught few tourists in its snare; the town was bracketed by two bigger towns with much better beaches, so the tourists mostly drove through here instead of stopping here. Strangers here tended to stick out.

"Afternoon," Jane said to Ray, who owned the bakery with his wife Rae. Jane thought for the hundredth time that there had to have been a better name for the bakery than Knead when you had a Ray and a Rae owning the place. Port Fletcher embraced punny store names, although most of them were painfully bad. Rae and Ray. Binary? Binaray Bakery?

"Afternoon, Jane," Ray said. He nudged his wife, who was putting pastries into the front case. "Our famous author's here."

"Oh, stop," Jane said. She wasn't a blusher, but wished she could blush on command. She felt like that's what folks expected of her.

"The usual?" Rae said as Ray got Jane's medium coffee to go.

"Please. Oh, and add a cupcake. Any of the frosted ones." Good thing about being a regular is it cut down on needless chitchat.

Rae boxed up the goods — a maple-frosted cupcake

plus Jane's usual dozen mini-muffins, which served as five days of breakfast when coupled with bananas — while Ray rang her up. Jane put the change in the paper tip cup on the counter.

"Big night tomorrow night," Ray said, tipping his chin toward a bulletin board that had a flyer for Jane's book launch event tomorrow night.

"I'm not sure why folks still come to the launches," Jane said. "This is book 18, after all. And it's much easier to buy the book online."

"Don't be coy. You're the biggest celebrity this town's got," Rae chirped from behind the counter. "Well, there was that ballplayer who almost made it to the majors. And that lady who's almost a hundred."

"Port Fletcher — a town of almosts," Ray huffed.

"That's why we fit in, dear," Rae added.

Jane forced out a genuine-sounding chuckle, although Ray was right — nothing much went on in Port Fletcher. "I'm blessed to live here. We all are."

She stopped at the CVS for a few essentials, then walked home, dropping the empty coffee cup into the fire pit in her back yard before ensuring that the red thread on the door was still in place. Good. Inside, she put the muffins away and checked the tape on the windows.

All good. It always was. But you never know.

JANE NAPPED FOR A FEW HOURS, then listened to the blues on the local college radio station as she lightly cleaned, paid a few bills, and made dinner for one. She checked her cell — no calls or texts. She looked reflexively at the spot on the counter where she'd had a landline and answering machine, but she'd given those up months ago after keeping track of every call her landline had received for a month and finding that they were all marketing calls, even though she was on the "do not call" list, which served as the "please spam me" list. A better list would be the "please leave me alone" list. She'd sign up twice for that.

After her dinner for one, she read for a while, checked all the locks, then went to the kitchen. Out came the cupcake, which she put on a white plate and placed on the four-person kitchen table that had rarely seen four people. Then came a fork and napkin, then a lighter and candle.

From the stove drawer, where most people keep cookie sheets and oversized pans, she took out a velvet bag and withdrew a framed picture of Kate, the estranged daughter she'd given up for adoption thirty years ago. Jane had taken the picture when the two of them were at a bar when her daughter had turned twenty-one. She'd seen Kate twice since then. She propped the frame against the fruit bowl centered on the table, then poured herself a shot of bourbon.

She sat, stuck the candle in the cupcake and lit it, then raised the shot glass to Kate's picture and slugged the bourbon, relishing the burn.

"Happy 60th birthday to me," she said to Kate's picture, then blew out the candle.

Day 2 (Monday)

MORNING ARRIVED WITH A DOORBELL RING, knocking Jane out of a dream where she was being chased, or maybe chasing someone. Her first thought was that she hoped she'd been chasing someone — being chased was no fun. Her second thought was: who the fuck was ringing her bell before seven?

She fumbled her way downstairs and checked through the front door peephole. Nobody there. She moved to unlock the door, then stopped. Instead, she padded in bare feet, stopping at every window to glance out quickly and listen. Nothing at the back door, either. She checked her taped windows. All good.

She padded back upstairs for her cell. No messages, including no messages from Kate.

Back downstairs, she palmed a Phillips screwdriver, then unlocked the front door.

There was a FedEx box on the stoop. She scooped it up, feeling the heft, then went inside, locked the door behind her, and squinted at the label.

Right. The books.

She knifed open the box and lifted out the books, a dozen hardcovers of her new Beachcomber Belle release, *Death Under the Boardwalk*, along with a note and the return shipping label. The hardcover run was for libraries, or people who wanted to overpay for books — most of her print sales were for the paperback. And way more people bought the ebook instead of print. The ebook-only people, Jane thought, were animals, although she was grateful for the royalties.

The note read, *Jane! So excited for this new Belle story!! Hope the party tonight goes great!!! ~ Margo.* Classic, spunky, glass-half-full Margo. Jane loved everything about her agent, except that the longer Margo wrote, the more exclamation points she used. Good thing Margo didn't write fiction.

She texted Margo that she'd received the books, cursing FedEx's efficient yet too-early delivery, then made some coffee and ate a few of the mini muffins along with a banana.

After a quick shower, Jane dutifully signed the books, sealed the box, and affixed the label. She'd drop it off after her stop at the shelter to see Rigsby and donate some food.

The drive to Take A Paws — the no-kill shelter sported possibly the worst of Port Fletcher's punny business names — was short. Once inside, Jane hoisted the 25-pound bag of puppy chow onto the counter.

Kendall, a dowdy middle-aged woman who helped run the place and had blonde hair and a long nose that made her look like a golden retriever, was at the counter. "I have great news, Jane. Rigsby got adopted! She left yesterday. Such nice owners. They have a big back yard and two kids. Rigsby will be a perfect fit for them."

Kendall droned on, but Jane didn't hear much past, "Rigsby got adopted."

Jane had been dragging her heels on deciding about

adopting Rigsby, and she certainly had no claim to the collie, but over the last month or so, she'd bonded with the dog, had imagined Rigsby sleeping on the couch, sleeping on her bed, curled at her feet while Jane wrote another Beachcomber Belle mystery.

Jane tried to make her face look happy, but more likely she looked like she'd just sat down too hard on a bicycle seat.

Along with happiness for the dog (sincere) and sadness that she wouldn't see Rigsby again (also sincere), Jane quickly pictured tracking down the new owners, slitting their throats, then clamping a hand over their wounds to feel their hot blood pump against her palm as the life emptied out of their eyes. That thought took all of two seconds. It was also sincere.

She pushed the daydream away. "I'm thrilled that Rigsby found her forever home," she said, her voice catching.

Kendall must have seen through Jane's mask, because she patted Jane's hand and replied, "She really took to you. And thank you again for coming in each week. Maybe you'll find your forever friend here. We've got some new arrivals, plus the long-term residents would still love to find a home. You want to come back and take a look?"

She'd go without a dog forever. She'd stop donating food. She'd spend the rest of her life alone — just like she had for the past 20 years. Fuck this place, and especially fuck Rigsby's new owners. She hoped that their big back yard developed a sink hole and took the house with it. Rigsby, of course, would have sensed it coming and escaped. She was a smart dog.

"I've got to run, Kendall, but of course I'll be back. Every dog needs a home."

"And every home needs a dog," Kendall twittered, then added hastily, "Or a cat. Are you interested in a cat?"

God no. "I'll see you soon."

She strode slowly to her car, got inside, made sure the windows were rolled up, then beat her hands against the steering wheel until the meat of her palms turned scarlet.

JANE STEWED about Rigsby through the afternoon, feeling restless, trying and failing to write, puttering with words but without results. She abandoned the writing and picked out an outfit for the night's book signing, slacks and a conservative blouse, then tried a few hairstyles. Should she wear her shoulder-length gray hair loose? No, it was too poufy, and she looked like she just woke up. Ponytail? No, she wasn't trying to masquerade as an eight-year-old. Messy bun piled high? Sultry, but she didn't want sultry, plus today it looked like a mound of wet newspaper. She went with clipping it all back, looking for all the world like a dowdy sixty-year-old mystery novelist.

She made sure she had two good author Sharpies — not all pens worked well for signing books — then grabbed a sweater, as yesterday's summer-feel weather had turned back to mid-spring chill. She shot a middle finger at Donald's picture without looking at his ugly face behind the candles and left for the event at six. The signing started at seven and she wanted to be sure there were no hiccups, not that it would matter, plus she had nothing else to do.

Seaside Books wasn't big enough to have its own event manager, so Jane worked with Bree, the owner slash manager slash events coordinator slash horrible delegator. Bree had coned off a parking spot for Jane, who slid her Honda Accord into the designated space in the lot next to

Bree's shiny new Tesla. Jane had no need for a vehicle with all those fancy electronics that tracked your every breath. Her old Accord did its job. Plus, who knows what someone could do with all that tracking information?

Bree met her inside. "We've set it up like last time," she snapped, marching Jane toward the back of the store. Whenever Bree said "We've," it meant "I've."

"Plenty of chairs," Bree continued, "here's your table, wine and cheese and crackers over there." She pointed to another table along the Science and Reference shelving. "I ordered extra copies of your first book in case we get some new Jane Hawkins fans who want to start at the beginning."

"This looks great," Jane said to Bree. "Thank you so much for your hard work."

Bree took Jane's hands in her own. "How are you feeling about this? Nervous? Excited?"

Jane forced a smile. "It'll be great. I've done enough of them to no longer be nervous. Thanks so much for hosting. I'm sure the night will go well."

Book events were the worst part of being an author. She'd rather write, send the manuscript off, then give herself a month's break before starting the new one. She didn't like mingling, or small talk, or remembering to laugh graciously. Being in the spotlight was not in her wheelhouse. It felt like posing. Not just because Jane was a typical introverted writer. It was more that the longer she was in front of people, the better the chance that her past might come up. Most people were polite, but there could be someone who wanted the spotlight for themself, someone who wanted nothing more than to dig for dirt. Everyone had dirt, but Jane had truckloads. Hence the bourbon, and a handful of Tic Tacs to quash the smell, accompanying her dinner of pasta salad earlier.

As seven ticked closer, the space filled with attendees. Soon, every chair was taken, and folks lined the walls, boxing Jane in, flooding the space with murmur and laughter and heat. It was time to play the grateful author.

At the stroke of seven, Bree clanged an old-timey ship's bell to silence the chatter and draw attention to herself. "Thank you all for coming tonight," she started as the crowd hushed. "Our author tonight needs no introduction, but I'll give her one anyway." The newbies in the crowd laughed. Bree turned to address Jane directly. "Jane Hawkins, author extraordinaire, you've put Port Fletcher on the map, and it is such an honor to have you here tonight." Turning back to the crowd, she added, "Jane will read from newest book, *Death Under the Boardwalk*. Then she'll take some questions, and then she'll sign your books." Bree spent another five minutes pointing out where the food was, how to pick up pre-ordered books, what Jane would and wouldn't sign (Jane always ignored that and signed whatever people brought up), and a litany of do's, don'ts, where's, and when's.

As always happened at the events, when Bree spoke, the attendees looked at Jane instead, so she did her best to freeze a slight smile on her face as Bree finished up.

Jane read all of chapter 1 — she wrote short chapters, so that took all of five minutes. Then came applause. Then came fifteen minutes of questions, the same ones that she answered at every book event, and then came Bree taking another five minutes showing people where to line up and how to approach the table. She then stood behind Jane, who was seated at the table.

It was nice to see her fans. Actually, that wasn't true. It was nice to know she had fans; if only there was a way to never see them. Most professions didn't allow for public fandom, so these people showing up just to see her still felt overwhelming. She limited herself to one event per book, so after tonight, she wouldn't be in the spotlight again until next year, after the next book was done.

Bill Ramsford muscled his way to be first in line. "Jane," he said, offering her his hardcover with two hands like it was something to be sacrificed at the altar. "You are such a blessing for our town."

"Why, thank you, Bill," she said. "It's so good of you to come." She signed his book *To Bill — you are such a help! Enjoy!* The way he was looking at her made her glad she hadn't gone with the sultry hair.

Bree, standing to the side, took Bill's arm. "Thank you for coming, Detective. I'll show you to the wine."

Jane signed, said "thank you for coming" to everyone, posed for selfies (which she hated but expected), and the line chugged along until there were a dozen folks left.

"Could you sign this for me?" a man asked, placing a book in front of her.

This wasn't one of Jane's books. It was a non-fiction book, a hardcover entitled *Bay State Butchers: Massachusetts Serial Killers in the 20th Century* by Esmir Roux. Jane started, then caught herself.

"I'm sorry, this isn't one of my books," she said to the man. He looked to be in his early 40s, with thinning hair, and gave off an Ichabod Crane vibe.

He chortled. "Oh, my apologies. I meant these." He added three of Jane's books to the pile — books one, two, and the newest.

"Two signings per customer," Bree said, stepping forward.

Jane waved her away. "It's fine." It was not fine. Her stomach churned — something here felt off. "Just my signature, or personalized?"

"Personalized," the man said. "It's Esmir. Esmir

Roux." He spelled it, then tapped the serial killer book. "This is my book, by the way. And I'm so glad to finally meet you, Jane Hawkins."

Jane pinned a smile to her face as she wrote "To Esmir" in each of her three books and signed her name. Why did he bring his own serial killer book? She pushed the books back to him, tamping down the urge to bolt out of the shop.

"I'd love to talk sometime," Roux said. "I'm the host of the podcast Mass*Murderers." He stopped, looking like he expected her to fawn over him.

"I don't listen to podcasts, Mr. Roux. But I know what they are. What is your podcast about?"

"Massachusetts murders, unsolved ones, and how some of the murders might tie together. My downloads have been impressive." He spouted off some numbers in the tens of thousands, numbers that meant nothing to Jane. She barely knew the sales figures of her own books.

"Jane," Bree said, reaching over and tapping the table, "we've got more guests waiting."

"If I could," Roux said before Jane could reply, "I am a fan of yours, but I'd also love to interview you for my podcast. Your husband ... his is one of the cases that I'm looking into. It's been twenty years, and his case is still unsolved."

The attendees within earshot fell silent. Jane's stomach went from churning to dropping out of her body and hitting the floor with a wet *thwack*. For twenty years, since the police had declared the case cold, she'd been fearful of someone probing into Donald's murder. Now that the time was here, her mind went dark.

"That," she started, "was a long time ago, Mr. Roux. It was a very painful time for me, but I've moved on. I'm not interested in talking more about Donald's murder. Please."

"Let's go," Bree said. "Ms. Hawkins has signed your books."

"Through crowdsourcing," Roux said as he picked up his books, "and new investigative techniques, we can solve these long-cold murders and bring whoever committed them to justice."

"I'm not interested in talking, but thank you," Jane said. God, he sounded full of himself. And confident. Too confident.

The bourbon, pasta salad, and Tic Tacs from earlier threatened to reappear.

"Here's my card," Roux said as Bree led him away. "We really should talk."

Jane's mouth was open and she was ready to respond, but instead, she shook her head, then dropped his card into her purse.

The next person in line stammered, "Hi, umm, I'm a really big fan."

BREE RETURNED AND CONSOLED JANE, who signed, posed, and smiled for the rest of the event, but all in a blur, her veins icy, her insides shaky. Roux had left, but the room still felt cold.

Jane took two glasses of wine into the restroom, chugged them, then splashed cold water on her face.

"Fuck," she said, tossing the glasses into the trash. "Fuck, fuck, fuck." She forced the wine and her dinner to stay down.

Esmir Roux? What kind of name was that? And the gall, to show up with one of his own books.

Maybe he'd wanted her signature as a handwriting sample? No, that was all twenty years ago. And she'd signed enough books over the years that it couldn't be that hard to find her signature out there.

Investigating old murders was definitely not what she wanted to hear tonight.

Someone knocked on the restroom door. "Just a minute," she said, tamping down the urge to say "Shit your pants out there" instead.

She leaned against the wall. She hadn't felt this rattled in a long time. It was like Esmir Roux had seen her scuttling on a counter and trapped her under a glass. She'd talked to the man for all of two minutes, and now she felt old, queasy, little.

Okay, take those in order.

- Old. Well, you just turned sixty. But that's not *really* old.
- Queasy. What he'd said had shocked you, sure. But he wasn't the police. He probably knew nothing about you. Just a curious fan with a crush on serial killer stories.
- Little. That's how you feel whenever you're scared. Little. You'd been scared plenty when you were little. You'd been scared plenty more when you were married. You'd taken care of it. You'll take care of it now.

SHE BRACED both hands on the sink, looked at herself, and said, "You are Jane Hawkins. Get out of your head and get back out there." Which she did.

After the last guest left, Bree locked the front door, then ordered a few staff members to break down the event tables and clear the food. She sauntered over to Jane.

"You had a good night," Bree said. "Sold all your books, even the early ones."

"Thank you so much. It did go well."

Bree huffed. "Except for that one guy. I'm sorry you had to go through that."

It wasn't a secret that Jane's husband Donald had been murdered 20 years ago during what the police had called a botched burglary. It wasn't a secret that no one had been caught, or that the police had no leads. The investigation had dried up long ago, and Jane was fine with that. More than fine.

What was a secret for now, one Jane intended to uncover, was why Esmir Roux wanted to talk to her about it.

Jane packed up her things, then walked outside. One light off the side of the building illuminated the few cars in the lot, keeping the end of the lot bathed in darkness. She paced quickly to her car, keys in hand.

From behind her she heard, "Jane."

She whirled around, startled, her bag hitting her in the opposite shoulder. Esmir Roux walked out of the shadows from behind the bookstore.

He held up both hands. "I just want to talk."

Jane clenched the keys in her fist, making sure the Accord's key, the longest on her chain, poked out between her pointer and middle fingers. She focused on the hollow of Roux's exposed neck as he walked closer.

"I have nothing to say to you," she said, stopping next to the hood of her car, keeping her voice low and deliberate. A quick glance to the store. No one else was coming. "And what a thing, to come here tonight to bring up my husband's murder."

"It's more than your husband," Roux said, stopping six feet from her, his hands still raised. "It's a series of murders. They're old, twenty years, at least. Ten of them. Including your husband. I think they were committed by the same person."

Jane's stomach somersaulted. Ten. She leaned against the hood, hoping the move looked casual. "Ten murders. Twenty years old. And you need me … for what?"

Roux's face was cloaked by the light in back of him, but Jane knew he was smiling. "Ten victims. No witnesses. Dead ends all around, according to the police. I can look at things differently. I'm good at it. I can find answers. I can give you closure."

Jane gripped the keys tighter. "It's been twenty years. Time has given me closure."

Roux dropped his hands, opened his arms as if beckoning her to approach. "Then answers. This could be a serial killer. A monster took your husband's life, took nine other lives. Answers for you. Answers for their families. Answers for the community. That's all I want. Answers."

"I don't care," Jane started, paused, then continued. "What I mean is, I don't care about answers at this point. Not for Donald. Not for nine other murders that don't concern me."

"Don't they?" he asked.

That icy feeling in her veins again. "Come again?"

"I mean," he said slowly, "that no one affected by any of these ten murders can truly know peace until the monster" — that word again — "is caught."

"I'm not interested in helping you, Mr. Roux."

He raised his arms again. His shadow, splashed across the hood of her car, looked skeletal. "Think about it. That's all I ask. You have my card. On the record, off the record, anything will help. Both of us."

He turned, then walked back around the store and disappeared.

Jane wondered three things as she braced herself against her car: where he'd parked, how much force she'd need to puncture his throat with a car key, and how she'd make him pay for calling her a monster.

∼

SHE DROVE HOME SLOWLY, carefully, checking her rearview for the headlights of cars following her, one of many old habits that she thought she'd left in her past but now she'd have to dust off.

Back at home, her house quiet and serene, the tape and thread undisturbed, Jane shed her purse and coat, then sat in her living room, in the dark, for five minutes, regulating her breathing, trying but failing to think of nothing. She could feel it bubbling up inside of her, that Jane of the Past feeling, the chaos and rage. She missed that feeling, but she couldn't let it loose again. Jane of the Past needed to stay in the past.

She slipped off her shoes, then, the house still cloaked in darkness, she padded to the kitchen, poured herself a shot of bourbon, and took the stairs down to the basement. No problem snapping the lights on here — she'd long ago blacked out the basement windows.

She dragged a sheet of plywood over to one of the unfinished walls and tented it against the concrete, then dug around in late Donald's workbench until she found a rubber mallet.

She pounded the plywood with the mallet, over and over, screaming and grunting, releasing, doing damage to neither the wood nor herself, until, panting, she felt empty, as well as sore. If the neighbors had heard, well, too bad.

She showered, twenty minutes of hot water trying and failing to wash away the icky feeling coating her — Esmir Roux and ten unsolved murders and Rigsby's new owners. She slipped on some sweatpants and a long-sleeved tee, poured another bourbon, this time cut with water and ice, and went into her office.

She turned on her computer. It was a ten-year-old tower, long in the tooth, but she didn't want to replace it. She knew what worked and what didn't, could fly on the old keyboard, didn't mind the older monitor outfitted with a bulky webcam. She'd thought about getting a laptop, but her routine was write at home, here, in the office. A new computer would be great, so why replace something that worked? But it was temperamental, like her, and it was being temperamental right now — refusing to boot up properly. She gave the tower a smack, which solved the issue.

She'd been considering ending her Beachcomber Belle series. Belle had solved enough kooky murders (the killings themselves never shown on the page, since they were cozy mysteries) to last her fictional small town for decades. Maybe it was time to do something different. Something darker. She'd have to push Belle the character to the side-lines — or would she? Nah, her readers enjoyed Belle's spunk and fearlessness and goofiness. They didn't want her to change. Belle couldn't set out on a bloody revenge tour. And she definitely couldn't be the murderess.

Jane was behind, deadline-wise; agent Margo was expecting a first draft, at least a synopsis, in the next month. Jane had never let her down, and honestly, after eighteen books, sending Belle out into the world was all muscle memory. She'd hit her deadline. But she didn't have a plot yet.

She pawed through some index cards, each with a

high-level Belle plot idea, all viable if not quite believable. Sigh. She plucked out one of the more promising ones — in Belle's quaint seaside village, a candy store owner fallen on hard times is forced to sell his business, and the new owner seems shady, and rumors start flying that he's in the Chechen mafia, and curious Belle does her curious Belle thing, and hijinks and danger ensue, and it all gets wrapped up in 60,000 tidy, cutesy words.

If only the real world worked like that.

Speaking of which — a little research on Esmir Roux. She plucked out his business card to make sure she got his name right. She started at his Wikipedia page. Hmm. It had been recently edited. Esmir was forty-five years old, born in New York City, got his undergrad at Lafayette, and was never married as far as she could tell. No children, either. There wasn't much info on his life before he got into writing and podcasts. The bio and success stories were glowing, so he probably had written the page himself. He'd published two books, the one he showed her and a dense-sounding tome about investigative techniques in the nineteenth century. He'd listed some plaudits about the Mass*Murderers podcast, download numbers and reach and listener hours, but Jane didn't know enough about podcasts to know if those were braggable. She'd never listened to a podcast. Maybe she needed to start.

On to Amazon. The reviews for *Bay State Butchers* were mixed. The hardcore true crime fans panned it for occasional factual errors and a clunky writing style. Some of those folks seemed to know more about the murders than the murderer probably did. Good to remember. But other readers were pleased with the book, mostly New England readers who liked the local flavor. There were few reviews for the dense academic book — it appeared to be self-published, so maybe all the university presses, which loved dense academic work, weren't all that interested, even the local ones.

She didn't want to spend any more time on Roux tonight. But his time would come.

Jane got to work on the Belle candy store Chechen plot, the bourbon loosening her mind, pushing Roux to the background, where he stood, smirking. Jane gave him the finger as she typed.

Day 3 (Tuesday)

JANE WROTE until three in the morning, then collapsed into bed, sleeping until nine, waking up disoriented and pissed off.

She brewed some coffee, took her first cup black with a shot of brandy, ate two muffins and a banana, then thought through her day. It would be a busy one. She had errands to run. Important errands.

Fog had rolled in last night, blanketing Port Fletcher, and had stuck around, adding some rain to the mix. She dressed frumpish on purpose, slacks and a button-down sweater, needing to look the part of the unassuming widow. She made sure the house was secure with locks, thread, and tape, then headed to the bank, where she sat for a few minutes in the lot, the engine running as she thought things through.

The urge to come here today was strong, and she'd given in to it. But was it too soon after the Roux incident? She didn't want to draw attention to herself, but she needed the confidence boost that the bank visit would give her. Plus she did need some cash.

She also needed to settle down. One shot of feeling like Jane of the Past last night for a hot minute, and she already craved the chaos and rage like a junkie needs a fix.

She couldn't give into it. She had to be better. Stronger.

She put the car into gear and drove out of the lot, then changed her mind and took an immediate right back into the lot into her same space, where she parked, the engine still running.

She slammed her palms on the steering wheel. Damn. Was she unable to make even a simple decision now? Had Roux rattled her that much?

Talking to herself would help. So she started.

"Pros and cons. Pros first. You need cash, so get cash. And the other part? You need that, too. You need to remember who you are. Who you really are. It's like you said to yourself last night at the bookstore — you are fucking Jane Hawkins. So be Jane Hawkins. Be confident."

So far, so good.

"Now the cons. You need to keep a low profile. It's a new world. Things have changed a lot in twenty years. Cameras everywhere. If someone suspects, it'll lead to questions. Be cautious. Get the cash, but don't do the other thing. Everything in there, you've committed it to memory. It's all safe. You don't need to look at it."

Valid points. But Pros had something else to say.

"You've played it safe for twenty years, Jane. And it's worked. But you are losing yourself. You are forgetting who you are. Like you said: you are Jane Hawkins. Start acting like her. If this Roux is really a threat, he's not going away because you stuck your head in the sand."

Jane turned to Cons. "Those are good points. You got anything else?"

Cons shook its head. "Besides play it safe? Nope. Just remember what I said. Someone is always watching."

Pros said to Cons, "Pussy."

Jane hurried inside, dodging the wetness, smiling at one of the tellers, who'd been at the event last night.

"See?" Cons said from inside her head. "Someone is always watching."

"Fuck off!" Jane said out loud. The few customers in line turned. She met their gaze while holding up her phone. "Sorry, you know how those videos auto play? It's really annoying, isn't it?"

When it was her turn, she asked to withdraw eight hundred dollars in hundreds and fifties.

"Anything else?" the teller asked.

Cons said, "Nope."

Pros said, "Yep."

Pros won. Jane said, "I'd like to access my safe deposit box."

"Great. Step over to the side, and I'll get someone to help you."

The teller called someone, and a moment later a harried-looking woman about Jane's age stepped out of an office. "Safe deposit box?" she said.

Jane nodded and presented the woman with her license. "504."

"Give me a minute." The woman took the license and stepped back into her office, did whatever she needed to verify that Jane was Jane, and came back out, ushering Jane into a secure room. Jane and the woman inserted their keys to unlock the box.

The woman indicated a door. "There are a table and two chairs in that little room," she said. "Take all the time you need. When you're done, close the box and let me know that you're through."

Jane took her box to the privacy room and closed the door. She placed the box on the table, took a seat, and rested her hands on the box, her eyes closed.

What's inside here gives you power, she thought. Power over your doubts. You come here when you doubt yourself, and you always leave stronger. Be careful, but more importantly, be who you really are.

She opened the box and took out a pair of leather gloves, which she donned. Then she took out the only other thing in the box. A three-ring binder, like you'd find in any office.

Inside were twenty pages, each page a clear pocket. In ten of the pockets were a small item.

Ten pockets, ten items. No names, no dates. She didn't need them. She flipped from page to page, running a gloved fingertip over each pocket, feeling each token through the layers of leather and plastic.

Each pocket held a story.

In the first pocket was a playing card, the Jack of Clubs.

In the third pocket was a half-smoked cigarette, Donald's last tobacco. Jane absently rubbed the back of her left calf, up near her ass, and felt the dimples from two of her cigarette burns. Donald, you wife-beating bastard, you got what you deserved.

The last souvenir was a necklace, a silver chain with the famous "Harley-Davidson" logo on the bar, "Motor" above it, "Cycles" below it.

Jane had "retired" after obtaining that necklace. Into the binder it had gone, joining the nine other souvenirs. She liked thinking of them as souvenirs. The press would call them "trophies," but she hated that term. They weren't symbols of victory, not really. They were symbols of what had needed to be done.

She came here to feel strong, and she felt strong now. Whatever Roux knew, or whatever he thought he knew, it wouldn't matter. She was stronger than him. She'd been stronger than these ten assholes, that's for sure.

She put the binder back in the box, followed by the gloves, then closed the box. She found the harried manager, then the box went back to its slot.

Back in the car, she sat for a moment before heading out. Her heart rate was back to normal, and she no longer felt annoyed. She felt peaceful. She'd make today a great day.

Speaking of Harleys, Jane headed to the next stop, a computer shop called Byte Junction a few towns and thirty minutes away. Harley Hawley was the owner. Stupidest name on the planet. He insisted that everyone call him Flounder. Stupidest nickname on the planet. He didn't have lopsided eyes, didn't fish that she knew of. Maybe he had the nickname because he smelled like low tide.

She parked, then opened the shop door, startled as usual at the tinkly bell above the door announcing a patron. Byte Junction was dark and cramped, with unidentifiable computer parts pegged to two walls and an assortment of new and used computers and monitors stacked on tables near the counter. She didn't see Flounder, but he'd pop out from his office soon, as always. There was one other customer, an annoyed-looking guy who looked like he rarely saw sunlight. He was comparing an image on his phone to different pieces of computer crap, sighing whenever he didn't find a match.

The office door behind the counter opened, then out popped Flounder. "Jane!" he exclaimed, beaming. Flounder had black curly hair, a patchy beard that looked forever incomplete, and an oily complexion that made him look like he not only lived on potato chips, he used them as an exfoliant.

"Time to upgrade the computer?" he continued, palms on the counter. "I've got just the thing."

"Not the computer, not just yet," Jane began, then looked behind her at Annoyed Guy, then back to Flounder and added in a low voice, "I'm looking for some C-RAM."

At that, Annoyed Guy turned. "There is no such thing as C-RAM."

"Keep browsing, Larry," Flounder snapped at the guy. "It's a local term." He then turned to Jane. "You've never needed that type of … memory … before. I don't think it's compatible with your system."

"I have my reasons."

He swept an arm toward the back room. "Then come on back. I've got what you need in my office."

Jane stepped around the counter into Flounder's office, which featured piles of hardware, paper, and trash on the floor, causing her to step as if they were landmines. Flounder swept a pile of junk off of a chair. "Have a seat."

"I'll stand, thank you." She had no desire to get something sticky on her clothes.

Flounder swung the door closed. A monitor above the door showed the storefront, Annoyed Guy continuing his quest for some elusive cable.

"You've never bought from me before," Flounder started. "Didn't even know you know about this."

"I'm a mystery author," Jane said. "I've learned to put two and two together."

"You just don't seem like the … C-RAM type, is all."

"Let's say it's for a friend."

Flounder laughed. It sounded like someone dragging a rusty shovel over uncured cement. "Coming from anyone else, I'd call that bullshit, pardon my French, but coming from you, I almost believe it."

He drummed his fingers on the desk. "I gotta ask, you being tight with the police and all…"

"This isn't a sting operation. Like I said, I have my reasons." Jane clutched her purse tight to her. "And this is a onetime transaction."

Flounder laughed again. Jane shuddered. "Sorry," he said. "I just can't picture you with product. Just with you and that purse and you being so proper, you remind me of some TV character I can't quite recall, you know, the little old lady who solved mysteries."

Jane gave a little shrug. She'd lied to Flounder — the "C-RAM" wasn't for a friend, it was for her, but she had no intention of using it. She wanted to feel what it was like to buy, plus a little voice inside her, most likely Pros, thought it'd be a good idea to have a little insurance policy. You never know when insurance will come in handy.

"How much are we talking?" Flounder asked.

Jane dug out four of the hundred-dollar bills. "This much."

Flounder raised his unkempt eyebrows. "I can do that." He turned, then stopped. "You know what? Promise me that when you upgrade your computer, you'll come to me first. Promise me that, and I'll give you this for no charge."

"I've got the money," she said. "I'm paying."

Flounder waved the money away. "This business is all about service and loyalty. I provide good service, which keeps you — I mean your friend — loyal. Plus I know a lot of secrets. That keeps people loyal, too."

He crouched, then yanked up a panel set into the floor. He lifted out a sealed plastic tub and balanced it on the desk, sorted through some clear pouches containing a white powder, then put one in another plastic baggie and handed it to Jane. "This is three grams. Price is going up, going down, going crazy lately."

"I've read about fentanyl. Does this have fentanyl in it?"

Flounder laughed, a phlegmy bray that Jane was sure could be heard in the showroom, as he put the tub away. "I don't deal that stuff."

"But would you even know?"

"No one's died from this batch yet."

The bell tinkled, and on the monitor, a teen girl and who could be her mom entered the store. Flounder smoothed his shirt as he licked his lips, staring at the monitor. "Gotta go. Lemme know about the computer. And I hope your 'friend' enjoys this shit." He opened the door and walked out of the office.

Jane plunked the four hundred dollars on his desk chair, then weighted the bills down with an old hard drive. Never be indebted to anyone.

THE TEMPERATURE HAD DROPPED five degrees since Jane had started her day, the rain now irritatingly chilly. She drove to one of Port Fletcher's two public beaches, parking along a row of scrubby pines, and left the motor running. Hers was the only car in the lot.

From here, she could see the ocean, choppy and gray, the water not nearly as violent as it'd be on the Outer Cape or facing the Atlantic dead on, the sand brown from the rain, the air tinged with salt, the kind of day that drove all but the hardiest of locals back inside.

Her calm at spending time with her binder had worn off. Fucking Esmir Roux. The past was supposed to stay in the past. The chill she felt in her bones was from far more than the weather.

She moved to the passenger side for the extra room,

then reclined the seat all the way back, cracking the window open just a bit so she could hear the ocean.

Calm. She needed to embrace the calm.

Esmir Roux didn't know anything. She'd kept her secrets for over twenty years. The past wasn't going to claw its way out of the earth to grab her by the ankle and drag her into the dirt.

Calm.

She startled a few minutes later when someone knocked on the window.

Her eyes were gummy. She must have dozed. Who was knocking? And why had they knocked so loudly? She squinted. A dark shape was outside the car on the driver's side. Her first thought was that it was her mailman, but that made no sense. She had no mailbox at the beach.

"Get out of here!" she yelled. She saw that whoever it was hadn't just knocked — they'd spiderwebbed her window with something.

The guy — she could see now that it was a guy — ran over to her side and yanked open her door. "You get the fuck out of this car!" he shouted, waving whatever that thing was — a screwdriver? — in her face.

"It's my car, asshole!" she shouted back, pissed that this was happening and pissed that her voice had just gotten really high.

When Jane was angry — really angry — she didn't see red like a stereotypical book character. It was more navy blue, shimmery, punctuated with pulsing starbursts like from a cheesy 1960s sci-fi flick.

Things went blue now. Real blue.

The man grabbed at her right arm with his left hand and yanked her out of the car. He's a lefty, she thought, and he was yanking her directly toward his body.

She managed to do two things: get one foot on the

ground while wheeling her left elbow at his chin. She connected before going down to the pavement, skidding on her knees.

She saw his legs buckle, then his feet move toward her. He launched a kick at her face, but she saw it coming and turned, his boot hitting her in the left shoulder instead. Pain shot through her shoulder and down her arm.

She was still looking at his feet. He made to run, so she looped a hand under one of his boots and drove her arm up, pushing him to the ground.

The rain beat harder.

Her knees were screaming from the asphalt, but as he scrambled to get up, she did the same.

He wheeled around and arced the screwdriver toward her face. She saw it coming a mile away and threw her forearm up, catching him on the wrist and staving off the blow.

The screwdriver rattled to the wet pavement.

Her first instinct was to scream, but her second, stronger instinct was to fight silently and let the blue take over.

He threw a punch, landing it on her cheek. She cartwheeled to the ground on purpose, on top of the screwdriver.

Someone yelled, but she couldn't figure where it had come from.

The man kicked her in the same shoulder with his thick boot, and her left arm deadened again.

Her right arm did not.

Now in a crouch, she pivoted from her hips, launching herself up and high, and drove the screwdriver just under the guy's jaw.

Her hand slicked with geysering hot blood, but she held her grip on the screwdriver. He clutched his neck, staggered, the blood fountaining as her momentum took her to the ground.

Whoever had yelled before was yelling again, closer. She heard someone running, getting closer.

A dog barked.

The guy fell to the pavement, his blood still pumping out of his body. His face flashed fear, confusion, fear, then understanding as his legs drummed on the asphalt.

The footsteps splashed closer.

The guy gurgled, a hand still pressed to his neck.

Jane swung a leg over the guy's stomach, pinning his arms between her legs, drew her arm back, and drove the screwdriver into the soft V below his Adam's apple. For a moment, his face changed into Esmir Roux's face, and the screwdriver became her car key, then it was back to the guy's face, which was now ashen, and she braced a hand on his chest and spit in his face and watched him die.

More barking, and now the footsteps were next to her. Hands on her shoulders, helping her up. Instead, she slumped, covering the dead man, not purely from exhaustion but so she could slip a ring from his dead finger and into her sock.

Then she accepted the aid from whoever was next to her as the barking and the shouts for help mixed with the patter of the rain. Before she was helped up, she whispered in the dead man's ear, "Asshole."

THREE COP CARS, each driven solo by local officers Jane knew by sight, wheeled into the parking lot, followed closely by an ambulance, then another, then, curiously, a fire truck. The rain and remote location kept the lookie-loos to a minimum at first, but the cops hurriedly taped off a big chunk of the parking lot and threw a sheet over the dead guy's body as the scene drew attention.

One of the officers took a statement from the one witness, a dog walker who Jane didn't recognize. The woman looked distraught, while the dog, a Lab mix, looked thrilled.

Two photographers showed up — an officer from neighboring Yarmouth and toting a camera was ushered through, while a newsie was blocked from taking snaps of Jane and anything close to the body.

Through all this, Jane sat inside one of the ambulances, watching the scene unfold through the open rear door. She had a cut on her cheek, scraped knees and palms, and a cut on her forearm that she hadn't felt and didn't remember getting, and her left shoulder still felt both dead and on fire. Someone swabbed her hands, which were heavy with the guy's blood, and took pictures before the EMTs cleaned her up and bandaged her arm, which didn't look bad at all now and wouldn't need stitches. Her heart still hammered from the adrenaline rush. She hadn't felt a rush like that in decades.

It felt really, really good.

Another car rolled up, its grill lights strobing. A pretty woman, a black knit cap atop her shoulder-length brown hair and wearing a tan brush jacket, black jeans, and sneakers, got out, surveyed the scene, talked to the officers, and peeked under the sheet. One of the officers pointed to the ambulance, and the woman strode over, climbed in, and took a seat across from Jane.

"Detective Sophia Perez," the woman said, taking off her cap and wiping her face with it. She took in Jane's injuries. "You're the writer. Heard about you. Pleasure to meet you."

Jane forced a *this-is-all-too-much* look. She was shaken —

most people would be after taking a life — but she was also feeling more like herself, her old self, than she had in a long time. She'd better bury it. "Good to meet you, Detective. I … I don't know where to start. I don't know what happened." She knew exactly what had happened.

"Take me through it. If you're ready." The woman was brusque, to the point. Jane didn't know this Perez, didn't know the name, didn't know that Port Fletcher even had two detectives. She must be new.

Jane walked her through the attack, which was clear as glass in her head, but she faked some fog, added some confusion and doubt because it had happened so fast, after all. She'd slipped the ring farther down into her sock, under her heel, and hoped they wouldn't search her.

She'd driven here to think, she told Perez. There was nothing shady about that. She lived in a beach town, and people here went to the beach. Maybe the guy had followed her — she'd been at the bank, and maybe he'd seen her withdraw the cash.

"How much cash do you have on you?" Perez asked.

"Four hundred dollars." Perez would verify that she'd taken out eight hundred, Jane knew. If Perez fished around and found out that she'd visited Flounder before coming here, he'd say that she put a cash deposit on a computer with the other four hundred — Jane had no doubt that Flounder excelled at self-preservation. Hopefully, it wouldn't come to that. "I like to pay in cash when possible. I'm old school."

Perez chuckled. "I get that."

The attack had taken maybe ninety seconds from start to finish — in the dead guy's case, finish meant Finished — and except for the second thrust to the neck, which no one had seen in its entirety except for maybe the dog walker, all of Jane's actions had been warranted.

"You were really lucky," Perez said. "Or really skilled, fighting off an asshole like that. Not even sure I could have done it."

Skill had nothing to do with it. It was all muscle memory. She shook off Perez's statement. "I wanted to get away, but he kept coming at me," Jane said, adding a quiver. "If I can't park at the beach in my own town without someone trying to rape me or steal my car, then I don't know what this world's come to."

Perez looked satisfied, but Jane didn't know if that look meant she really was satisfied. "The witness saw most of it, but from a distance," the detective said. "I don't know yet who the guy was. There's no other car here, so maybe it was about that, him trying to steal your car. Maybe he didn't know you were in it."

Jane went to say something but then remembered one of her rules, "shut up more often," so she nodded and tried to look frail.

Perez asked a few more questions, went over things again, this time taking notes. "Self-defense," she said, "is what this looks like. I'll investigate, but right now, all of this looks to be pure self-defense. No ID on the guy. Between us and the Yarmouth officer we called in for backup, we'll figure out who he is. The State Police will be involved." She walked through the rest of what Jane would have to do, including coming to the station, but promised she'd keep it to a minimum.

"I'll need to keep your car," Perez said. "It's okay if you take out what you need, but leave the car key and take your other keys."

Jane responded with more nodding. She hated being without a car, but she'd rent something.

"Let's get you home," Perez said. "Clean up, rest, try to put this aside. I'll walk you to your car, then I'll drive you home in mine. You live with anyone? Got any family close by?"

"I live alone. I've got neighbors. We keep an eye out for each other."

"Someone should stay with you."

"I'll be fine." Typical New England stoicism. Jane remembered looking through her grandmother's hand-written diaries when she was in grade school, deciphering the lives of people she'd never met from small leather-bound five-year journals, the handwriting formal, full of stoicism and buried emotions. *July 29, 1916. Ethel Cooper from next door died. Sunny weather. Picked beans.*

Perez sighed. "If you say so." She nodded her chin toward Jane. "That eye's going black."

Jane met her gaze, held it. "I've had black eyes before."

Perez raised an eyebrow, then led them to the car, where Jane retrieved her purse with the cocaine inside and handed Perez the car key, then they climbed into Perez's car and navigated past the onlookers to Jane's house.

The five-minute ride was quiet, which Jane appreciated.

"I'll walk you in," Perez said when they parked. Maybe she felt protective. Maybe she wanted to be sure there were no bad guys here. Maybe she wanted a look around to get a sense of Jane.

Perez was probing, Jane knew, but on the sly. She seemed to accept Jane's story, but the detective had given her a few looks, a few long beats of silence after Jane answered questions … things would have gone smoother if Bill Ramsford had been the detective. He'd have eaten out of Jane's hand.

She'd have to learn more about Sophia Perez. Where she'd come from. What made her tick. Would she be a friend. Would she be a foe. All the normal things one does when they're trying to keep their past a secret but they kill a guy in a parking lot.

Perez handed Jane her business card, asked her to call if she needed anything, and said she'd be in touch soon. She'd let Jane know who the guy was once they ID'ed him. Maybe Jane knew him. Probably not. She also said that she'd ask the press to leave Jane alone. She'd been through enough.

Perez drove away, leaving Jane alone. The house was quiet save for the rain beating against the windows. Dark. Gloomy. It fit Jane's mood.

She sat on the kitchen floor, her back against the cabinet corners, and closed her eyes. She thought about the day so far. Bank, cash, safe deposit box. Cocaine.

Attack.

The guy ... let's see. He'd been wearing a dark gray hoodie and blue jeans. No gloves. His face ... she didn't know him. Hadn't seen him before. He hadn't been at the bank, she was sure. The Cape was full of guys who looked like him — white, scruffy facial hair, lean, compact. The Cape also had a rampant drug problem. He'd been a blue-collar worker, if he worked at all. He looked like a local movie extra fresh from central casting.

He'd had no car, so where had he come from?

Could he be tied to Esmir Roux? Coincidences meant that you weren't seeing a connection. But Jane couldn't connect what Esmir had said, what he wanted, to this. It didn't make sense. Or it didn't make sense yet.

With all the little things out of the way, she focused on the big thing.

She'd killed a man an hour ago with a screwdriver.

This was a learning moment. There was what she *should* feel, and there was what she *did* feel.

What she should feel: unsafe, distraught, shock, fear,

horror. An indelible mark. A life-changing event. A clear division between Jane before the attack and Jane after.

She didn't feel any of that.

What she did feel: sore. Tired. Satisfaction. Glee.

Satisfaction, because she had protected herself. Glee, because she hadn't lost who she was after twenty years. More glee, because you do not fuck with Jane Hawkins.

So: what was the lesson from this learning moment?

Act like you should act, but inside, feel how you want to feel.

She silenced her phone, then stretched out on the couch and dozed, dreamless, for hours.

The weather hadn't changed when she woke up. The rain still beat hard outside, and inside, the house was just as gloomy.

The shoulder where she'd gotten kicked ached. She peeled down her sleeve. Her skin was red and purple now, and it'd go through all the colors of the rainbow before running its course. Her knees hurt, her palms hurt, but the scrapes weren't as bad as she'd first thought.

She snapped on the bathroom light and took a long look at herself in the mirror. Perez was right. That eye might go black, or maybe the swollen cheek would be her only visible trophy. She stuck her tongue out at herself, and that made her smile.

Speaking of trophies … she sat on the toilet, then plumbed around her sock until she found the guy's ring. It was silver, hefty, one thick line circling the perimeter and etched in black, or maybe it was only filthy. There was nothing inscribed on the inside. It wasn't a wedding band, or at least it hadn't been on his wedding band finger. She'd taken it off his right hand, but she couldn't remember which finger. She slipped it on her thumb, the only finger it came close to fitting, then noticed the blood on the ring, then the blood under her nails. She looked down and saw blood on her sock, probably from when she'd jammed the souvenir there.

She stood and got close to the mirror again, this time angling her face to take it all in. There. A spot of the guy's blood on her temple. She kissed one of her fingers, then put the finger on the spot of blood.

She took three Advil, washing them down with cold coffee, then went upstairs to her office. She typed out the details of the attack, blow by blow, as best she could remember. They might come in handy for Belle in the next book. Not that Belle would jam a tool into a guy's throat. Belle didn't work like that. But maybe she should. It would really make her feel alive.

She stripped off her clothes and threw them in the trash, then drew a bath. She soaked for thirty minutes, smoking two cigarettes while the water cooled, flicking the ash and the spent butts into the tub with her. She didn't usually smoke in the house, as she wanted to keep her vices private and to herself, not that she got visitors who'd notice, but between the rain and the day's events, why not? She deserved a treat.

The Advil had worked its magic, but she was still sore. Sixty-year-old authors can't fight to the death in a rainy parking lot without paying a price. At least she had won this time.

After drying off and changing into the loosest, softest clothes she could find, she pulled out Esmir Roux's card and poured herself a bourbon.

"This is Jane Hawkins," she said when Roux picked up. "Let's meet tomorrow. I'm ready to talk."

Day 4 (Wednesday)

IN THE MORNING, Jane called a rental car place and arranged for a vehicle to be dropped off at her house. Was a small SUV okay? They were out of sedans. She'd never driven an SUV, but sure.

She peered outside. The rain had stopped, and now thin, high clouds scalloped the blue sky. A better day, weather-wise, than yesterday. And maybe a better day all around, if she wasn't carjacked again.

She hadn't turned her phone ringer back on since yesterday, so she'd missed some calls. Two calls were from the *Cape Cod Crier*, the local alarmist weekly, wanting comment. She wouldn't return those calls — she wanted to stay out of the press, plus there was nothing to say. One from the Port Fletcher police — she'd need to come down and go over her statement. She probably should return that. Later.

One from Perez — they'd ID'ed the guy as Jonas Ferrier, a drifter who'd been arrested for previous carjackings, break-ins, and other mid-level crimes. He'd been convicted a few times, but he'd never done enough time to make a difference, this being bleeding-heart Massachusetts. Perez sounded annoyed in the message, like her job would be much more enjoyable if lowlifes didn't exist. Couldn't argue with that. Oh, and they'd bring her car back after the window got fixed — a local place had already agreed to fix it for free after hearing that it was the local author Jane Hawkins who got attacked. Perez had ended the call with, "Nice to have friends in high places."

Nothing from Roux. They'd set up the meeting last night. He was in Boston, she was on the Cape, so they'd meet halfway, off-Cape, in Plymouth at Brewster Gardens, a park near the waterfront. She wanted somewhere public yet somewhat private.

Jane took stock of her injuries. Her shoulder still ached, but it was manageable. The cut on her forearm looked okay after a peek under the bandage, which she'd totally gotten wet yesterday in the bath, going against instructions. Oh well. Her cheek didn't look bad, and her eye hadn't gone dark. Donald had smacked her around enough back in the day that maybe the cheek and eye no longer cared. Her knees were scabby, her palms the same, but again, nothing terrible. All in all, she'd gotten out of it in decent shape.

She'd slept well for having killed someone. No feverish dreams beyond her normal ones.

Probably should keep that to herself.

She'd head to the senior center later for some volunteering, but she had an hour to kill, so she'd spend some time with fictional Belle first. She turned on the computer, but nothing happened. She gave the tower a smack. Nothing. The monitor powered on okay, giving her the same blank stare she was giving the tower, but the computer itself seemed dead.

She considered calling Flounder, this time for a legal

transaction, but it was too early to deal with his voice and smell.

The doorbell rang, and she hurried downstairs to take a look out the window. She saw her rental car — actually two cars, an SUV and another car so that the rental car driver wasn't stranded. She took care of the paperwork, thanked them profusely, and took the keys. A cute Chevy something or other SUV, not too big, a non-conspicuous gray. Perfect.

She went inside to clean up, secured the house, then headed out to the rental. She'd be early for the senior center, but it's not like they'd turn her away. She was a volunteer. You didn't turn someone away who was willingly giving you their time for free.

Before she got to the rental, someone shouted "Jane!" Why did people keep startling her like that? This time, it was Ellen Bligh from next door — the better neighbor, not the evil leaf guy on the other side.

Ellen hurried over. "I just heard," Ellen said when she got within range, clutching at Jane's arm.

Jane winced. "Careful. I got cut there. Heard what?"

Ellen huffed. "About the attack! It's all over the news. They said your name. I'm surprised there aren't a flock of reporters out here. They said that a man died!"

"He did. The whole thing was sad. I'd rather not talk about it right now."

Ellen nodded profusely, as she was prone to do. She was a tiny thing, Asian — Jane had never bothered to get more specific than that and would never apologize for not asking or not caring — with a whiplash assortment of personalities. Ellen was always one hundred percent some-thing. Happy. Pissed off. Worried. For someone so small, she did everything large.

Ellen was now one hundred percent divorced, from

Ben, a pear-shaped, doughy, meek guy who worked a lot and had made only rare appearances in Jane's life. Ellen and Ben had split up late last year, Jane never knowing why definitively but, again, not really caring. Keep your yard neat and don't make a lot of noise — all she wanted from a neighbor.

There'd been signs, of course — Ellen's job, some vague medical position, not a doctor or a nurse but something — had not gone virtual during the pandemic. Ben's had — what he did for work was vague as well to Jane, but something to do with importing, or exporting, or procurement. Big changes like people being home when they were never home full-time before had put a strain on nearly everybody's family dynamic. And once Ellen and Ben's son Ryan had gone back to in-person learning at the high school, Ben had been home alone, and Jane had seen the same woman park the same car in their driveway many times. Maybe it had been a work thing. Maybe the woman and Ben had been fucking, although looking at Ben, Jane could never figure out what Ellen had seen in Ben, let alone what some other woman would see. Picturing a naked Ben made her queasy. Again, whatever — their drama, not hers.

Ellen gave her a pouty frown. "If you need any help — *anything* — you let me know."

Ellen, although feisty, would never punch a screwdriver into anyone's throat, so she couldn't help with "anything."

"That is so sweet," Jane said. "Thank you."

Then she had a thought. "Is Ryan home? I've got a computer question." Ryan was a college kid and the Blighs' only child, and he'd beaten Ben's pear-shape gene, turning out tall and good-looking, although gawky.

Ellen looked pleased that she could be of immediate help. "You need Ryan for something? I'll get him." Jane didn't mean now, but Ellen did. She marched over to the house, and a minute later came out with Ryan, a backpack slung over his shoulder.

"Hi, Ms. Hawkins," he said. "Mom says you have a computer question."

Jane had babysat Ryan dozens of times, but that had ended years ago. Back then, he'd been a happy, if quiet and shy, kid, pleased to be by himself. He was still polite, on the rare times Jane saw and spoke to him now, but he usually came across as sullen. Maybe all teen boys nowadays were sullen. Maybe it was the divorce. Maybe it was because Ellen was a hover-parent, all up in his business. Maybe she needed to be, as a single mom. Maybe Jane didn't care.

"My old computer is either dead or dying. I'd get a new one, but I want to be sure I don't lose anything." Ryan had helped her automatically back up all her work a few months ago but had noted that her computer was obsolete and she should think about getting something current.

"I can help, but I've got class, I won't be back until tonight." His voice had gotten so deep. All grown up. Just like Kate.

"I've got some things to do as well, so tonight is fine, or whenever. I need to get to writing, but it's not an emergency."

"Okay, I'll look for you later," he said, then added in a rush, "Mom said you got attacked at the beach. I'm so sorry to hear that. I hope that you're okay."

That was a lot of words from Ryan. He seemed to be purposefully avoiding looking at her bruised cheek. Good manners for not being obvious and mentioning it. Jane would have.

"I'm fine," she said. "I'll look for you later."

They said their goodbyes, then Jane left, arriving five

minutes later at the Port Fletcher Senior Center, where local elderly folks came, sometimes every day, for community and help. Jane wasn't that far off from joining them, age-wise, although she'd rather die in a vat of acid than center her life around coming to a senior center. Not that the place was depressing — the town had done a good job making the new building feel bright and lively.

There was a good crowd today, and as usual, the early birds had plowed through the coffee and pastries. The room was a sea of white hair, gray hair, blue hair, and no hair. Jane handed out word search puzzles, watched but did not participate in a brief exercise class, and helped where she needed to help. Some of the seniors had heard about the attack yesterday, so she spent too much time reassuring them she was fine while dodging discussing the details. She even signed a few Beachcomber Belle books, too — her book launch event on Monday night had started after some of these people's bedtimes.

Everything went as normal, except for what Jane termed the Visitations. She hadn't had a Visitation in twenty years, since she hadn't killed anyone in twenty years. She saw Jonas Ferrier everywhere in the senior center — huddled in a corner, shuffling across the room using a walker, doing stretches during exercise class. Everywhere she looked, she saw his hoodie, his blank eyes, and his thick work boots, wet from the non-existent rain. Then she'd blink, and he'd be gone. She'd expected to see him today, and hoped that he'd be gone by tomorrow, like the others always had.

Jonas Ferrier, get back to the morgue where you belong.

The oversized wall clock showed it was coming up on noon. She'd planned to meet Esmir Roux at one, and it'd take about an hour to get to Plymouth.

"Jane!" a voice from behind her came. She rolled her eyes. The third time in two days that someone had felt it necessary to shout out her name.

She turned, forcing a welcoming smile. It was Bettina Yothers, another volunteer. Bettina was about Jane's age, tall and reedy. Jane hadn't seen Bettina in a while. She was nice enough, but perpetually mopey.

Bettina glanced around the room, then in a low voice, "Can we talk?"

Ugh. "Of course." She didn't have the time. But keeping up appearances was important.

Bettina led her to a storage room, flicked on the light, and closed the door. "First off, I heard about what happened to you."

Jane waved her off. "I'm fine. Are you fine, Bettina?" She'd been working on using first names more and being less brusque. Usually, she wanted people to get right to the point and ditch the small talk, like Detective Perez had done yesterday. Efficiency is a virtue.

"It's about Yip. Things are … well, bad at home."

Jane let her continue. Yip, Bettina's husband, the name short for something that Jane never knew, was a surly bastard, nice enough in two-minute doses the first time you met him, then his assholeness always popped out like a whack-a-mole and you'd cross the street to avoid talking to him.

"Whatever I can do, Bettina. Talk to me."

Bettina swallowed. "I don't know if you've heard anything. Everyone knows you, and you must hear a lot. Not saying you're gossipy, because you're not. You're just so good with people. They trust you."

She'd fooled Bettina, at least. "Thank you, dear. Now about Yip."

"I think he's having an affair. I should say, *another* affair.

It's like a switch got turned on recently, and I don't know why. He's turned mean. Verbally mean, physically mean. With me. I can't take this marriage any longer."

She thinks the switch *just* got turned on? Yip Yothers had always been like this, at least since Jane had met him years ago. Bettina was a "saver" — she'd met Yip, then thought she could change him. The Yips of the world never changed, but good luck telling the Bettinas that.

Jane had never been a saver. But when she'd first met Yip, he'd seemed a clone of Donald. Brothers from another mother. Everyone loved them, except for those they should have loved. Donald as Yip, Yip as Donald. Life of the party, unless it was just him and you partying.

Jane forced an understanding face, making herself smile without humor. It hurt, in a way, faking this much honesty and compassion. Especially when the conversation carried on far too long. Now, if Bettina had said, "Yip's an ass. He's fucking his way across the Cape. And when I confront him about it, he whacks me," then turned and left, that's all Jane would need to know. Don't let words get in the way of a good story.

Bettina went on, supplying no other relevant information, so at a logical stopping point, Jane cut in. "Bettina, my advice is that you carry on. If you want to leave him, and I've got to be honest, that is probably best for you, you have my support." Needed to amend that. "You have the support from *all* of us." The vague, collective "us" was better than giving Bettina the impression that Jane wanted to shoulder the burden of help by herself.

Relief washed over Bettina's face. "Thank you for listening. I don't know what to do. I don't know what you can do or what anyone can do. This has been eating me up. I just wanted you know, if I've been coming across as sulky lately."

Lately? "I'm here for you." She patted Bettina's arm. "Now go out there and make those peoples' days. They need you."

A bit later, Jane hurried out of the senior center, for a moment looking for her Accord and then not remembering what the rental looked like, then she spotted it. She climbed in and started it up, then looked down at her hands and shrieked. Both hands were covered in blood. Then they weren't.

She checked the back seat for a ghostly Jonas Ferrier. Nope. She'd be riding alone. Thankfully.

BETWEEN TALKING to Bettina and road work on Route 3, which was a typical Massachusetts Highway That Was Never Finished, she pulled into Brewster Gardens in Plymouth ten minutes later than she'd planned. There were a few cars in the lot. School was still in session, and tourist season hadn't begun, so this was the quiet before the storm.

She spotted Roux on a bench overlooking the creek that split the gardens. She palmed the Chevy's key fob, but fancy new tech made for an inferior weapon, so she sighed and dropped it into her purse. A good old-fashioned key, now you could do some damage with that. Eyeballs were soft. Throats were soft. What could she do with a key fob if she were attacked — unlock the guy?

There would be no hunting here anyway, key or no key. Not physical hunting anyway. But information hunting, that was on the menu. What does Roux know? What is he wrong about? Hopefully, plenty of the latter and little of the former.

She circled around the bench. "Mr. Roux."

He stood. "Jane." He offered her a hand, which she refused. He peered closer. "Sorry. Your face. What happened?"

She assumed he'd have heard about the carjacking attempt, but why would he? "Got into a bit of a tussle. You should see the other guy."

He laughed. She didn't blink. He cleared his throat.

"Well then." He sat back down. "Let's talk here."

She sat, taking in the sun.

He began, both of them looking at the creek instead of each other. "Thanks for meeting me here, Jane. I wanted to follow up on our conversation the other night." Not *apologize for scaring the shit out of you the other night and being an ass by bringing up your dead husband*, she noted. "For this season of my podcast, I'm digging into a series of old murders, back in the late 1990s and into 2003. All unsolved. I think I can tie them to one person, a serial killer who hunted Massachusetts for decades." He turned to her, and she to him.

She gave him no reaction. The "decades" part was wrong. More like "several years."

"Go on, Mr. Roux. But I'm not sure why you are talking to me about this."

"One of the victims is your husband. Donald Hawkins was killed during a botched burglary in 2001. But I don't think it was a botched burglary. I think he was targeted. Killed by the same person as the other nine."

Keeping her face devoid of emotion was hard. But then, that wasn't the right move, was it? She had to show some emotion. Pain. Shock. Those would be right. Her first instinct was annoyance, though, and that wouldn't do. Her second was to drag Roux into the creek and bash him on the temple with a river rock. That wouldn't do either.

She put a hand to her throat. "Mr. Roux, the police investigated all this years ago. It was a burglary gone wrong. They never caught the person, of course, but I … I've moved on. I told you this at the book launch. I've worked hard, really hard, to keep the past in the past." At least that part was true.

She continued, choosing her words deliberately. "But you think Donald was … a victim … of a serial killer? I don't know, Mr. Roux."

Excitement crossed Roux's face. "These murders. There's a pattern. Your husband, Donald, he wasn't the first, he wasn't the last. But there was a first, and there was a last. The methods of each murder — I apologize if this is coming across as insensitive."

"I write mystery novels, Mr. Roux. I don't have delicate sensibilities."

"Of course." He seemed eager to please. Excited, almost. "Each murder is different, yet they're also similar. The police investigations were rote. A botched drug deal, a botched robbery. I want to dive into each case, figure out the connections. It's been a long time, but it's not impossible. I'm starting to see the patterns. The timing. The victims. Something, someone, ties them all together."

She kept her face blank as if allowing him to continue. There had been no pattern, not in timing, not in method. She'd made sure of that.

"So, Mr. Roux—"

"Esmir. Please."

"Mr. Roux, you think that my Donald was one of this man's victims? A serial killer?"

Roux leaned back. "I didn't say that the killer was a he. I don't want to presume. There are female serial killers. They don't have the notoriety of male serial killers, but there have been plenty of them. Books, articles, a lot has been written about them. FSKs, they're called. Female serial killers. Women can be as deadly as men."

Some women certainly could be.

"Even if this were true," Jane said, "why talk to me about it? I told you that the past is the past. Nothing will bring Donald back. I'm not up to reliving his murder. And if there were a pattern, surely the police would have found it by now." All true.

Roux shook his head at the last statement. Clearly, he thought himself superior. "I'd like to have you on my podcast," he said. "Have you listened to it?"

"I'm a writer. I prefer my entertainment in written form. Even the most tawdry of tales."

"Tawdry." He chuckled. "Well, I've read your books. Not all of them, but Belle, I enjoy her. She falls into trouble, then wiggles out of it and solves cases the police can't or won't solve. She's always a step ahead. Like you."

Jane turned to the creek. "That's not my world, Mr. Roux. I invented Belle, and I invent her investigations and cases. It's all imagination. I do talk to the police when I need authenticity, but what I write is entertainment. It's not based on fact." She turned to him. "It's not real life."

Roux nodded. "You should give the podcast a listen. Last season was good. But this season will be incredible."

No response needed. Let him fill the dead air. She knew he would. Never trust anyone who can't abide silence.

"Anyway," he said after a beat, "think about it. I'll cover Donald's murder in episode 3. I've recorded the first episode, covering the first of the ten murders, and I'll go in order. I'm releasing episode 1 on Friday, two days from now. I think you'll be pleased."

"And why would I be pleased?"

"Closure, Jane. Closure for the families of the victims. If not from me, then maybe this will spur the police to do their jobs better. Go through their cold cases, find answers. I want to find the monster who did this."

There's that word again. Monster.

"I'm not comfortable with this, Mr. Roux. I'm not comfortable with you digging through the past, bringing me into this. Let Donald rest in peace after all these years."

"I'm surprised. I thought that you'd want closure. Because Donald isn't resting in peace. His killer is still out there. Same for the other nine families."

This was getting very cat-and-mouse. He knew more than he was letting on, but what? If he had anything concrete about her, he'd have led with it. It was obvious that pride is what drove him. He'd have based a whole podcast season about her, if he had any evidence. But he had no evidence. He had a pattern, or at least he thought there was a pattern. He hadn't found it yet. He had nothing.

"Are you hounding the other families to be on your podcast as well?"

He chuckled. "Some. It would be boring to have just me talk for an hour every episode. So of course I'm interviewing whoever I can. Families, police. Going over old news reports. Reviewing what I can. But yes, there will be family members on each episode, I hope."

He angled his body toward her. "But you, you're different. You're smart, you're well read, well spoken. You're a name. You'd make for a great guest. I think that there's so much more to you than meets the eye."

That felt like a loaded statement. How to react?

She shook her head slowly. "I'm a middle-aged writer, a widow for over 20 years, and I've moved on. Yes, I might be a name, someone with a bit of fame who could boost your podcast. But I don't want to be used like that. My writing, what I do, isn't about this. I didn't even start writing until after Donald was … gone. It started out as something cathartic, but I was always a reader, Mr. Roux. Now I'm a writer. A writer, a widow, and someone who wishes to be left alone. Someone who wants the past to stay in the past."

He raised his brows. "We're at an impasse. You don't have to come on, of course, but I'm free to talk about you. I wanted background on Donald, but I can fall back on plenty of public information. I want you to be able to tell your side of the story."

"I don't have a side. Because there are no sides. Donald is gone. I've moved on."

"Perhaps I was indelicate," he said. "By side, I mean you should be able to tell your story. It could help catch whoever committed these murders. And even if I'm wrong, even if they weren't committed by a serial killer, well, I'd rather bring ten people to justice for ten murders than no one."

He blew out a breath before continuing. "I might not have all the answers, Jane. I might not be doing this the way you'd want me to do this. But I have listeners. Listeners hungry for justice. Other families hungry for justice. And through crowdsourcing, presenting all the information about these cases, someone might remember something. Someone might come forward with new information I can build on."

"You mean the police can build on."

"Yes, yes," he rushed, "of course the police are the ones who will eventually bring this killer to justice. And if I can help that along, I will."

Be the cat, not the mouse. "I will think about it, Mr. Roux."

"That's all I can ask, Ms. Hawkins. I'd need to record you, if you agree, within the week. As soon as possible."

She stood, not offering a hand. "I will consider it."

~

SHE DROVE a mile down the road to a salad place and parked in the back corner of the lot. It looked attack-free. Shouldn't she be wary of remote parking spaces, after what had happened yesterday? Shouldn't she be traumatized, perhaps for a lifetime? How would normal people feel? She didn't know. She just wanted privacy and a salad.

She went in, ate, came back to the car, and thought about Esmir Roux. What had he said that was true, and what had he said that was not?

He thought that ten unsolved murders from twenty-plus years ago were connected. Ten was a magic number. Was he talking about the same ten murders? At least one of them was — Donald's. And he said Donald's wasn't the first and wasn't the last. That was all true.

He thought there was a pattern. Location, timing. Was that true? She didn't know. She didn't think so, but tonight, she'd go over it.

He thought ten people were killed by the same person. Depends on which murders. So, maybe true.

He didn't say that his presumed killer was a man. He said it could be a woman. He didn't know who the killer was. If it was even the same killer.

He didn't think the police had done a great job investigating. That was certainly true.

Then she thought about his subtext. Words and phrases with potentially two meanings.

She's always a step ahead. Like you.
I want to find the monster who did this.
Tell your side of the story.
There's so much more to you than meets the eye.

Too early to tell, but if there was going to be a hunt, she'd be the hunter, not the hunted.

Her thoughts were clear, crisp, focused. No blood on her hands, no Jonas Ferrier lurking behind every corner. She felt like the lioness basking after a successful kill, now with a full belly, her mission accomplished.

She drove, a straight shot down Route 3, then up and over the ancient Sagamore Bridge, the Cape Cod Canal leaden and choppy below her, then Route 3 ended and she picked up Route 6, the Mid-Cape Highway, which was always jammed during tourist season but empty enough now that she flew home.

She parked in the driveway, got to the front door. And stopped.

The red thread had moved.

She'd left the house like normal. Ellen. She'd run into Ellen after securing the house. Did she go back inside after Ellen? No, she'd brought everything she needed with her before the senior center and left right after Ellen left.

Had she placed the thread, or hadn't she?

She crept backwards, to the lawn, then turned. No cars on the street, nothing seeming out of place. Then she crept along the side of the house. The shades were still drawn. Good. Except she couldn't see if anyone was inside. Bad.

She inched around to the back of the house and stopped at the corner, listening. Nothing. The house felt empty, even from the outside. From experience, a house *feeling* empty and a house *being* empty were two different things.

She considered texting Ellen to see if she'd seen anything unusual, but that would come with a whole lot of talking and explanation.

She crept back to the front door. Thought about what she had in her purse. The key fob would be of no use. Her house key would be in her hand, but it would also be in the lock.

She picked up a softball-sized rock from along the foundation, then trod softly up the steps. She inserted the key with her left hand, while keeping the rock in her dominant right hand.

She raised the rock high as she turned the key, unlocking the door and shoving it open with her ass, then launched into the house with an "A-ha!"

She stood, frozen, rock still held high, listening. Nothing. The house felt empty. Her adrenaline surged, then stopped flowing. Relief mixed with disappointment. No hunt today.

She lobbed the rock back outside, then checked the windows. All fine. Nothing out of place. She'd forgotten to properly attach the thread, was all.

Lesson learned. She needed to be better. She needed to be *exacting*.

Also, she needed to ask Ryan about home security cameras.

She tried the computer again. It was still dead. She could type on her phone, but she hated doing that. Beachcomber Belle and the Chechen candy lord would have to wait.

The heat inside the house was still on, but Jane shivered. Her kicked shoulder was still achy, so she downed more Advil, then sat at the kitchen table and made a list of supplies she needed.

These purchases needed to be untraceable, not that anything was untraceable in this day and age. She couldn't worry about store security cameras — they were everywhere. But she could make things harder.

She triple-checked the house before she left, checking the thread so many times that it bordered on stupidity.

This was no way to live. But it was thrilling to think that someday, maybe soon, she might come home and see the thread moved and catch someone inside. Hence the need for these errands.

She shouldn't buy any of this in Port Fletcher. She probably should have thought about this list before meeting Roux, as she could have done it all in Plymouth, but that seemed too far away to drive to now. Hyannis, a half-hour drive, probably had everything she needed and would give her some anonymity.

Speaking of which ... she shouldn't look like herself. In the basement, she dragged some boxes out, burrowed through them, found the red-hair wig. That had been a big help back in the day. She tried it on — her hair was longer now, and the wig didn't fit like she'd hoped, but it would do. She'd dress like a dirtbag anyway.

Underneath the wig were half a dozen eyeglass frames, the lenses non-corrective. Just for looks. The biggest of the frames, woefully out of date and not coming back into style, would draw attention away from her bruised cheek, she hoped.

Upstairs, she dug through her gardening clothes, the stuff with rips and tears and stains, and found a beat-up hoodie, one quite similar to what Jonas Ferrier had been wearing, except this one had no blood on it.

Ferrier. She closed her eyes, wondering if he'd appear in the room when she opened them. Nope. Gone, but not forgotten. His ring was safe, at least.

On went the wig, on went the hoodie, on went blue jeans and sneakers, on went the glasses. She adjusted the wig, getting close to the bathroom mirror. She looked ridiculously trashy. Perfect.

She found an old fanny pack in the basement. Those might never come back into fashion, but they served a purpose. Don't throw away anything you might need in the future. In went the cash. Now she was cashy trashy.

On to Hyannis, not the mall but the outskirts, where things could get a little sketchy and lot more anonymous.

From a dusty cookware store, she bought a set of steak knives. Eight in all, enough for any surprise guests.

From a medical supply store, she bought a box of syringes tipped with needles. This caused some raised eyebrows — real drug users probably knew where to get these for free, so she added a "These work so well for fine detail work on my paintings!" for the clerk, who didn't seem to care at all.

From an independent hardware store, she picked up a Leatherman multi-tool, thought about it, then added a second to her basket, along with some contractor-strength black garbage bags, zip ties, a box of 100 blue nitrile gloves, and a small bottle of bleach. Definitely a stereotypical serial killer's receipt, although this clerk didn't care either.

Back in her car, she surveyed her purchases, thinking it through. Rope? Duct tape? Nah. If it got to that, she'd make do. This wasn't about holding anyone hostage. This was about preparation. She stuffed everything into the largest of the store bags.

In Massachusetts, you couldn't swing a dead cat without hitting a Dunkin' Donuts, so she hit the first one she saw and treated herself to a large iced coffee with plenty of sugar.

Once back in her driveway, she ditched the wig and glasses in the big bag in case Ellen or Leaf Guy were peeping, then carried everything to the front door. The thread was in place. The house was secure.

Before she unlocked the door, she remembered what she'd forgotten to put on the list. Screwdrivers. She could explain away needing those, so she got back into the Chevy, wig-free, drove to the local hardware store and picked up a set of six screwdrivers with generic black handles. Satisfied she had everything, she drove back home and spread the purchases on the table. Good enough.

She pawed through the back of her closet until she found an old purse, unused for years, more of a cotton bag with a magnetic clasp. She wasn't sure where she'd gotten it, but it would do. She stuck in three screwdrivers and a handful of empty syringes, along with two of the steak knives. She then emptied a half-full spray bottle of Shout! stain remover into a smaller spray bottle, then added some ammonia for a kick and made sure the bottle was sealed tightly. Hopefully the mixture wouldn't explode.

On to some house modifications. She found a length of white-painted board in the basement, a relic of Donald's puttering at his workbench, which had lain mostly dormant for 20 years. She brought it upstairs, placed it on a few walls until she found a suitable space, then drilled two pilot holes and screwed the board to a wall near the front entryway. She brought out the last three screwdrivers. They were longer than she thought, but maybe they'd do. She drilled three holes in the new board and into the wall, angled slightly downward, then jammed in the screwdrivers. Nice. At a quick glance, it looked like a rustic coat rack. She draped the cotton kill bag over one of the screwdriver handles. Easy access.

She put two knives under her mattress, then one in each bathroom, taped to the back of each toilet. She reconsidered, then put the upstairs one in the shower instead, next to her shampoo bottle. If someone came for her while she was on the toilet and made it all the way upstairs, she deserved whatever was coming to her for being that unprepared.

She dropped one multi-tool in her purse and put the second in a kitchen drawer.

The syringes. She hadn't used syringes in two decades. She filled a few with bleach, testing them out. She figured they'd be okay without too much leaking, but they'd get jostled and she didn't want to be caught with empties if things turned bad. Table carrying around the syringes for now.

Good work like this deserved a reward, so she poured out a bourbon, took it outside, set up a lawn chair in the back, flush to the house, lit a cigarette, and closed her eyes, embracing the late afternoon chill. Good work all around.

Then she remembered. One more thing to check. She crushed out her cigarette, drained the bourbon, went back inside and into the kitchen. She rooted around in the freezer and brought out a yellowed plastic food storage container with a masking tape label reading "Mom's Meatballs."

Mom had never made meatballs. Mom had died a few years before Donald had. Dad had passed years before then. She hadn't missed them then, and she certainly didn't miss them now. They had listened to her first complain about Donald, then, later, plea for help to get out of the marriage. They were of little help. "He's a good provider," they'd said. "Life of the party. Who else would marry you?"

They hadn't broken her. She'd already been broken. Maybe she'd always been. But conversations like that, with Mom Who Didn't Make Meatballs and Dad Who Didn't Give A Shit, had sealed the deal. Her parents had not earned any mourning.

She ran a finger over the masking tape label, remembering exactly when she'd written it. Exactly why she'd written it. Exactly when she'd gotten her hands on what was inside.

She cracked open the lid, which was stubborn from years of closure, and lifted out the bottle. She was sure that what was inside was long expired. Would it still work all these years later? If she had a working computer, she could look up the shelf life of phenytoin and pentobarbital. It had worked wonders providing a humane death for beloved pets at the veterinary clinic back in the day, when she'd been scrubbing floors and mopping up shit and no one took notice of a key missing for five minutes. It had worked wonders providing a not so humane death for non-beloved humans, too. Powerful stuff. Probably spoilt by now. But it couldn't have gone fully dormant after twenty years. It'd probably do something.

Dormant. She'd gone dormant for twenty years. Kinda funny, actually. You and me, bottle — let's see if either of us still works.

Ellen from next door texted. Ryan was home from class, he was eating dinner, how was she feeling, does she need anything, Ryan will come over in thirty minutes, hope you're doing okay!

She checked the time — just shy of six. She texted back, all friendly-like, that anytime would be great and she'd be ready for him.

Mom's Meatballs went back into the freezer.

A knock at the front door. Ryan.

"Hey, Ms. Hawkins," he started. "Mom said it was fine to come right over."

"Of course, dear. Come on upstairs. That's where the computer is. You want a drink or something?"

"I'm good."

She led the way to the office. She pulled up a side chair

while Ryan sat behind the desk, looking things over, then under the desk he went, checking stuff out.

"This is pretty old," he said. "Let me try a few things. Is it not turning on at all?"

She explained that it needed a shove to power up, that it was slow and sometimes made a vibrating sound.

"What do you use it for?" he asked. "Besides your writing."

"Just going online."

"Is it backing up your data okay?"

Who knew? Backups were invisible. She thought about the prompts and alerts the computer had given her over the last few weeks. "Yes. I need what's on there, but it's backing up." Hopefully that was true. "I use it for research, writing of course, and normal things. Email. You know." God, she really was computer illiterate. She could probably make her life a lot easier if she put in the time to learn this stuff.

Ryan spent a few minutes trying a few things, then got the computer to turn on, causing them both to say "Yay!" in unison. But it looked all different. "I got this to boot up in what's called Safe Mode. It's on, but not like it usually is. That's good. Something's definitely wrong, though. I think … I mean, sorry, is it okay if…"

Don't apologize when you've done nothing wrong. Between Ben never growing a pair and Ellen's constant hovering, Ryan was afraid to do anything, especially anything wrong. "What do you need, Ryan?"

"Is it okay if I take the tower with me? I have a few ideas on how to fix this, but I need to take it apart."

Was it okay? All of her books were on that computer. Her research, not that there was a lot of it. The start of the next book. Photos, but not a ton. She had no one to take pictures of. Problem was, without the computer, she wouldn't do any writing.

"Of course. I appreciate the help."

"I promise I won't lose any of your data, Ms. Hawkins. I'll be really careful."

"You are doing me a favor."

Roux.

"One more thing," she added as Ryan disconnected the monitor and keyboard. "What do you know about security cameras?"

"You mean, on the computer, or for your house?"

"House. You know, after the attack…"

"Yeah, that stuff is easy now. It's all wireless. You can look at the camera feeds on your phone or on the computer."

"Do you know of a place I could get one?"

"We get a student discount at the tech store at my school. I'm pretty sure that they carry security cameras. Computers too."

He yanked out his phone and browsed his school's tech store site, showing Jane what he thought might work. The cameras were wireless, easy to install, and she could work it all through her phone and computer, like he said. She hadn't thought about security cameras since the old days. She knew enough to avoid them, but that had been easy since the cameras were easy to spot back then, bulky and intermittent, not omnipresent and tiny like now.

They agreed on five cameras, two to cover the front and back of the house and one each for the basement, first floor, and second floor.

"I'll stop by the store tomorrow between classes," he said. "I'll have to pay for them myself to get the student discount."

"You are so helpful, Ryan." Truly. She wouldn't have

known what to look for herself. "And I'll give you the money upfront."

"You could Venmo me."

She'd heard the word before, but didn't know what it meant. "Now you're making up verbs."

He laughed. "It's a way to send money to each other through a phone."

New world. "Then I guess I don't Venmo. Cash?"

He hesitated. "Sure."

"Wait here."

She had a few hundred left from the withdrawal the other day, but she'd keep that in her purse. She needed to visit her emergency stash.

She cleared the books off of the lowest shelf of the built-in case in the living room, then lifted off the plank and withdrew a shoebox. Fifties and twenties should do. She put the box back, replaced the shelf and books, then went back upstairs to the office. She handed Ryan five hundred dollars.

"This is too much," he said.

"I'm paying you for your time. I couldn't do this by myself. Treat yourself."

He replied with profuse thanks, tinged with apology. Balls. Needed. Now.

He lugged the tower downstairs, promising to be in touch tomorrow or the day after. That'd be fine. She had the itch to write, but she also had the itch to get other important things done. Beachcomber Belle could wait.

With Ryan gone, Jane heated up some leftover pasta for dinner, then headed back up to her office.

The whiteboard mounted behind her desk would work well. She erased her Beachcomber Belle notes — nothing there she couldn't replicate — then, after making sure all the doors were locked and all the shades were still drawn, she got to work.

In one column, she wrote the numbers 1 through 10. That's all she needed. No names, locations, methods. Just the numbers. Each held a story, a story only she knew.

This was all so long ago, like having a decades-old surgery scar on your forearm. You could run your finger over it, feel it, acknowledge it, but the emotions, the pain, from the original incident, those had long passed. You gained objectivity. The lesson? Appreciate that you were still here, and they weren't, because if they were still here, you most likely wouldn't be.

She assumed that Esmir Roux had a high-level snapshot — dates, names, and locations of each murder. So what did he see that she didn't know? What connections was he making that she wasn't?

Searching for info on the Internet without a computer pissed her off. Her phone screen was too small. But she gave it a go and looked up Massachusetts unsolved murders.

Hmm. One site said that for the forty-year period starting in 1980, Massachusetts had almost 10,000 murders, and more than 3,500 of those were unsolved. So it wasn't like there were only ten unsolved murders. Roux could have picked any subset of murders. Why these ten, if he was even looking at the same ten?

Shit. She didn't want to see or hear from Roux again, but she'd have to talk to him, learn what he knew.

Maybe he was looking only at dirtbags who'd been murdered. The ten people represented by these ten numbers certainly fit *that* description. Could you filter murders by dirtbag level?

She pulled up another site, one that listed Massachusetts cold case murders, and scrolled through, peering at the thumbnail images and descriptions.

There were plenty of well-known serial killers from the area, she already knew. You had the most well-known, the Boston Strangler, but that case had been solved a long time ago, although there were still questions from the fringe folks. Albert DeSalvo had killed 13 women in the 1960s. Some said he couldn't have done it alone, or that someone else had committed a share of the killings pinned on DeSalvo.

Then you had the New Bedford Highway Serial Killer — a terrible name — and that was unsolved. Again, all the victims were women. Not relevant here. You had the Cape Cod serial killer, Tony Costa, again decades ago. He had killed four women. No, that wasn't right. She went downstairs to her bookcase and pulled out a book published a few years ago. Right. Costa had probably killed eight women, people thought.

All the victims in these cases were women.

She spun the word "victims" around in her mouth, tasting it. Victims. Death was death, she knew. Murder was murder. But these women taken by these serial killers, she considered them victims. The ten people represented by the ten numbers on the board, she considered them to be ... not victims. She didn't consider herself to be a victim, either — exception made in Dead Donald's case. He'd victimized *her*. Some of the others had, too, but Donald was the nexus. Without him, none of this would have happened.

Maybe.

She continued scrolling through the tiny pictures of murder victims. These were all too recent. Why wasn't Roux focusing on recent murders?

So many of the unsolved murders on the site weren't

like the ten on the board. First, so many were killed by guns. Jane didn't own a gun and had never used a gun, except for when she'd gotten her license to carry. Maybe that was what Roux was looking at? Murders by means other than guns — stabbings, poisonings, asphyxiation. She didn't see a way to sort by method, however.

She turned the phone sideways to make the pictures bigger, then figured out how to navigate through the pages. Could you sort by date? You could. Her heart beat faster. This was getting someplace.

Then she stopped. Should she be doing this on her own phone? Was that information trackable? Add it to the ask-Ryan list. Well, she was already here. She could claim, if anyone ever asked, that she was trying to figure out what Esmir Roux — and he had approached *her*, not the other way around — was talking about. That much was true, maybe true with an asterisk, but true enough. May as well continue.

Her ten victims: nine men and one woman. The years in question: 2000 through 2003. All white, or at least she thought if she had to pick a race, it'd be white. There was no way to sort by race or gender, at least that she could find. But you could filter by date.

Interesting. Seven of her ten were listed on this website. Not Donald. And why not? Maybe these sites weren't exhaustive. There was probably no central database of murder. Just the cases that made it in front of whoever built the site.

But seven out of ten. Not bad.

Her breath caught in excitement as she browsed the seven. "Hello, old friends."

Day 5 (Thursday)

JANE AWOKE FIDGETY. She couldn't write until she got her computer back. Well, she could, but writing out an entire book in longhand? Not how she worked.

She needed to ground herself. She knew where she had to go.

After a quick muffin/banana breakfast and an even quicker shower, she headed out to Truro, a thirty-minute drive up the Cape's thin east peninsula, halfway up the arm of Massachusetts.

She parked in the church's lot. Attending the occasional AA meeting helped keep her steady, even if she never stopped drinking and whatever she talked about, it was never about alcohol. She kept her anonymity by not attending meetings in Port Fletcher, her charming sad little town with a name that didn't even reflect the place's history — there was no evidence that it had ever seen a port. Maybe early descendent of the Pilgrims had high hopes, but who'd build a port in the middle of the Cape, where the bay was so shallow you could walk a half mile out at low tide?

A little distance, a little anonymous socialization, was what she needed, and these meetings gave that to her. You couldn't live your life fully devoid of human connection, even if those connections, however tenuous, were built on lies.

Inside the church meeting room, there was the stereotypical circle of folding chairs, styrofoam coffee cups, and despair. The leader, a gangly thin-haired guy named Mike, looking weary even at this early hour, led them off with a few minutes of inspirational talk that hit home for no one. The group was quiet today. One woman mumbled her way through a few minutes of sharing, and when no one else spoke, Jane stepped up.

"Hi, I'm Jane." A tired sounding "Hi, Jane" from the group. "It's been, let's see, almost twenty years since my last, well, you know." A few chuckles. If only they really knew.

"I've worked hard to keep my problems in my past," she continued. "I'm not proud of my past, I don't like talking about my past. I don't like talking at all, actually. This is probably the most I'll talk to anyone this week."

A few more eyes looked at her instead of the floor. "I recognize my past, but I don't honor it. I've tamped it down. Moved forward. I don't look back. It's hard work. I know what's following me. But this week, something changed. My past is walking with me, not my choice, and I don't like it. I don't need my past to be a partner walking with me. What I need is for the past to be left where it is. Dead and buried."

All eyes on her now. "I'm tempted this week. I feel the pull. The ache. One more taste. To remember. To feel that response, a whole-body response, mind and matter. To feel alive again. For me, these last twenty years have been the best twenty years of my life. I've found myself. But I haven't found joy. I've been flat, but I haven't been bad. I haven't strayed.

"And these last twenty years have also been my worst. I'd like to say that everything changed since the last time, that I'm happy as a clam, that the sunshine chased away all the shadows and I sleep in peace every night knowing my demons are at rest. I wish I could say that. I don't need to look behind my shoulder, because I know what's keeping pace back there. I know what I'll see. Who I'll see. Me. From back then. A miserable, scared, ruinous, dangerous woman. But also a woman so much more alive than the woman before you today."

She paused, the room silent, before continuing. "Like all of you, I'm a secret keeper. We keep our secrets here. We've all kept, or tried to keep, heavier secrets. I have. I'm the queen of secret keeping, the undisputed champ. I'd rather die than tell my whole truth. I don't know what that makes me. A good person, a bad person. Someone to be envied. Someone to be pitied. I've thought about it a lot. I don't think it makes me anything other than a *person*. A person who doesn't want to look back, who's afraid to look forward, but who keeps moving anyway. For too long, I've been standing still. If change is coming, then I'll greet it at the front door, usher it in, and kick it between the legs if it gets too handsy."

Laughter. "I'll use this week to find myself. Hopefully I won't give in to temptation. Hopefully I'll keep my streak going." Ferrier was an exception. She hadn't planned for him, so he didn't count. "And if not … you all know, it's not the end of the world. It just means that the next day, I have to get up and continue doing the work. Pushing forward. Keeping the past in the past."

Jane sat through the other monologues, nodding but not really listening, her thoughts consumed with people she currently hated. That fucking Esmir Roux. That fucking Jonas Ferrier. The newest addition: that fucking Yip Yothers for leading Bettina down the path of emotional collapse. Keeping those demons at bay would be hard work. So: should she try, or should she unleash them?

At the meeting's end, she dropped her cup of cold coffee into the oversized trash barrel, said a few "Thank you for what you said" to people whose words she hadn't listened to, and went outside.

From behind her came, "Jane?" Again with people talking from behind her. She needed to watch her back more carefully.

A bald guy, maybe 45, with a goatee and a three-day beard, wearing boots and jeans and a worn jacket, looking fit and outdoorsy like he worked on a commercial fishing boat, leaned against the church wall, smoking a cigarette. He'd not talked inside during the meeting. Jane strode over when she didn't get immediate Ferrier or Roux vibes from the guy (although she'd stay alert for them).

"Yes, I'm Jane."

"Scottie." He took a final drag of his cigarette, then crushed it out. "Just wanted to say, what you said in there, it hit home for me." He looked away, focused on something distant. Maybe the horizon. "The past." His New England accent was thick, like he'd been born in the sands of the Cape and never left.

"The past," she echoed.

"I've been coming here for a few months now, every week. I've seen you a few times."

She studied the lines in his face and saw that they were carved from sadness. He might be a lot younger than forty-five. Hard to tell with those guys who spend their days in the sun and the salt and the wind anyway, but sadness is what really ages a person.

"These meetings help," he continued. "Don't know what'll happen if I miss a week, if I don't try each day." He chuckled. "Actually, I do know. I'll get shitfaced. Lose my job. Don't want to go back to that life."

He offered her a cigarette. She accepted. He lit her up, took a second for himself, and she leaned against the wall to his left as they smoked.

"The pull can be powerful," she said. The pull she was talking about was much more powerful than drinking, than any drug. But let him think she was talking about booze.

"I've lost a lot," he said. "Nearly lost everything, including my daughter." He pronounced it *DAW-duh*, like all good Massachusetts people do. "But what you said, it's made me think. Maybe I can't be so disappointed in myself if I slip. It's not starting over. It's all about moving forward even if you fuck up."

"I get the good that these groups do." She took a deep drag, then blew out a stream of smoke. "Everyone's journey is different, and if we fuck up, we fuck up. I've fucked up. Many times. But I never start over from day one when I do fuck up. If I did the chip thing, say 20 years, and I had one bad day, I'd still carry that motherfucker proudly in my pocket. Twenty years good, one day bad. Forget the bad day. Don't start over. Accept the bad day and keep moving."

Scott gave her an odd look. She couldn't tell if it was bemusement or disgust. "So to you, all the work here to get through each day, leading to each week, each month, each year, you can mess up for a day and not start over? Pretend it never happened?"

"That's what works for me, Scottie. Not saying it should work for everybody."

He looked to the horizon. "I'm gonna think about that. Think about how I can keep moving forward and feel better about myself, maybe not worry so much about staying perfect."

Then he met her gaze, looking like he had more to say but wasn't sure if he should say it.

She smiled. "Glad I met you, Scottie." She was in no mood to make a new friend, and from Scottie's gaze, he wanted a new friend at the least.

He smiled back. "I was thinking, I don't start work until the afternoon, if you wanna talk more, get some better coffee than they have here…"

Her phone buzzed before she could respond. She held up a finger as she checked. A text from Roux. *We need to meet. I have important information for you.*

She didn't need a reclamation project, had no interest in dating, even casually. Also, she might have just destroyed his carefully trod path to sobriety. Well, what worked for her, worked for her. No guarantee it would work for anyone else.

What had she said in the meeting, anyway? *Pushing forward. Keep the past in the past.* Best to take her own advice.

"Maybe next time," she said, then gave his arm a squeeze, a longer than normal one since he looked so disappointed. They exchanged numbers anyway, then she added, "Gotta go. My past is calling."

She took a last drag from the cigarette and flicked the butt onto the parking lot as she walked to her car. Once inside, she called Roux.

"Mr. Roux," she said when he answered. "You're getting to be a daily habit. And a bad habit."

"Jane, I've got some important information for you." He sounded smug. "We need to talk. In person."

"What is this about?"

"It's about your husband's murder. Too long to discuss

over the phone. I'm driving to the Cape. You tell me where to meet, I'll meet you there."

"We aren't partners, Roux. We aren't anything. Maybe I'm not using the right words. I don't want daily updates on your life. Leave my past in my past."

"You'll want to hear this. I promise. It will change everything."

She recalled her whiteboard exercise. She needed to know what he knew. Too bad she had to keep seeing him in person to do so.

"Fine."

She gave him directions to a public beach in Brewster, a town bordering Port Fletcher, unrelated to Brewster Gardens in Plymouth. So much of New England had the same names for entirely different places. She told him where to park and that she'd be waiting for him, then hung up and drove off.

Thirty minutes later, she was in the lot nestled at the end of a pretty residential street. No other cars. Hopefully she wouldn't get carjacked again. The beaches here were delightful, especially off-season when the tourists were away. Today was partly cloudy, the wind alternating between off-shore and on-shore, typical Cape air moving randomly, undecided if it was warm or cold or which direction it should blow.

She slipped off her shoes and carried them as she walked to the shoreline, the cold sand squishing beneath her toes. High tide, with small waves typical for a north-facing Cape beach. From here, on clear days, you could look twenty or so miles across the bay to the north and see Pilgrim Monument in Provincetown, usually a dark line jutting out of the otherwise flat horizon. But not today. The ocean, a dark gray-blue, extended seamlessly into the sky.

What could Roux say that would "change everything"? If he knew anything, he could trap her. She half expected to turn and find a line of police cars rocketing down the street, penning her in, forcing her into the ocean to escape.

Some locals strolled past on the beach, a few walking their dogs, which were allowed on the beach off-season, and an elderly couple pacing fast, probably getting in their steps, the same route every day, weather be damned.

The cold sand felt good on her feet. The cold air felt good on her face. She loved this time of year, the offseason when winter had left but summer hadn't arrived. The Cape would soon bloom into heat and people and activity. This was the calm before the storm.

She walked back toward her car and saw Roux pull into a spot next to her car. He rolled down the window of his black Acura, beckoning her over. She got into the passenger seat.

"Nice day for the beach," he said. Facetious? He looked down at her feet. "You've got sand all over your feet."

She knocked her feet against the floor mat, then wiped the top of each foot with her hand. "Now I don't."

He blinked. "Is there a bathroom I could use? Long drive."

"It's off season." She indicated the bushes bordering the lot. "There's your bathroom."

"Then I'll hold it." He paused. Considering something? What?

"You asked me here, Mr. Roux. Get on with it."

"Sorry." This was not yesterday's confident Roux. Or Monday's pushy, smarmy Roux. This was a new Roux. So what had changed?

He started again. "Did you see the news?"

She didn't follow the news all that closely. Most of it didn't apply to her. Why waste the time? "I did not."

"Ah." Now he seemed pleased. Or was that really pleasure? A little disappointment at first? "Then I can be the first to tell you. There have been some new murders."

"It's Massachusetts. People hate other people here, like in every state. It happens."

"Agreed. Otherwise, I wouldn't have a job."

She didn't give him the satisfaction of answering such a stupid response. But she would give him no more than thirty seconds to get to the point before she left.

"Anyway," he continued, "you know those ten murders I've talked about? The unsolved ones?"

"Not specifically, except for Donald's, but you did mention ten unsolved murders. Several times." She wouldn't give him anything except annoyance.

Excitement took over his face. He seemed almost giddy. "In the last week, there have been three particular new murders in the state. Each unsolved. Each seemingly unrelated. But here's the kicker — those ten murders from before? These new three are copycats of the first three of those original ten. Including the murder of your husband Donald."

She gasped. Not what she was expecting. She immediately hated herself for giving him the satisfaction, for not holding back her emotion.

But her surprise was valid. Copycats? Time to cover. She put a hand to her mouth. "Those poor, poor people." Then she forced a frown. "Three ... are you saying that someone is mimicking old murders?"

"I am." He sounded too proud. "The police haven't connected the past kills and the new kills. Yet. The locations aren't exact, of course, not to the house level. That would make connections easy. And the method for each is close. Not exact to the old murders, but close enough. I told you that this would change everything."

He was right about that. Maybe. He hadn't pointed a finger at her. Actually, he hadn't ever said he suspected her. Or had he? She thought back to their meetings. The book event, the parking lot after, and the meeting in Plymouth. He hadn't said much of anything about these ten old unsolved murders, the only specific being that Donald's murder was one of them. She already knew all about *that* murder.

But what he *had* done so far is show a lot of curiosity about her, about Donald's murder. Was he pestering the families of the other murder victims this much?

Time to play stupid and find out what he knows.

"I'm not sure I'm following you. You say that there are ten old murders you think you can tie together. And three new murders that are copycats of the first three of those ten. And one of them is Donald's murder?"

She needed some hysterics. Problem was, she couldn't cry on command. She rarely cried when she was sad. The more raw the emotion needed, the more fake it looked when she tried to … fake it.

She bent forward, as if in the throes of emotion, gripping her legs. She discreetly clutched her lower leg near the bare foot and swiped up, hoping she'd feel some sand. She did. She then buried her face in her hands while opening her eyes wide, pressing the sand and her palm flesh against her eyeballs. The pain was cathartic.

She withdrew her face and turned to Roux, feeling hot tears roll down her cheeks. "Are you saying … that there's been a murder at my house?"

Through her fake-globby eyes, Roux looked like he had to assemble an Ikea dresser without the instructions, his mouth open, seemingly unsure of what to do. "No," he stammered, "not at … no. There was a murder in Port Fletcher, which is why I'm here."

Jane sniffled, not having to fake it with sand in her eyes. She'd taken it too far. Now her nose was running. "I don't know what to … and the other murders…"

"One was in Wareham, the other in Orleans. All three in the last week or so. The Port Fletcher one was late last night."

Maybe she should check the news more often. Also, having no real social circle meant that no one would gossip to her unless she was standing in front of them. Except for Ellen. When Ellen got on a tear, she divulged everything.

The locations … Grrr. The locations were correct. Someone *was* mimicking old murders.

Her murders.

She told him she needed a moment, that this was too shocking to take in all at once.

Really, she needed a minute to think.

And double really, for maybe three seconds, she thought about killing Roux, right here. But that wouldn't end the copycat murders. It wouldn't do anything except get her caught. Plus there was no real reason to kill him that she could think of.

She'd worked so hard to bury what it felt like to kill. Then Jonas Ferrier had to give in to *his* demons. Now Roux — no, he was just the message bearer — now *someone* had dug up the coffin she'd buried those feelings in, was cackling while they wiped away the dirt on top, grinning as they raised the lid…

Screw this.

After enough time passed where she could have reasonably composed herself, she said, "This is painful, Mr. Roux. Nearly too painful to continue. But tell me. Tell me about these new murders and why you think they're connected to the past murders."

"The first recent murder was in Wareham," Roux started. The victim, a fifty-three-year-old divorced woman, had been poisoned in her duplex ten days ago.

She nodded along as he spoke, but she didn't care about the rest of the details.

The location was right. Wareham, over the bridge and on the mainland, a blue-collar southeastern Massachusetts town of maybe 25,000. Lots of drugs, lots of cranberries. Lots of dirtbags.

The poisoning was correct. The gender wasn't. The first victim, back in 2000, had been a man.

RICHARD EIDENBERG. An asshole's asshole. A drinking buddy of Donald's. He mistreated his dog. That was bad enough, and for Jane, more than enough to warrant murder. But there was more. He knocked his wife around — she was always sporting a black eye and must have been incredibly clumsy to have fallen down the stairs or hit her face on an open cabinet door so many times. He was a fat slob with no redeeming value, unless you counted the ability to drive people from a room due to his body odor.

Eidenberg had egged Donald on, told him that he needed to control his wife better. Donald hadn't needed the extra urging.

There were times, she thought as Roux droned on, that she hated who she'd been far more than she hated who she'd become. She didn't think of herself as a victim. If she were caught, she wouldn't play that card. She'd own up. But she also knew she wouldn't be caught.

Eidenberg hadn't met his maker because he smelled or

because he slapped around his wife. There had been another reason.

One November night in 2000, back when Jane was mired in a years-long depression for giving up her daughter, every day like staring into a black tunnel with no way to go back and no reason to go ahead, dirtbag Richard "Richie" Eidenberg had been over, sitting out back of their house, the same house she lived in now, he and Donald going through a case of cheap beer like it was water for a castaway on a desert island. Donald had been growing angrier at Jane, not that he'd ever been a bastion of patience since he'd forced Jane to give up Kate, and Richard would have none of it. Control your woman, he'd say, or something like that, only far less eloquent. Control your woman. Show her that you're the boss.

She'd been seething, mad at herself for staying, mad at Donald for existing, shamed beyond shame for enduring what Donald had done to her, and heartbroken for giving up Kate. She had no friends to call, no family for support. She'd been alone. And trapped.

The Jane of today, as she liked to think of herself, she'd never have let things get close to being what they'd been. But she also knew that she'd never be Jane of Today without having gone through being Jane of the Past.

Anyway, she'd been seething, listening to the two of them as they smoked and drank and belched in the back yard, her crouching in the bathroom under the open window, eavesdropping because she had nothing else to do, the room dark, every heartbeat a change from fear to anger to sadness, letting her emotions trap her and feeling so, so not proud of that.

She thought she'd been careful. She thought they couldn't hear her, that they didn't know she was listening to them. Maybe they'd heard her crying, although like now, she hadn't been a crier back then.

Now Donald, he already thought of himself as the boss. Her boss. Through his drunkenness, he cut Richard off, said he'd show him, that he'd made sure to mark Jane as his property. Eidenberg laughed it off, not realizing that Donald was being literal.

She heard them get up, heard them come into the house, and realized she was trapped, literally now, and maybe if she'd run, maybe if she'd done anything except cower, then she wouldn't be sitting in this car with Roux today. But what would the alternative have been? Stay with Donald?

Water under the bridge at this point.

So yes, she hadn't been proud of it, but she had cowered. Frozen. Then the lights snapped on, Donald's rough hands pulling her up, her screaming, the smell of his dangling Winston and the beer on his breath, and Richard, behind Donald, looking amused, bored, and excited all at once, Donald dragging her, literally dragging her, into the living room, throwing her on the couch, yanking down her pants.

Pointing at the cigarette burns on her ass.

"I marked her, the dumb bitch," he said. Proud. He was a man who could control his woman, after all. "You want a turn?" He handed Richard his lit cigarette.

"I'll kill you!" she screamed, but it was muffled because her face was buried in a couch cushion. The next scream was from the pain.

She hadn't killed Richard Eidenberg for vengeance. She was no Caped Crusader. But that cigarette, that fire, broke something inside her.

The "I'll kill you!" was for them both. For Donald, because in that moment, she knew it was her only way to truly escape. And for Richard, because if she was going to kill Donald, she needed to get it right.

She needed to practice.

A few weeks later, she was in Wareham, at the Twisted Pickle, a crappy dive bar that looked and smelled like every crappy dive bar. Crappy clientele, crappy parking lot, crappy beer, crappy music. Even the sign was crappy, a tipsy-looking cartoon pickle downing a drink, its googly eyes a clear indication that this was not the pickle's first drink of the night.

Donald, and by association Richard, were cheap. They'd cozy up to the bar, playing cards, and every hour they'd take turns hitting the men's room and going outside for a smoke, solo, the other watching their stools in case someone tried to steal their beer, which of course had never happened. They also carried their cards out with them, because they each knew the other was an inveterate cheater.

The first time Richard had come out, night had long fallen. Jane had taken a few steps forward, still cloaked in darkness from her hiding spot near a dumpster. This was the moment, she'd thought. But a waitress had joined Richard, her smoke break timing giving the asshole at least another hour of life. Jane had retreated back to the shadows, anger replacing fear. Now they were wasting *her* time.

An hour later, Donald had come out, leaned against the side of the building, smoked, crushed it out, and took a leak against the wall. In the dim light, he looked skeletal, which was odd, she'd thought, considering he'd gone flabby. She shot him a silent middle finger from the dark.

As Donald left, she'd crept to the side of the bar. The shadows would keep her hidden, unless Richard decided to circle the building. Unlikely. Like Donald, he was a creature of habit and shunned extra steps. Emphasis on creature.

Richard came out as expected, his turn to smoke, coming around the side of the building to just about where Donald had been. No other voices that she could hear, just the click of his lighter. Donald wouldn't be coming out. Someone had to guard their Budweisers, although who'd steal half a draft of straw-colored, straw-tasting swill from a couple of lowlifes like Donald and Richard was a question best left unasked and unanswered.

Richard was a fast smoker, starting and finishing a cigarette in about four minutes.

Plenty of time.

Now was the time.

She'd planned on creeping over. Fuck that. She walked confidently. He wasn't looking, didn't seem to hear her footsteps until she was almost on top of him.

He turned, squinting. In one hand, he held his playing cards. Of course. Don't want Donald to cheat. "Jane?"

"Hey, Richard." She stood in front of him, smiled, a big one, reached a hand to his face, his look of confusion perfect. Be confused in your last moments, Richard. Did you not see this coming?

She palmed his cheek with her gloved left hand. Then she drove the syringe into his neck, just under his jawline, angled upward, pushing the plunger down.

He drove his arms up, knocking her back, his cigarette flying to the side, along with the playing cards, the syringe sticking out of his neck like a new appendage. He slapped at it but missed, turned a full circle, said something she couldn't understand, then fell forward, cracking his forehead on the wall. He leaned there for a moment, enough time for her to take out the syringe, bend down and pocket one of the fallen cards, and run to the dumpster. She'd parked next door, in the lot of an auto parts place closed for the night. She needed to beat Donald home.

Once she got to her car, she bent over, feeling sick, and retched, but nothing came out. She peeled out of the parking lot, heading for the highway and the bridge, traffic light, dark night, and the nausea cleared. She felt so, so right.

That had been the unexpected part. Feeling right. She felt lighter, woozy but in a good way, like after a strong orgasm.

She could do this. And it had felt fantastic.

"THE SECOND WAS IN ORLEANS," Roux said. "A landscaper, in his thirties, found bludgeoned five days ago."

Two for two. Orleans was correct, bludgeoning was correct, male was correct.

Actually, "bludgeoning" seemed too ostentatious a word. When she thought of bludgeoning, the act connoted, for her, the use of something specific and formal from an Agatha Christie novel — a candelabra perhaps, or a statuette. Maybe a vintage paperweight.

The crowbar she'd used didn't seem like a bludgeoning tool.

Sal Lomasio. February, 2001, an icy night. Donald had become less physical and more sullen after Richard had been murdered. Maybe it was the interruption to his drinking and urination routine. Jane hadn't gone to the funeral. The police had grilled Donald, him being the last person to see Richard alive — second to last person, she'd silently corrected — but it seemed like it was just one of those things, maybe a robbery gone wrong. Jane had already retreated from devouring the news, figuring the less she knew, the more she could deny knowing and maybe come across as truthful. The cops had asked her a few perfunctory questions when they'd followed up with Donald. She knew of him, she'd said. He'd been over. She didn't really know him. She'd shown no grief, because there was no grief for her to give.

She'd gotten away with it. But she needed to be sure. She gave in to the need for one more practice kill. Gave in to the need to feel *that* again.

She'd read once that most serial killers don't arrive on the scene fully formed. They experiment. They build their way up. Stereotypically, this meant animal cruelty, an escalation of violence. Baby steps, but always following a straight line.

She'd never hurt an animal, wasps excepted. She had no interest in taking baby steps or walking in a straight line. She'd arrive fully formed.

Back to Sal Lomasio. He was an area child abuser, at least according to the rumors. A Level II sex offender, which was no rumor. He'd brought a cat to the vet clinic where she'd worked part-time cleaning floors and restocking supplies, including the end-of-life cocktail she'd used on Richard Eidenberg. Whispers among the staff. Some said that they'd heard from a friend of a friend of a friend that he'd bragged about his predilections. She knew that the rumor tree was often wrong, but didn't all rumors start with a kernel of truth?

Ear to the ground. She spent some time in the local library, honing her research skills, looking at microfiched newspapers and public information. Arrests, sentencing, delays, lawyers. Typical Massachusetts red tape.

She needed to know. She forced herself to have a conversation with the man in a local park, feeling like she was on the set of a hackneyed TV crime drama — the pedo in the park, literally licking his lips as his eyes darted, no lust in his eyes for her, but lust in eyes for something. Maybe those kids on the swings. Or maybe their mothers.

She decided. If she had to practice on someone, Sal Lomasio was as good a choice as anyone.

He had been ... easy. A late-night knock on his door. A package left at the foot of his stairs, bringing him outside. A hedge for her to hide behind. A crowbar to the neck, a second blow to the back of his skull as he was hunched over, half dead already. A soundless kill. He hadn't had time to say a word. She yanked the lace from his sneaker as a souvenir. It had been pink. She'd actually strolled back to her car, driven back to Port Fletcher, past her empty house — Donald had taken to working second shift — to a Burger King parking lot to dispose of the crowbar and to think.

The surprising thing to her wasn't what she felt, but what she hadn't felt — guilt fear, remorse. What she had felt was empty, but not drained. More like blank. Objective. Mission accomplished.

She knew that she'd crossed a line. Had crossed it when she'd decided about Richard. She'd moved from beaten, timid wife to killer in plain sight. No turning back from that. She'd also felt lighter, focused. She'd started tooling around with writing, some short stories, some ideas for longer stuff, the plots all focused on crimes that needed solving.

Later, she felt focused. Energized. But not swallowed up by the feeling. Another part of her, the rational part, threw its hands in the air and said that there's no going back, you serial killer, so if you're going to do this, do it well. Don't make mistakes.

That consumed her. The fear that she'd fucked up. Been seen. Left something behind.

She hadn't. No one talked to her about Sal Lomasio. If someone had, maybe they'd wonder why she'd seemed so … alive.

~

"AND THE THIRD was in Port Fletcher. Last night. A retired plastic surgeon. Stabbed in his house. Three times. Probably incapacitated before that with some drug."

No use dredging up the play-by-play of Donald's murder. She'd done that hundreds of times. It used to bring her euphoria. Now she thought of it as her divorce.

Roux continued. "He was found in his house by a neighbor who saw the open front door." He pulled out his reporter's notebook and told her the address. She didn't recognize the street. Roux didn't have a name for the victim.

She hoped she'd been keeping an interested or blank face while he'd recited details of the new murders and while she'd been stewing in her own memories.

"Horrible," she said. "No matter who it was. I hope I don't know the person, not that that matters, I guess. So close to home … maybe I should get back, see if there's anything I can do to help the family."

Roux furrowed his brows. "Don't you see?" He let out a sigh. Frustration? "These kills, they're copycats. All three of them. Including that of your husband." He paused, maybe waiting for her to join in his enthusiasm. When she didn't, he added, "This will be a huge story."

For him.

She wiped the last of her sand-induced tears away, then chose her words carefully. "Thank you, Mr. Roux, for filling me in. I don't know what to make of all this. It's bringing up some very old and very raw emotions. I don't know who'd do something like this. I need some time alone. I feel so, so badly for those whose loved ones have lost their lives."

Not really.

Roux looked at her closely, like he was searching her face for something she didn't know was lost. Then she had a thought.

"You say these are copycat murders," she said. "The original killer was never caught, and that's *if* all those old murders were done by the same person. Maybe the original killer is back, replicating their own kills."

"I don't think so," he said, shaking his head and looking self-satisfied. "That wouldn't make sense."

"It would make as much sense as someone copycatting old murders that no one besides you seems to have connected."

A sly smile crept across his face. "Fair point. I have my reasons for the copycat theory. I'm not ready to share them. I'm still working things through." He sat back, smug, then continued. "Jane, you don't know me. You don't like me. I get that. And you haven't listened to my podcast, so you don't know this: I'm really good at investigating. This isn't just my passion. It's my calling. I want a murderer brought to justice."

"Don't you mean two murderers? The old one, and the new one?"

Something dark crossed his face for a moment. "Two murderers. I want everyone who killed without reason brought to justice."

And you want to break the story. Lead the charge.

"Thanks for the meeting." She clapped her shoes together, adding more sand to the mix on his mat, then slipped them on. "I've got to get going."

SHE DROVE with the windows down, needing the air after meeting with Roux. Thinking.

Those were her murders. How had someone tied them together? For one, they weren't gunshot victims. That's how most murderers dispatched their victims, so maybe these murders stuck out. Gun murders were quick. Efficient. But loud. She'd thought about that last night. Would that be enough to tie the murders together? Doubtful. More than doubtful. No.

Couple that with the proximity. Draw a circle around, say, Port Fletcher, and all of her kills were within, say, thirty miles in any direction. That'd be close to 3,000 square miles, but much of that, most of that actually, was ocean. The Cape was skinny. So maybe 1,000 square miles of land. Unless she'd killed on a boat, which she hadn't.

Maybe Roux was onto something. That would be unfortunate.

She angled through Port Fletcher, finding the street of the murder. The head of the road was taped off, police cars preventing anyone from leaving or entering. It looked like the murder house was a biggish Colonial, white with black shutters and manicured grounds, about four houses down on the left. She idled at the cross street and watched people walking in the house, walking out, taking pictures, carrying evidence bags, chatting. No ambulance, no sirens. Peaceful. Now.

Until someone knocked on her passenger side window, startling her into accidentally pressing down on the SUV's horn.

Perez. She indicated that Jane should roll down the window.

"Ms. Hawkins," Perez said, leaning in. "Are you lost?"

"I … heard about what happened here on the news. I didn't know him, but it's such a shame. And so close to home. The news said there'd been a stabbing here. And in the same town, the same way, as … my husband … I was curious."

"Or morbid," Perez added. The detective's dark eyes narrowed. Suspicious. Of her?

"I…" Talk less. Listen more. She needed to stick to that rule. She shut up.

"Go home, Ms. Hawkins," Perez said slowly. "Right now."

BACK HOME, she downed a shot of bourbon, then paced the first floor. The house was quiet, and normally she loved that. But now, the hum of the fridge, the ticking of a clock … they were deafeningly loud, as if everything in the house was chanting, "You are a lonely, widowed serial killer, and you'll die alone here."

Fuck you, house.

Rigsby would have helped. Dogs made a house a home. She felt the twinge of regret, for not deciding about the dog sooner, for not having connections to any other living creature. For not trying harder with Kate. Not that Kate herself wanted to try.

Although whatever Perez had said to the press had worked. Two days in, and no reporters or TV cameras had showed up outside her house, begging for a shot or a story. Perez deserved a medal for keeping away that kind of companionship.

She turned on the radio, a jazz station to drown out the house's chanting. She had lots to think about.

Three new murders, echoing three past murders. One right here in Port Fletcher.

Esmir Roux calling her daily, and her giving in and meeting him. Every time, he delivered bad news, but it was news she needed to hear. Things were so much better when they were left buried. Now it was like the sea was dragging her into the deep by her legs, her fingers digging into the sand in a failed attempt to prevent it.

She wasn't going to drown. Not after all this time.

And she couldn't even write her Beachcomber Belle book as a diversion. No computer. Ryan was a busy college kid, and it had been less than 24 hours, but still, that wrinkle needed to get ironed out.

Things could come to a head. She'd do whatever it took to protect her past, her secrets. But she was woefully out of practice.

And out of shape.

She decided to change into workout clothes, which she didn't own, so that meant a tee shirt and stained sweatpants she found in the corner of her closet, and sneakers, then she ponytailed her hair. Five minutes until noon. She could work out for an hour, then shower and treat herself to lunch out, then take the afternoon to think, to calm. A good plan.

Stretching, sit-ups, hand weights. Easy. She could go for an hour.

Ten minutes in, covered in sweat and annoyance and a complete lack of motivation, she gave up and flopped on the couch with a cigarette. Woefully out of practice indeed.

The doorbell. She was not dressed for visitors.

She peered through the peephole. Perez. Holding a bag.

This day was going downhill but fast. She let the detective in.

"Glad to see you took my advice and came home," Perez said as she entered, Jane following. The detective sniffed. "You smoke?"

"Only after I kill a man in a parking lot."

"Hard habit to break."

Most of them are. The good ones, anyway. She assumed Perez meant the smoking, not the killing.

"Ignore my workout clothes," Jane said as Perez eyed the ratty sweats. "I need to get back in shape."

She led the detective to the kitchen, where they sat, Perez doing her detective thing and taking in her surroundings.

Perez indicated the bag. "For you. Courtesy of Knead. I brought two things. This is the first. And the best."

Hardly know you, and you're already bringing me gifts. Jane opened the bag, which contained a small box, which contained a small cake, pink frosting, no inscription.

"A 'hope you're doing okay after you killed a guy in a parking lot' offering," Perez said with a hint of a smile.

"Thank you, Detective."

"I'm assuming you can eat it. I hope you aren't gluten-free, sugar-free, or pink-free."

Jane laughed. "I appreciate it. A piece for each? I've got coffee on."

They dug into the cake and coffee, both of which were delicious, neither talking at first. A prelude.

Perez set her fork down halfway through her piece. "The second thing. I also bring a warning."

Jane set her fork down. Interesting. "A warning."

Perez took a swig of coffee, then leaned back. "I looked up your husband's murder. Two days ago. Not this morning. Yes, it's similar."

This didn't sound like a warning. Jane eased a little inside.

Perez continued. "I won't share details of the new murder. That's the warning."

She paused, strong eye contact. Jane held her gaze. No warning in there she could see.

Perez sighed. "There were no news reports, Jane. The press knew nothing about that murder. I made sure of it. Yet you showed up there and said that you heard about it on the news. A murder similar to your husband's murder over twenty years ago. An unsolved murder. You knew that he'd been stabbed before almost anyone did. How?"

Again with the eye contact. This woman could stare down a tree until it burst into flames.

Hmm. Her addled senior citizen persona wouldn't work. Grieving widow? Perez had already seen through that.

May as well default to the truth, or at least some truth. "I lied about the news, Detective. Someone told me about the murder. This morning. As soon as I heard, I drove over. I don't know why. Just felt I had to. Needed to."

Perez narrowed her eyes. "Not good form to lie to a detective. Is your friend a cop? Because cops and EMTs and one neighbor are the only ones who could have told you."

Her heart squeezed like it was caught in a vise. How to step aside gracefully here?

"The … person who told me about this isn't a friend. Isn't a cop. Isn't an EMT or a neighbor."

Not enough for Perez, who waited for her to continue, and when Jane didn't, the detective pounced. "If the station has a leak, I need to know about it. I'm so sick of this shit. People who don't need to know about things shouldn't know about things. And here I was, bringing you a good-will cake."

Jane's turn to sigh. "There's this podcaster, Esmir

102

Roux." Perez grimaced. At the name? Or the occupation? "He approached me at my book event the other night, told me he was working on a series of episodes about unsolved murders. He mentioned Donald's murder. Yesterday, he wanted to meet, and we did, and he told me that he thinks these old murders he's investigating were committed by the same person. Today, he insisted that we meet again, and he said that there were new murders copying the old ones. He's the one who told me about the murder here. He gave me the address."

Too much? The rule about talk less, shut up more seemed to not apply here. She'd dug the hole — now she needed to wriggle out of it.

Perez had held onto her grimace through Jane's spiel, her compact body tightening. "I know Esmir Roux. Well, know of him. He's a pain in the ass. And obviously he's got friends in the wrong places if he knew about that murder so soon."

"That's all I know. He drove down to the Cape this morning, so he must have heard about it early. When did the murder occur?"

Perez shook her head. "Not telling you that. What else did he say?"

"That the victim had been stabbed three times, like Donald. That's why he was so insistent to meet me. He also said that maybe there were drugs involved. To knock the victim out. Incapacitate, he put it."

"Well, shit. No one was supposed to know that." Perez loosened up, shaking her head. She held up her empty coffee mug. "I'm going to need a refill. And one of your cigarettes."

They moved outside, sitting side by side on the stoop, finishing their coffee and smoking. Perez gazed at her cigarette. "Been a long time since I had one of these. Don't want to start riding the smoking train again. But this situation…" She flicked her ash. "This Roux, I'll tell him to leave you alone if you want. You don't need to get dragged into this."

Dragged *back* into this. "I can handle Roux. I just don't understand what's going on. Who would do this?"

"Don't know. For this murder, I have the how, the where, the when, but no idea about the why. It's early. Something will turn up. We'll get camera footage from any houses. There are some street cameras in Port Fletcher, and most people don't know where they are. It's a connected world now. Hard to get away with things." One of the reasons Jane had stopped killing. All those cameras.

"We're also, discreetly, taking pictures and video of the people who showed up," Perez continued. "You've probably heard that sometimes the killer shows up at the scene. You never know."

Jane had heard that. Actually, Beachcomber Belle was very aware of that. She'd caught a few bad guys and gals by combing through crowd footage. Killers inserting themselves into the scene? Or worse, into the investigation? A rookie move, Jane knew.

She said to Perez, "I'm sorry about lying earlier. In the car. I was flustered. I wasn't thinking clearly. Don't look at the street cameras — I drove there way too fast."

Perez laughed, then crushed out her cigarette. Jane indicated she could leave the butt on the ground. "Thanks for letting me bum one," Perez said. "You're a bad influence."

If you only knew.

Perez continued. "Gonna be a complicated day. Murder isn't something that happens here. At least, not very often. I'm already getting pressure to solve this, and fast. Tourist season is coming up."

The detective turned to Jane. "You have a license to carry." A statement, not a question. Perez was good at those. She'd know if Jane had a gun or a license. No use lying. No need to, either.

"I do. I needed to understand the process for one of my books, so I went ahead and got it. I don't own a gun. I took my safety course. I didn't enjoy it. But I needed to understand it. I needed to feel what it was like to shoot."

"And how did it feel to shoot?"

"Scary." Which was true. "And thrilling." Also true. "But I haven't shot a gun since my training."

Perez nodded. "Do you feel safe here?"

She did. She felt even safer after her purchases the other day. But a gun in the house? She'd rather have a dog. "I don't know, Detective. I don't think I need one."

"It might make you feel safe. Safer. I'm not going ageist or sexist here, but you're a widow, living alone, and a scumbag podcaster is hounding you, and another scumbag just murdered an innocent man — I'm going with innocent, I don't know that much about him yet, he could be a scumbag himself — in a way that could — *could* — be copying your husband's murder. Think about it."

Perez's phone pinged, and she took it out. "Gotta go. Back to the scene. You know Trigger City?"

Jane nodded. She'd driven past it plenty of times but hadn't been inside. A firearms retailer and gun range in Hyannis.

"You ask for Boss. Tell him I sent you. He'll cut you a deal, won't sell you any crap. If you're interested."

"I appreciate it. And thank you, Detective. For the talk. And for the cake."

Perez put down her mug, then stood. "You are welcome. I always have time for cake."

~

JANE WENT BACK INSIDE, placed the mugs in the sink, bundled up the remains of the cake, then slammed her hands on the table. "Fuck!"

She liked Perez, but liked her better at arms' length.

She hated Esmir Roux.

She called him. "You're an asshole," she said when he picked up.

"Jane Hawkins," he replied. "Long time, no talk."

She pictured kneeling on his chest, then taking her coffee spoon and plucking out his eyeball. "I went to the murder scene."

"I didn't ask you to do that. I only gave you the address."

And there goes the other eye. "How did you know about the murder? A detective stopped me, asked me why I was there. I told them I'd heard about it on the news. But there was no news. Not yet. I felt like an idiot, having to lie."

"Maybe you're not a good liar. Besides, I didn't say I heard about the murder on the news."

So smarmy. "You put me in a bad position, Mr. Roux. I don't belong near any of this. Leave me alone."

She was about to end the call when he responded. "I apologize for putting you in a bad position. In my opinion, you needed to know what's going on."

"You still didn't answer how you knew about it."

"I've got a source. That's all I'm saying about it."

Perez would be pissed if she learned it was a police source. But was this Jane's news to share?

"I don't know what you want from me, Roux. You gave me shady information. I told you I want to be left alone. So leave me alone." He wouldn't leave her alone. She was sure of it. And that was okay, she realized.

"I'll be finishing up the episode about your husband's murder on Sunday. I have an office in Boston. I'll text you the address and the times I'll be there. I'd love to interview you and get your side of the story."

"My side of the story is that someone killed my husband two decades ago and I've moved on. I've got nothing more to say."

"And that's okay, even if that's *all* you say." He paused. Muffled noises. Driving? "I need you, Jane. This story is huge. Yes, I'm being selfish. You'd be helping me. I'm not helping you."

"I make no promises. But I'll think about it."

She hung up, then texted Ryan, asking nicely if he had any updates on her computer. Then she cleared the books off of her stash shelf and took out the money shoebox. She kept her cannabis in there. An excellent hiding place.

Why hide it? Pot was legal in Massachusetts. She was an adult. She could leave it on her kitchen table and it would be fine.

But she liked keeping her vices, her past, everything about herself, hidden. Kind of like with Perez and the smoking. This was her house — who cares if she smokes in it? But her tendency, at least since she'd lived her alone, was to continue to hide things and pretend to be the kindly, straight arrow, drab writer the world thought she was.

Best to keep vices, and secrets, hidden away.

She went upstairs to the bathroom, which had a ventilation fan at least, closed the door, sat on the toilet, and lighted a joint. She stared up the ceiling, watching the smoke whirl, then get sucked into oblivion.

"Kate," she said to no one as her high took hold, "we need to talk."

She took a deep drag, exhaled, took another, held it, then broke off the lit end of the joint as she blew the smoke out. Two hits were enough tonight. Weed was much stronger now than it had been when she'd been growing up.

If only Kate knew how much Jane talked to her. If only Kate knew how much Jane depended on her to keep her sane.

"I don't understand this Esmir Roux, honey. He knows too much, not everything, but it's all information I need, too, and I wouldn't get any of it without him. I'm torn, Kate. I'm torn between wanting the past kept buried and needing the past with me now to understand what's happening. Donald's murder … the details were splashed all over the news back then. Then as the days and months went on and they didn't catch me, it disappeared. Which is what I wanted and needed. Now it's back."

It was impossible for her to make new connections with all these moving pieces when she was high. But she needed to feel numb right now.

"If I could go back in time … well, that's a loaded statement. There's so much I would have done differently, or not at all. You know that. But here's one thing. I wouldn't have stabbed Donald three times. In the moment, it made sense — three cigarette burns on my ass, three stab wounds, and him the third victim. Trinity. But if I could, I'd go back and tell myself to not be clever. The euthanasia drugs would have been enough. I gotta tell you, Kate, in the moment, in the moment — I was so pissed. And thrilled. I wanted him dead. So many ways."

She smiled, then held it for a few seconds, thinking about how it felt. Killing, for her, was like that first cigarette of the day, when your body craves nicotine and you give it nicotine and it floods your body with a delicious thank you.

She dropped the smile when she thought more about the trinity.

"So: who's doing this? Who's copying my kills? And why? I have to keep Roux close, don't I? And I have to keep Perez close as well. I was happier when I was alone."

No tears, as pot beat the emotions out of her.

"Today was a lousy day. I lied in my AA meeting. Going there is a lie in itself. I lied to Esmir Roux. I lied to Detective Perez. All I do is lie, or not tell the whole truth. I don't like this part of me, honey, but I can't give it up. I can't stop lying. Stop hiding. But right now, I have to worry only about me."

And you.

"And I just lied to you. Happier when I was alone? I didn't mean that, Kate. The house was so quiet today. You know, in another life, I would have had you but with a different man. Not Donald, and not your real father, but someone different. I'd have raised you. Held you. The house would have been alive with your noise and your mess and our laughter. We'd be a family, the three of us, or maybe just you and me. I need someone in my life. Something. I can't even adopt a dog correctly."

She laughed. "Speaking of which, let me tell you about Rigsby. She was such a good girl. She would have fit in perfectly here."

Day 6 (Friday)

WHATEVER PEREZ HAD SAID to the newsies to keep them at bay had worn off. In the morning, Jane was greeted by three TV news trucks camped outside her home, along with some gawking neighbors.

Ellen Bligh from next door had alerted her by sneaking into her back yard and tapping at the kitchen window. Jane heard the tapping from her bedroom, wondering what was going on now. When she got down to the kitchen, she looked around, only after a bit noticing the top of Ellen's head. She ushered her inside.

"TV people!" Ellen started.

Jane sighed. "They were told to stay away." She texted Perez, who didn't answer right away, about it.

"They're fuckers, all of them," Ellen said, then put a hand to her mouth. "I'm sorry about the swearing. Is there anything — *anything* — I can do?"

How about finding out who's replicating my old kills? "Thank you, but I'm fine. Honest. I'll go out and tell them I have no comment, then ask them politely to leave."

Ellen's eyes narrowed. "What if they don't leave? I can

go out and say something to them. Next thing you know, they'll be blocking my driveway, too."

The last time Jane had dealt with the press was after Donald's murder. She thought at the time that she'd handled it well, but looking back, she probably did just enough to not appear guilty under their lights. Those trucks had been parked right where these were now, only back then, there were a lot more of them.

"If I'm going to not stay blocked in all day so I can run some errands, they'll have to leave. It's not a good look for the neighborhood, I know. I'll take care of them."

The doorbell rang. Jane looked through the peephole. A TV reporter, obviously, the woman looking way too glamorous for this neighborhood and this time of day, a bearded camera guy about ten paces back, his camera trained on the door.

Jane cracked the door open, making sure to stay out of the camera guy's line of sight. "No comment."

"Ms. Hawkins, Trish Harrier, Channel 8 News," the reporter started, her microphone held forward like she was challenging Jane to a sword duel. "I'd like to—"

"No comment."

"There are some disturbing—"

"No comment."

The reporter talked over Jane, who consistently interrupted. "There are some disturbing (No comment) and shocking similarities between (No comment) the murder yesterday in Port (No comment) Fletcher and the murder of your (No comment) husband Donald many years back (No comment). And we've learned that you were almost carjacked (No comment) two days ago. Do you think that the incidents are related?"

"No comment."

They both paused for breath. "What's your name again?" Jane asked.

"Trish Harrier, Channel 8 News," the TV woman said proudly.

Jane let that hang in the air, as the competing newsies hurried toward the stairs, cameras in tow. Jane made sure they were ready to capture the exchange before continuing, then she stepped into the doorway in full sight, ruing, but only slightly, that she was dressed like trailer park trash.

"Trish Harrier. You're the one who used to do the weather on weekends, right?" Trish smiled, perhaps sensing she'd worn the old widow down. Who didn't love a fan? "Then I do have a comment. I remember that time you were at the rotary during the blizzard, live on camera, and a passing car splashed slush in your face. All that makeup running down your cheeks? I never thought that you needed that much makeup. But I can see now that I was wrong."

Trish's eyes narrowed. As Jane shut the door, she heard a murmured "Asshole" from the reporter.

"Good news. The trucks are leaving," she told Ellen.

Perez texted back, saying she'd send a car over if the TV people were causing problems, but it was a public street and there wasn't much she could do about it unless they were backing traffic up.

Jane texted back that they'd given up. All good.

She ushered Ellen out the back door, then brewed some coffee. Tried the exercising again. Gave up after eight minutes. Hit the shower. Finished off the muffins.

Now what? She couldn't write. Channel 8 was taking its sweet time leaving the street. She still had the rental car. Her own car should be ready soon. How long does it take to replace a window? Perez would know. Maybe she'd text her about it later.

She hated feeling antsy. Not that she had much to do besides errands. And figuring out what was going on with these murders.

She went upstairs to her office, gazing at the whiteboard, which still sported the numbers one through ten. No help there. She still felt a little gauzy after the pot last night. What she needed to sharpen her mind and wake up was writing. Let Beachcomber Belle lead the way. But she still had no computer.

She texted Ryan. He responded right away; he had an early class, but he'd come over around dinnertime with news about the computer and the security system. So no writing today.

Time for some research. She fired up her phone's browser to search for news about the new murders. Annoying, the small screen, but it beat doing nothing.

Then she stopped. Could they track her searches? Then she stopped again. Who was "they"? Perez wouldn't care if she looked for information. It was natural. So Perez wasn't the "they." Maybe there was no "they." Or maybe there was.

She texted Ryan again: *I'll give you twenty dollars if you can tell me how to make my web searches private on an iPhone right now.*

His response was immediate: Tap the little square-on-a-square icon, hit the down pointy thing next to where it says tabs, then open a new private window. Like she could have ever found that on her own.

But it worked. How private was it? Who knew? She assumed that nothing was private when it came to the online world.

"Port Fletcher murder" brought up links to news about the murder. Douglas MacGonagle, a retired plastic surgeon, living alone, had been stabbed three times.

Nothing about incapacitating drugs. How was Roux getting his info so fast? Who was giving it to him?

The other two murders, the ones in Wareham and Orleans, were pretty much as Roux had described. A woman poisoned. A man bludgeoned. No leads. Three unsolved murders on or near the Cape in the last two weeks.

She tried searching for "old murders," but those results were all over the place. She had that website, the one with all the unsolved murders, but that wasn't news. Maybe Ryan could show her how to refine her searches.

How could she get him to show her how to search for something that she didn't want anyone to know she was searching for? No idea. One thing was clear — she needed more coffee.

What if the answer was in Roux's podcasts? Not that she relished hearing that man's oily voice. But she'd learn what he knew if she listened. Pretty sure his ego wouldn't allow him to *not* regurgitate everything he knew.

She'd pay Ryan to show her how to download podcasts and play them in the car. He was getting rich off of her.

PROBABLY SHOULDN'T BE DRINKING every morning, she thought as she downed a shot of bourbon. She probably shouldn't be doing a lot of things.

Wispy clouds danced across the sky. She'd rather walk to town than drive, but there was someplace she needed to visit later this afternoon. A contingency plan, one she'd need the car for.

For this trip, she'd drive into town, then walk the rest of the way. She wanted to visit the scene of the last murder, but this time, not in a car. She didn't know if the street was still taped off. It might look ultra-suspicious for her to visit the scene twice and in the same car. Walking would let her fit in better. Plus the exercise would do her good. She couldn't give up *that* after eight minutes.

She grabbed her purse, locked the house, and drove to the center of Port Fletcher. She parked behind Knead, then started the walk, an easy series of rights and lefts angling away from town.

It was a pleasant day. She touched her cheek. It felt almost normal. She rotated her shoulder. Better.

That reminded her of Jonas Ferrier. Any news about him? She stopped, leaned against a tree, and opened a private browsing window. Jonas Ferrier ... the news articles about the carjacking basically all copied from each other. His family piled on the plaudits — *he was a wonderful son, he'd been troubled, he'd turned his life around.* His wake, she saw, was tonight, and the funeral was tomorrow. She would not be attending.

Halfway to the murder house, she saw three teen boys and their bikes stopped outside a run-of-the-mill ranch with a shoulder-high chain-link fence. They looked young enough to still be in high school. It was a school day, so maybe they'd skipped. The boys were guffawing. As she walked closer, she saw why.

There was a dog in the yard, a little white terrier thing leashed to a run. One boy dropped a Doritos chip into the yard, and the dog ran to the chip but got yanked back. The boys laughed, then another flipped a Dorito into another part of the yard. Run, yank back, laughter.

Things went blue. Real blue.

As she neared the boys, she felt around for the multitool she'd dropped into her purse yesterday. She unsheathed it.

"Hey boys," she said, making her voice full of fake cheer. "Is this your house?"

The boys turned, each with an expression resembling post-lobotomization. Don't give me any ideas. I've got a knife with me.

"No," mumbled one boy. A second held a chip out, seemingly unsure whether to tease the dog more or eat the chip. The third held her gaze, giving back a lot of attitude.

"Then let me give you a little advice." She rested a hand on Attitude Boy's shoulder and spoke low to the group. "If you tease that dog again, and I mean ever, I'll hunt you down, peel the flesh from your bones, and cut it into pieces so small that even the ants won't bother to scrape your rotting molecules from the sidewalk."

It was fun when people visibly paled. These boys visibly paled. This walk really had been a good idea after all.

A woman, chunky, her long brown hair trailing after her, hurried out of the house. A little late, Jane thought. "What's wrong?" the woman snapped. "What are you doing to my dog?"

"Nothing," the boys mumbled, a sullen chorus.

"Let's just go to the park," the first chip boy whined to the other two.

"I was walking and just admiring your sweet doggo," Jane said. She caught the woman's eye, shook her head slightly. "These boys dropped their chips. Guess your pup wanted some. Don't worry, they're leaving now."

The woman unleashed the dog and scooped it up as the boys got on their bikes and began pedaling away. Attitude Boy circled back after a few pumps, caught Jane's eye, gave her a middle finger, then circled back to rejoin his friends. "Wrinkled old grandma," she heard one of the kids say.

"Those kids," the woman said, stroking her dog. "Haven't seen them here before."

"You won't be seeing them again," Jane reassured her.

∿

TEN MINUTES LATER, she stood on the sidewalk outside of the murder house. The tape had been cleared, although the home's front door was still sealed off. Jane took in the house. It seemed so normal. Why this house? Why this man? She crossed her arms and continued her gazing and thinking.

A "Hello!" from behind startled her. This again? She turned. A neighbor from across the street walked toward her. He was older, maybe seventy, and stooped. His yard was pin neat. Probably picked up every leaf as it fell in the fall. He should give yard work lessons to Leaf Guy.

"Can I help you?" the man asked as he stood next to her on the sidewalk.

"Such a shock," Jane said, shaking her head. "I heard about Dr. MacGonagle. On the news. I couldn't believe it."

The man grimaced. "Terrible. I feel so badly that I didn't see or hear anything. Such a nice man. Kept to himself. Quiet."

That's what they say about serial killers. Such a nice man. Or nice woman. Kept to themself. Quiet. You'd never think something like that could happen here.

"Did you know him well?" the man added.

"Oh, not really," she said. "I'd had a consultation many years ago. My late husband, he used to…" She turned away. He used to live. Now he was dead. "The doctor said to drop by his office any time, or his house. I never took him up on that offer. The husband is long gone. I just remember how nice the doctor was. How kind."

The man took in her swollen cheek but didn't say anything about it. "I don't know who'd do this to Doug. He had no enemies." He'd had at least one. "He was a great neighbor."

Jane sighed in agreement. "Such a shame. No one should get away with murder. This monster needs to be caught."

She said goodbye to the neighbor, then walked back to town via a different route, one that would take her past the town park.

She stood on the outskirts of the park. A basketball court to the left. Empty. The boys' three bikes leaned against the court's fence, along with some others. To the right, about fifty yards away, the three Doritos Boys were playing Frisbee with a number of other teens, braying as they made fun of each other in that I-don't-know-what-to-do-with-my-testosterone way that teen boys are drenched in.

The court was half in shadow. Perfect. She walked to the bikes, sure she had the right three, then got out the multi-tool and snipped their brake cables in places the kids wouldn't notice. If they weren't brake cables, they were something equally as important. Good enough.

She put a hand to her mouth and laughed. This really was turning out to be a pretty good day.

AS SHE WALKED BACK to the SUV, she took a call from an unknown number. The auto repair place had fixed her window and had dropped the car in her driveway. She thanked them profusely, then offered to pay. "No way," the repair guy said. "We take care of our own here in Port Fletcher."

Don't we ever. She had just taken care of three of Port Fletcher's own.

She called the rental place and asked nicely if they could swing by her house after six tonight or any time after that; her car was fixed and she was ready to hand back the SUV.

She got into the Chevy. It was almost three o'clock. Between belittling a TV reporter, investigating killings, visiting a murder house, and threatening teens, today was really flying by.

Five minutes later, she parked in back of John's Barber Shop, near the dumpster. John was close to retirement. His daughter Maura worked alongside him, as John was prepping to hand the business over to her. Jane hoped that Maura wasn't here. She liked Maura a lot and had heard that she was a much better barber than John ever was. But John was a fixture in town, so people kept coming to him, even if his barber skills were long past their prime.

She walked around to the front of the shop and entered. John was sweeping up. No Maura. Perfect. "Jane," he greeted warmly. "What can I do for you?"

"Just stopping in to say hello. Lovely day, isn't it?"

"It is." He stopped sweeping and took a seat in one of the two empty barber chairs, indicating the other for Jane. She sat.

"I hear," he said softly, "that someone attacked you the other day. What an awful thing. And that murder I heard about? What is this town coming to?"

They gossiped, Jane sharing little. John the Barber would share his Social Security number if it meant someone listening to him. She urged him to keep sweeping as they talked, and he obliged while gossiping about everyone and everything.

After a while, he flipped the *Open* sign to *Closed*. "That about does it for today," he said. "I'll lock the front door after you leave."

"I parked out back. No room along the curb when I got here."

"Fine by me." He locked the front door. "Just have to tally the register for the nightly deposit and take out the trash." He'd dragged a contractor-sized barrel out as he swept. It was overflowing with hair clippings.

"I'll take the trash to the dumpster on my way out while you handle your money," she said. "I'm going right past it."

"Jane Hawkins," he said, smiling. "What would this town do without you? Thank you. I'll take you up on that."

He bundled the big bag and handed it to her. They said their goodbyes, then Jane went out the back, depositing the bag of dozens of customers' hair into the back of the Chevy.

A good contingency plan.

BACK AT HOME, Jane put the bag of hair on top of some boxes stacked in the basement.

Now what?

A life of living alone suited her. She was used to it. It had been twenty-plus years now. Normally, to pass the time, she'd putter or read, and most days, she'd write, write, write. Not having a computer made her feel edgy.

She puttered until Ryan knocked at the door. He was carrying a paper shopping bag.

"Thanks for coming over," she said, handing him the promised twenty for the iPhone privacy call.

He smiled. It looked good on him. Better than the sullen.

"I've got your security cameras. We can set them up now. I just can't attach it to your computer yet."

She must have broadcast disappointment on her face, as his face fell and he quickly added, "I fixed the computer. Got it to start up. But something weird's going on with it. I want to keep it overnight. I'll bring it back in the morning. If that's not okay, I'll go get it right now."

At least he was no longer sullen. "You love working on this stuff, don't you?"

A shy smile. "It's fun. I mean, your computer's old. You really do need a new one. But it's a puzzle, you know? Figuring out what's wrong, putting the pieces together, stopping problems."

Story of her life. "That is fine, Ryan. Thank you for everything. And you're right. I should get on that." She thought about Flounder. He'd probably give her a good deal on a computer. As well as a leer. She indicated the bag he brought over. "That store at your school. This is where you bought this stuff?"

"Yeah. It's got everything."

"Computers, too?"

"Sure. Mostly Macs, but some others."

"Is the store open tomorrow? Or tonight?"

He went to his phone. Seemed like kids no longer knew anything, but they did know how to look everything up. "They open at eight tomorrow morning."

"I have an idea. If you buy me a new computer — a laptop is fine, a Mac is fine, although I've never used one — and you help me set it up, I'll pay you back for it, of course, and whatever it costs, I'll give you twenty percent on top of that."

He started and stopped talking a few times as he worked it through. "You're serious, Ms. Hawkins?"

"Totally. I need help, and you're the best person to do it."

She waved away his offer to give her change from the security system stuff as he laid the purchase out on the kitchen table. Five cameras, as promised. They were so little. You could put them anywhere. She'd have to remember that. Cameras could be anywhere.

Ryan scurried around, borrowing a few tools, and mounted cameras to cover the front and back of the house as well as Jane's office with a view of the hallway, a corner of the living room that also covered some of the kitchen, and the basement, aimed at the stairs.

"They're all charged," he said when he was done. "You have to charge them probably once a month."

He borrowed her phone, installed an app, did everything she couldn't do, and presented the phone back to her like it was a bar of gold.

Amazing. She could pick a camera, and it would show her the view, live. She went through all five, including the living room one, and they both waved to the camera as she saw them on the phone.

"The app can send you alerts when you're not home," he said. "If your phone's in the house, though, it won't, because it knows you're already here."

She could keep an eye on her house when she was out. Anyone could set this stuff up in a flash. It really was so much harder to get away with things now.

Ryan left, promising to come over tomorrow after he bought the laptop. Then came a whirlwind of activity. The auto repair guy dropped off her car, new window and all, and the car rental place came to pick up the Chevy. The rental car lady drove the car repair guy back, so they must have coordinated.

Jane ate an early dinner, read for a while, then laid out on the couch, thinking.

Esmir Roux had his finger on the pulse of these new murders. Jane needed him to keep her in the know, but she felt so dirty after talking to him. Could she cozy up to Perez? No, she didn't seem the type. Jane would have to follow the news like everyone else.

The murdered plastic surgeon seemed random. Maybe a home invasion turned deadly? If someone was copycatting her old kills, there had to be a reason. The three stab wounds, the same town — it was too coincidental.

She sat up.

She could prove that someone was copying her kills. She knew where the next murder would occur. Plymouth, the town over the bridge where she'd met Roux two days ago. And she knew how the murder would occur.

Poison.

Could she give that information to Perez? Right. *Detective, I happen to know where and how the next murder will occur. Can't tell you how I know. You just have to trust me.*

How would a normal person feel knowing that someone in a certain town would soon be killed, and how?

Who was she kidding — a normal person wouldn't have that information. Normal people didn't know about impending murders. They didn't kill people and hide in plain sight for twenty years, lying to everyone they met.

She lined up three shots — a whiskey, a vodka, a gin — and downed them all, boom boom boom, slamming each empty glass on the counter.

Normal. Normal. Normal. You need to act normal.

Day 7 (Saturday)

THE DOORBELL SHATTERED Jane's drunken sleep the next morning. Or what she assumed was morning. Her eyes refused to open. She forced them.

She'd slept on the couch, fully dressed. Now she remembered. Whiskey, vodka, gin. It had been the gin, she was sure, that had put her over the edge. Once she could find her way to the kitchen, which, from the ache in her body, might be never, she resolved to pour it down the drain and bury the bottle in the back yard.

The doorbell again. Something primal tried to claw its way into her brain to warn her. Run. They've found you.

But who is "they"? And if "they'd" found her, would "they" bother with the doorbell? Probably not.

A half-formed thought. Someone said they'd be here in the morning.

The doorbell a third time. "Just a minute," she croaked from the couch, realizing that it had come out sounding like she'd vomited in a well. Vomiting in a well sounded like a better idea than getting up.

But she did get up, stumbled to the door, and looked through the peephole. Ryan.

She unlocked the door, then opened it a crack. "Come in, be right back!" she said, walking to the bathroom before Ryan could answer.

She squeezed some toothpaste directly into her mouth, swished it around, spit it out, splashed cold water on her face, then headed back to Ryan.

"You had breakfast yet?" she asked.

"Umm…" He was looking at her like her hair was on fire. Her head was certainly on fire.

"Doesn't matter if you did. I'm making us eggs and coffee."

She changed into non-disgusting clothes, smoothed down her hair, which looked like it had been caught mid-explosion, then started the coffee while Ryan made a second trip back to his house, bringing back her old computer.

He unboxed the laptop. "Here's the new Mac," he started.

She held up a finger. "After coffee, after we eat."

The caffeine helped muffle the drumbeat in her head, and the eggs soaked up whatever alcohol was left inside of her. They ate in silence. If Ryan took offense, he didn't show it, but she had no talk in her yet.

Ryan cleared his plate first. "That was nice, Ms. Hawkins. Thank you."

"Eggs are eggs, Ryan. Simple."

"I meant the not talking."

She went to question him why but realized she already knew the answer. Ellen was a henpecker, a hoverer. And more than that, an incessant talker who always had to be right.

She nodded instead. "Meal talk is always welcome. I'm

used to eating alone, is all. And sometimes a meal is just a meal. No need to make it into *My Dinner With André*." He'd never heard of the movie, she was sure from his look. "Meaning there's no need to talk all the time. Eat in peace."

He smiled. She cleaned up while he brought everything up to her office.

"I transferred everything over from the old computer to the Mac," he said. A look of anguish? "I didn't look at anything," he added in a rush. "I mean, just the settings. Your files … I didn't look at your files."

"There's nothing wrong. Everything I need is on the Mac?" He nodded. "Perfect. That's what I wanted."

She had him bring out the receipts, then gave him a wad of bills from her stash. She'd need to replenish that soon.

"All there, plus your bonus," she said. "And Ryan: thank you."

He flipped through the bills. Probably the most cash he'd ever held. "You're welcome." He took a breath, maybe thinking things over. "Ms. Hawkins, can I ask you something?"

As long as it wasn't about murder. "Sure. Always."

"You like using cash, right? Isn't it easier to use a card? Or I could show you how to use an app to pay for things with your phone."

Jane chuckled. "Ryan, two things. First, I'm old. I do things the way I do them. Second, cash gives you anonymity. You buy something, you give them cash, no one else knows about it. It's not about keeping secrets" — it totally was — "but the world doesn't need to know every little thing you buy. Also, it's nice to touch money." She took the bills from him, fanned herself, gave them back. "See? Nice. Cash makes money real. It's not just a number on your phone. You work, you get something tangible."

"Okay." He looked amused as he put the cash away. "But I feel like a drug dealer."

Flounder. No need to buy computer equipment from him any longer. No need to see his oily face again.

Ryan showed her where her files were on the new laptop. She'd figure the rest out.

"Thank for this, Ryan. You're a lifesaver."

He smiled but look fiddly. "There's something else."

He hooked the old computer back up to the monitor but didn't turn it on. "I got all your files off this, set up everything, but I didn't hook this" — he pointed to the old computer — "up to the internet after I found what I found."

"What did you find?"

He gulped. "Spyware."

She was generally aware of what that word meant. Something on the computer that spied somehow, obviously. She'd even used the term in an earlier Beachcomber Belle book. Belle had deduced that the thief was using spyware to log people's keystrokes when they were banking online. Jane hadn't gotten more technical than that because she didn't know more and her readers didn't read her books for their technical accuracy.

But spyware on *her* computer? She hadn't done a lot of murder research on it, but still, her head started pounding again.

"I don't think you did anything wrong, Ms. Hawkins. You can get spyware from a lot of shady websites, but this looked like someone installed it on purpose. Who last worked on your computer?"

The only people who'd ever touched her computer, besides Ryan that one time, were her and Flounder. She'd brought it to him in November. He'd upgraded the hard drive. Apparently, he'd done more than that.

"I'm not sure. I can't recall right now."

"I can get rid of it. The spyware. I didn't in case you wanted to see it."

Did she? "What do you think this spyware was doing?"

He ticked things off on his fingers as he spoke. "Activate your camera without you knowing, recording audio without you knowing, keeping track of what websites you visited. I don't think it was keeping track of what you typed, but I can't be sure. It's bad stuff, Ms. Hawkins."

It's going to mean bad stuff for someone, that's for sure. "I don't have anything to hide, Ryan. The computer wasn't in the bedroom or anywhere else private, so whoever did this didn't get much of a show."

He looked relieved for her. "I can get rid of the computer. You don't need it, and I definitely wouldn't use it any more with that on there."

"I'm going to…" She stopped. Best to get rid of it. Destroy it. But maybe she had another use for it. "I'm going to keep it. As a memento. I've written so many of my books on it. But I'll keep it unplugged."

She slipped him an extra hundred dollars after they went back downstairs. "Bonus for the spyware."

He grinned. "You're making me rich, Ms. Hawkins."

"Money is for spending. And I have one more favor, a little one." She handed him her phone. "Show me how to get podcasts on this so I can play them in my car."

BEING mad at a shady computer guy for putting spyware on your computer is a little like being mad at your spouse not because they fucked your neighbor, but because the neighbor left their hair in the shower.

Harley "Flounder" Hawley was an awful person. Jane had been stupid for trusting an awful person. Awful people did awful things. No truer truism existed.

She pulled into Trigger City, the one-story, flat-roofed building sporting a crisp red, white, and blue sign exuding optimism and patriotism.

The inside was well lit, stuffed with locked display cases, looking more like a tiny Staples than a purveyor of death and protection. She made her way to the front and asked one of the folks for Boss.

She leaned against the counter to take the place in. Besides weaponry, there were all types of accessories, cases, other things she had no clue about, even a few racks of clothing. A one-stop kind of place.

Beachcomber Belle relied on her wits instead of bullets, although she wasn't averse to carrying some non-lethal protection. If Belle ever upped her game, Jane would come here for research.

A "You looking for me?" came from behind her. She turned to see a muscular man, probably in his fifties, lean, buzz cut. If he were in a movie, he'd be called Sarge.

"I take it you're Boss."

"I am. Welcome to Trigger City." He put his hands on the counter. "What can I do for you?"

"Sophia Perez sent me. I got carjacked a few days ago. It didn't end well for him, but Detective Perez suggested I come here if I want to feel safer."

Boss nodded. "Perez is a good customer. I trust her, and you should trust her. The carjacking — that was you? I read about that online. How are you doing after that?"

"I'm fine, thank you. I feel safe. But it's just me at home. You never know, right?"

"I'm glad you see it that way. Let's see your paperwork."

She'd brought her license to carry and everything else she could think of. Boss looked the paperwork over, then did some computer stuff before returning the documents.

"Tell me what you've used before," he started, "or what you own."

"Nothing and nothing. I got the license for research. I'm a writer. I never thought I'd ever need a gun. The only time I've shot one was when I took my safety class."

"Okay then." She liked his military precision. "You want to carry this with you at all times, sometimes, or just have something at home?"

Good question. She really didn't want to carry around a gun. But she felt safer at home than anywhere else now, since the carjacking and since Esmir Roux entered her life and since Flounder sealed his fate. You never know.

"I don't plan to carry, but I'd like the option."

Boss asked good questions, eventually steering her to what he called a "mouse gun" or "pocket gun," which he explained meant a small handgun.

"This," he said, sliding a handgun onto the counter, "might be perfect for you. The Ruger LCP Max. It's small enough that if you carry it around, you won't even notice the weight. Holds 10 rounds of .380 ammo." Enough rounds for most purposes, although she could get a different magazine that would hold 12, he explained. The lightweight ammo wouldn't rip anyone's head off necessarily, but it would be enough to put someone down and make them stay down if they were close.

He showed her how to load it, assuring her it wasn't loaded now, and had her hold it until she felt comfortable.

"It's so light," she said.

"Its best feature. That, and it works when you need it to work."

Boss led her to the store's inside range, fit her with protective equipment, and loaded six rounds into an empty magazine.

"It's got a kick, so you'll feel it in your wrist and up your arm. Use the grip I showed you. It's a tiny thing, and you don't want to accidentally have a finger in front of the barrel."

At her shooting lane, her ears and eyes protected, Boss set her up with a target about 15 yards away.

"Any farther than that, with you being new, you won't get close. But this will give you an idea of what you can expect."

She loved it. The gun did have a kick, one that traveled up her arm. More than two or three shots, she'd be all over the place. She nicked the target once. Good enough. She didn't plan on using the gun. But plans change.

"I'm in," she told Boss when she was back at the counter. "Now tell me about stun guns."

BETWEEN THE RUGER, the stun gun, a compact gun safe, and the ammo and other accessories, she'd expected to spend well over a thousand dollars and was pleased that it came in below that.

On to solving problems, she thought as she drove. She had more protection — between the weaponry and the security cameras, she'd made herself feel safer. The new laptop meant she could both write and not be worried about someone spying on her.

Someone meaning Flounder. She didn't need that

burden right now, not with Esmir Roux probing her old kills.

List of things to take care of, in order of importance: a) the Roux problem b) the Flounder problem c) the writing.

List of things to take care of, in order of ease: a) writing b) Flounder c) Roux.

The Roux issue was complex and happening too fast, and it felt partially out of her control. She still didn't know what he really knew or where he was going with all his questions and research. Flounder, that was much easier. And the writing, that would help ground her.

Focus on writing, and the rest of the world would become clearer.

Once at home, she tucked her purchases safely away.

She wrote, the afternoon passing in a blur of productivity. One on one, just her and her words. It only took her about ten minutes to get used to the laptop's keyboard. Ryan had done a fantastic job setting up folders and applications where she needed them, and she found all of her old files. If she wanted an assistant, she'd hire him. He knew what he was doing.

But did she know what *she* was doing? She felt like she'd been tossed in the deep end of the pool after only five minutes of swimming lessons. Too many moving pieces after too many years of complacency.

She slammed the desk with her palms. That was the problem. She'd done a great job of hiding in plain sight, keeping her past a secret, but she'd grown too used to the status quo of this new life. She wasn't Jane of the Past any longer, which was a good thing overall, but Jane of the Past knew how to get things solved fast and well.

She saved her writing, took a thirty-minute nap, showered, then decided to research Sophia Perez.

There were hundreds of people named Sophia Perez,

and at least one in every state, according to the top Google result. She added in filters like "police" and "Massachusetts" and eventually found a few relevant results. Between those and some meandering through Facebook and LinkedIn, she learned a few things.

Sophia Perez was 36 and had recently accepted an open detective position in Port Fletcher after several years of patrol in Springfield, a sometimes-rough, sometimes-charming city in western Massachusetts. She'd split time growing up between Springfield and Hartford, Connecticut. In the few pictures Jane had found, Perez looked stoic, unamused, and ready for action. And that was it.

Why Port Fletcher, a sleepy place as different from Springfield and Hartford as you could get? Maybe the higher rank. Or maybe she'd fallen in love with the ocean.

Maybe she just wanted a change. Or maybe change had been thrust upon her.

Jane returned to her writing. She'd painted Belle into a corner. Her amateur sleuth was trapped in the candy store after hours and was hiding in a supply closet. Belle had to access the store's computer and see what the Chechen warlord was hiding. Were there security cameras? Belle didn't know. She should have been more prepared. If Belle tripped an alarm, the Chechen would come running. But she needed the proof.

Jane stopped typing, then smiled. She needed the proof. Thank you, Belle. You just solved a problem for me.

After a quick dinner, she raced to a party goods store, found what she needed, drove back home to get ready, then headed toward Byte Junction. Flounder closed up his shop at eight, and she guessed that meant a hard eight. He probably had to head home for a night of spying on her while he fired up some porn.

She drove past the store. The lights were on, and a few

cars were parked out front. She thought she caught a glimpse of Flounder talking to someone at the counter. Closing time, she knew, would bring in the non-computer customers looking for a late-night fix of "C-RAM." Her plan wouldn't work unless someone was looking to party, and knowing the clientele who visited Byte Junction, she probably wouldn't have to wait for long.

She parked across the street and slid down the seat until she had a good view with just her head exposed. Driving while wearing a black full-body suit covering her head to toe had been annoying. At home, she'd discovered that she needed to wear the suit backwards. She couldn't zip the thing up comfortably and quickly. It looked stupid that way, and the arms were in the wrong place, constricting her movements, but she didn't care about looking stupid. Then she found that she could barely see, so she had to cut two eyeholes.

The store emptied out. She checked her phone. Ten minutes until closing. Flounder was tidying up, meaning pushing food crumbs off the counter to the floor, where presumably the Byte Junction fairies would magically sweep. What an unclean idiot.

Five minutes to go. Flounder was checking his phone and looking antsy. How could no one else want to party tonight?

At three minutes to, a car slid into an open space out front, and a weather-beaten guy shuffled toward the front door.

Jane dropped her phone and picked up the stun gun. It looked like a flashlight, and one of its three functions was a flashlight. They think of everything.

She ran across the street, keeping to the shadows, reaching the side of Byte Junction just as Shuffler opened the door.

The door. The tinkling of that bell. A problem.

Shuffler stood in the doorway. "You here, Flounder?" It was hard to miss Flounder, him being so portly and greasy, so maybe he'd gone to his office. Once the door closed, the bell would tinkle when she opened it.

Shuffler stepped into the store. The door was closing.

Jane made her decision. She hotfooted it toward the door and threw out a hand to prop the door open just enough that Flounder and Shuffler hopefully wouldn't notice it.

She risked popping her head up for a better look, but the mask had slipped, so now she saw mostly black nylon. Through the nylon, she saw Shuffler step around the counter as Flounder walked out of the bathroom next to his office. She heard Flounder say, "Jake, my man, what can we do for you tonight?" as the office door closed.

Okay. She strained to keep the door propped open as she drew herself up.

Headlights shone from behind her. The time was now.

She eased inside, dropped to the floor, and made sure the door closed quietly. Then she crawled to the bathroom in the rear and closed the door, keeping the light off. Which, from the smell, was a good thing.

Flounder was young enough to have a healthy bladder, she hoped, so he probably wouldn't be back in here tonight. Judging from the odor, he was in no hurry to clean before leaving.

She put an ear to the floor, holding in a swear when her cheek got damp. Who pees next to the door? If Flounder didn't deserve what was coming to him for the spyware, then the urine on her cheek had sealed it.

The gap below the door allowed for her to hear muffled voices and see a sliver of harsh fluorescent light from the store. She couldn't make out everything "Jake" said as Flounder walked him to the door after finalizing their transaction, but it was probably along the lines of, "Keep using."

Eventually, the sliver of light disappeared, then she heard the front door tinkle. She made to get up but stopped mid-crouch.

She didn't want to kill Flounder tonight. She wanted information. But what if he was still here? The store was prime spying territory, she assumed. The office afforded him privacy. He'd fire up his spyware here. Or would he? Maybe spying was his porn and he'd do that at home, naked and covered in potato chip grease. She shuddered, wishing she'd never imagined that. Whatever happened, this would be her last visit to Byte Junction.

After what she guessed was fifteen minutes of silence and darkness, she creaked open the bathroom door. The store felt empty. She palmed the stun gun as she reached for the office door.

The knob wouldn't turn. Flounder had locked his office.

She looked to the ceiling. She didn't see any tiny lights indicating equipment up there, but would security cameras nowadays have lights? They all used to back in the day, but that day had long passed. Everything now was micro this, wireless that, and the little spies were everywhere. And she knew there was at least one camera — she recalled Flounder licking his lips at the teen and mom the other day.

In for a penny, in for a pound. She flicked on the stun gun's flashlight and searched around the store until she found a heavy backup storage device, then whacked the locked knob with the drive until the door groaned open. She heaved the drive over the counter, where it clattered across the floor. She probably had at least a fifteen-minute head start before Flounder came, if he'd been alerted at all. Might as well cause a little chaos while she was here.

She pushed the office door closed and snapped on the overhead light. Flounder's office computer was humming, so she turned the monitor on. It showed his computer desktop, ready for action. No password protection? Figured. Flounder considered himself to be the king of the castle.

His castle was about to get stormed.

Five minutes in, she found what she was looking for. A folder nestled several layers deep. *Client Videos.* Really? He couldn't pick a more obvious name? Inside that folder were dozens of folders named … with exact client names. She shook her head. No way should anyone trust this guy with their computer.

The first folder she looked at was hers, of course. It contained several video files, automatically named with the date and time. She clicked open the most recent one. And there she was, typing away, her eyes darting around, her fingers presumably flying.

Flounder.

She was one of the few lucky ones. She learned that a lot of people kept computers in their bedrooms, because here was a woman splayed out on her bed masturbating, and here was a couple having sex. The videos weren't limited to the bedroom, either. Here was a family eating. Here was a child napping.

The shimmery blue curtain range hit with a vengeance. Flounder was going to pay.

She grabbed a large-capacity USB drive from the storefront and copied all the videos she could cram onto the device. Might as well save the evidence if she needed it down the road. While that was working, she clicked open Flounder's customer database program and created a new newsletter to be sent to All Clients, timing it to be sent late the next night, Sunday night.

What's a good newsletter message title? She decided on *I've Been Watching You*. That would result in some clicks. She attached several of the ickiest videos, added hers, told the program to send despite the large file sizes, and sent it off.

Flounder would not be having a good Sunday night.

She shut off the monitor, then decided it would be a good time to test out the stun gun. She stuck the gun's probes into the computer at the front counter and zapped it. That felt so good to her. Not so for the computer. The store alarm began screaming. Who cares. She zapped several brand-new computers as she walked past them, then strode out the front door, swinging the stun gun from its wrist strap and humming.

SHE PULLED into a Mobil gas station and swung around to the side, then climbed out of the car and stripped off the body suit. She'd worn only a tee shirt and her underwear under the suit. The freedom felt fantastic.

She checked the seat next to her. Phone, stun gun, balled-up suit, USB drive. She had everything she needed. And much more.

She was only a half hour or so from home. Maybe she had enough time to catch an episode of Mass*Murderers. She opened the podcast app that Ryan had shown her how to use. Her car was old enough to not connect to the phone, so she plunked the device between her legs as she drove.

"I'm Esmir Roux. Welcome to Mass*Murderers." Yuck. His voice was smarmy even on the podcast. His preamble was boring. Actually, most of the episode was boring. The man could not tell a story. But the facts were somewhat engaging. This episode was the one covering the old Sal Lomasio murder. He got a lot of it right. And a lot of it wrong. That's what happens when the case goes unsolved. You don't know which leads are real and which are false.

The ending, however, gave her chills.

"Listeners, I'm working on something special. This season is all about ten unsolved murders. And these are special murders. My investigative team and I" — she snorted at that; he had a team of one — "are working hard to show that these murders were all committed by the same person. You heard me. There was a serial killer loose in Massachusetts twenty years ago. And we *will* bring that person to justice."

She shut off the podcast and lobbed the phone on the seat, stewing in the silence until she parked in her driveway, where she idled.

Esmir Roux's pride and arrogance overshadowed everything else in that podcast. One star. Would not recommend. However … he'd stay at her number one position of important things to take care of.

Pride and arrogance. They so often lead to downfall.

Day 8 (Sunday)

THE NEXT MORNING, Jane bundled up for her weekly walk to Knead. The sky was a pasty gray, the wind from the north a reminder that summer might look close on the calendar but was still pretty far off in real life.

It had been quite the week since she'd last walked this route. She'd killed a carjacker, someone was copying her past kills, her little town had seen a new murder, she'd caught a slimy computer salesperson spying on her, and she'd bought some weaponry that she adored but never thought she'd need. Her hand and knee cuts were mostly healed, but her face was still a little lumpy, and her shoulder was still bothering her. She deserved a treat today.

At the bakery, Rae fussed over her — she'd heard about the carjacking — and Ray comped her the coffee and muffins.

"Did you hear what happened last night?" Rae said from behind the counter as she handed Jane the muffin bag.

What now? "Do you mean the murder here the other day?"

Rae blinked. "No, last night. Someone was murdered in Plymouth. They found a woman's body propped on her front steps."

Plymouth. Of course it was Plymouth. "Oh my, that's terrible. Who's the woman?"

Rae shrugged. "Some mom. That's all they know. A woman found dead on her front steps, but there's gotta be more, since the news called it a murder already."

Jane hurried out of the bakery, found a bench along the main drag, and pulled up the news on her phone. Rae had been correct. A local woman was found dead last night, suspicious, no obvious trauma.

She caught a little shiver of giddiness. She knew how the woman had been murdered — poison — before anyone else, except the murderer. It was weirdly exciting to know something that no one else knew. She should feel bad about that, she reasoned, but she didn't.

Unfortunately, she had bigger problems to deal with than a stranger's murder. Now there were four recent murders, all mimicking hers. And Esmir Roux was trying to tie them all together.

She shook her head as she hunched on the bench. Once she figured out who was doing this, she'd take care of the problem.

She walked back home, dropped off the muffins, kept the coffee, grabbed the Ruger, and drove to Trigger City. When you live near the beach, the horizon is vast, but she still felt the walls closing in. Not a good feeling. She needed to practice. And burn off some nervous energy.

At the range, she bought enough ammo to last her a lifetime, then the woman working the range helped her load and reload as Jane went through four magazines, her arm numb by the end, her wrist and shoulder aching, her spirit calmed.

She'd gotten better at hitting the target, and even had the woman move it back for the last magazine. What helped was mentally chanting "You" with each shot, "You" being whoever the copycat killer was. Die, You. Having the right mindset was so important to success.

As she stripped off her protective gear, her phone buzzed. A call from Roux.

"Jane," he started. "Where are you?"

She held the phone out so he could hear the sounds of shooting. "I'm working through a few issues."

A beat of silence, then, "I'm in Boston at the studio. We were scheduled to talk."

They were? "Hold on." She scrolled through her texts. There was the address. There were the times he'd be there. And she'd replied that she'd be there by now. "I can be there in three hours." More like 90 minutes.

Roux sighed. What a drama queen.

"I'm doing you a favor, Mr. Roux," Jane added. "I don't need to talk to you about anything. I don't need to talk about my husband's murder to anyone. I can also change my mind."

"No," he said sharply, then softened. "I just want to hear your story, Jane. I want the world to hear your story. Bring someone to justice. Bring closure to families. To you."

Driving to Boston would be a pain. But Roux was her best path forward to getting information and hopefully some answers. So she drove.

Traffic was a nightmare, parking was a nightmare, the price to park was a nightmare. But Boston looked wonderful, although a bit weary from the long winter. The city always had tourists, and those Jane passed as she walked to Roux's office, even those she bumped into when they came to sudden halts to take selfies with old buildings to prove to their faceless followers that they "loved" history, looked resigned to the fact that if they had waited just *two* more weeks to visit, they'd see a different Boston, one more vibrant, more green, and maybe less cold, but that last one was always a crap shoot.

Roux's studio was on the fifth floor of a six-floor brick building a few side streets off of Boston Common. There wasn't much foot traffic on the side streets, as tourists weren't interested in seeing where the natives worked. Jane was hungry, and Roux could wait, so she grabbed a Mediterranean bowl from a place a few blocks away, went back to Roux's building, and ate in the lobby, chatting to the guard, who didn't seem to have much to guard. She promised to send him one of her books. It was good to make friends with security guards. You never know when you might need a favor.

She'd kept Roux waiting long enough, so up she went to the third floor and knocked on the studio door. He opened it two seconds later, like he'd been leaning against it.

"Jane," he said, sweeping an arm to clear her passage like she was a grande dame.

"Mr. Roux."

The studio was nothing more than a big conference-sized room filled with equipment — microphones, headsets, cables running all over the place, a bank of computer monitors and other tech she didn't recognize, a big sign, *Mass*Murderers*, plastered on the far wall. You didn't need a sign for an audio podcast, but maybe it stroked his ego.

Roux today was dressed in jeans and a light blue dress shirt, the sleeves rolled up. He indicated a seat, which she took, then he started fiddling with a mic.

"Just so you know, Mr. Roux, I won't be recorded. I'm here to listen."

His face fell for a beat, then he recovered. "I see. Then I'd like to take notes, if that's okay."

"I'm fine with that. But no recording."

Roux flipped through a folder. He probably had everything memorized, so this was part of his show. "You were the one who found your husband."

A statement, not a question. "Yes."

"Tell me how that felt."

She'd answered hundreds of questions during the investigation. At the time, she strove to answer each question as truthfully as possible. Since no one had asked her "Did you kill Donald?" she'd been able to stay pretty truthful. She'd do so here as well.

"How that felt … have you ever found the dead body of your spouse, Mr. Roux?"

He shook his head. "No. I'm not married."

"Then imagine it. You see someone and they're alive, like they've been the million times you've seen them before. Then you see them and they're dead. Imagine the shock. Imagine what you'd feel. That's how I felt."

She'd been prepared for that question that wasn't a question: "Tell me how you felt." And she'd answered truthfully. It *had* been a shock to see Donald dead, once she'd killed him and realized he'd never be violent with her again. Her shock had dissipated quickly, water down the drain, and had been replaced with a dread that she'd be caught. But she hadn't been caught.

The real problem — one that she wouldn't discuss with Roux or anyone — is what happened to her *after* Donald. You don't start killing people for practice so that you can successfully kill your husband, then keep on killing, without a reason.

But she had.

Roux scribbled some notes. "Take me through it. The

five minutes before you found him, then after you found him."

Odd. "This is all in the police reports, I think."

"It is, to a degree. But I'd love to hear it from you."

Because it makes it more real. You want real? "Excuse me for a moment." She dug in her purse for a tissue, didn't find a tissue, but did find a McDonald's napkin. How long had that been in there? She dabbed her eyes with it. "I'd gone to sleep early that night. Our bedroom was on the second floor. Donald, he liked to stay up late, while I was more early to bed, early to rise back then." Mostly so that they could avoid talking to each other. Fewer cigarette burns that way. "I heard something. I didn't know what, just enough of a noise to stir me. The bedroom door was closed, but the house didn't feel right. I can't explain it. The lights were on, although later the police said it was only one light. The house seemed too bright. I called out his name, Donald's, and he didn't respond, although I heard something else. It didn't make sense. What could I be hearing, and why hadn't he responded? I hurried down the stairs. You take a left into our kitchen from the stairs."

She paused here, and Roux jumped in. "You still live in that house, correct?"

"I do."

She waited. Roux seemed to be waiting for her to continue. Let him.

She won the wait-it-out battle. He finally said, "What happened next?"

"Let me think."

She had gone to bed early that night but didn't sleep. She was waiting for Donald to pass out on the couch. Which he'd done. She'd planned for it to be that night. She had decided to be more goal oriented.

Once he'd passed out, things became simple. She'd

injected him with the doggie death drugs. But she gave him a small dose. She'd wanted him alive when he died. Wanted to look in his eyes, wanted him to struggle. Wanted him to know.

He did. He had.

He started blabbering, but his words didn't make sense. So she'd stabbed him three times, one for each cigarette burn, but she could have stabbed him a hundred times and that still wouldn't have been enough. The abuse. The rapes. He'd taken away who she was and forced her to be this new person. A survivor, but a shattered survivor.

She'd thought about killing herself afterward. Sticking that knife into her heart. She'd been ready. She'd even researched it. Can you stab yourself to death? Turns out you can. Not the neck. Too messy, even for her. She'd even drawn a little dot on the spot where she could drive the knife in. Just to the right of her sternum. Here's how it would have worked. You hold the butt of the knife against the wall. You push yourself into it, the point, then the tip, the blade, the spine and the edge. You ignore the pain, and you fight your body's instincts to survive.

She didn't think she could have made it all the way up the blade to the hilt, but if she'd done it right, she'd never know if she could have done more.

One thing had stopped her. Actually, two things. The first was how the sheer joy at seeing Donald die had rekindled how she'd felt at killing the previous two people. She'd been broken before, but killing Donald had shattered whatever was left of her old self.

Because of lust. The closest she could describe it. Better than drugs. Better than sex. Better than … anything. The power to take a life was so powerful that she could taste it back then. She could taste it even now.

The second thing was the chance, however small, of

making things right with Kate. But that still hadn't happened.

"My feeling at seeing Donald on the floor ... they were ... it's hard to describe. My world narrowed. If whoever did this was still in the house, I didn't care at that point. It's odd, Mr. Roux. The police asked me so many questions. Was the front door open or closed? What did you hear? Did you see whoever did this, even a glimpse? I don't know. I saw Donald on the floor. I knew without knowing that he was dead. I'm sure I touched him. The blood on my hands was evidence of that. But at that moment ... who I'd been, it was gone. I was never coming back. That was my first clear thought. That who I was had disappeared out that door along with the killer. He'd killed Donald and stolen my life. It didn't matter if the door was open or closed. Donald was gone. And so was I."

She dabbed at her eyes again. "I've moved on, Mr. Roux. It's been more than twenty years. Investigate those old murders if you must. But they're your white whale. Not mine."

She palmed the table, took a deep breath, and continued. "My husband was a complicated man. And also a simple one. His passion was being destructive. I didn't love him, not at the end. He was a terrible husband. He was a terrible person. But I'm not saying he deserved to die." He had totally deserved to die. She just wouldn't say it. Semantics. "I told the police all this. And in the end, it didn't matter, did it? They never caught the murderer. And now you're claiming that Donald's murder was part of a chain of nine other murders. Honestly, Mr. Roux? So be it. Find your justice. But I'm not walking alongside you while you do it."

Roux had stopped scribbling and was instead watching her. Intently.

He cleared his throat. "Let's, uh, let's take a break."

He showed her where the bathroom was, and she smoked a cigarette in there, breaking the rules while she leaned against the sink.

Roux. His questions were simple and direct; her answers were long and meandering. Exactly what she had *not* wanted to happen. Be Jane the secret keeper. Stop emoting.

Had she hung herself with her answers? No. Most of it was the truth. Her world *had* narrowed. She *had* touched Donald's dying body. She'd wanted to feel the blood pumping out of him. He'd closed his eyes as he died, and she thumbed his lids open to watch his eyes. She hadn't felt love for him, or remorse, or guilt, or even urgency. This was her home, this was her husband on the floor, this was his blood soaking onto the tiles and into the grout.

This was also her knife. And the one physical thing she'd had to deal with. That hidey-hole in the bookshelf had been there a long time. Even Donald didn't know about. The police had certainly never checked. They had no reason. They had a grieving, freshly minted widow standing right in front of them, a widow who'd been sobbing on the floor next to her dead husband when they'd arrived after she'd made the call.

Funny thing, tears. They can make joy and sorrow look an awful lot alike.

~

"LET'S walk through the four new murders," Roux said, "and how they line up with four past murders."

Oh, yes. Let's. She let him take the stage.

"Two weeks ago, a woman in her fifties was poisoned in Wareham. In 2000, a man was poisoned in the same town. Richard Eidenberg." He paused, looking up from his notes at her.

She shrugged. "Okay."

"And next, a landscaper was beaten to death in Orleans. This mirrors an Orleans man, Sal Lomasio, who was beaten to death with a pipe, police say, a few months after the Eidenberg murder."

Again with the pause and the look. Crowbar, pipe, pretty close.

"It sounds gruesome," she said, meeting his gaze. "There's so much evil in the world."

"Indeed."

She put a hand to her mouth, stifling a laugh, because he looked right then, to her, like a frog who'd gulped down something way too big for it to swallow. She had no idea where that image had come from, but she couldn't shake it. Then she pictured the frog holding a sign that read, *My name is Esmir Frog*, and the laugh escaped before she bit down.

"Excuse me," she said, wanting nothing more than to call him Esmir Frog right then. "I have a little frog in my throat. Can't seem to shake it. Can you get me some water?"

"Of course." He turned to open a mini fridge. She wiped away her laughter tears, then took a long swig from the water bottle he'd handed her.

He started again. "Okay, where were we?" He looked down at his notes. Surely he had all of this memorized. The man did love a show. "Within the last week, there have been two more murders in the area. Douglas MacGonagle, a retired doctor, was stabbed to death in his house. This mirrors the murder of your husband, Donald Hawkins. Both murders occurred in your hometown of Port Fletcher, twenty or so years apart. It's quite chilling, isn't it?"

MacGonagle had sounded like a nice man, according to his neighbor, but Jane didn't really care about his death. Donald, now *that* was a murder she'd really cared about.

Was there really a connection between the two murders? Humans look for patterns instinctually, even when there is no pattern. We see faces in Mars rocks, alien spaceships in ancient civilizations' cave doodles. We try to make sense of the world by falling back on patterns.

Here's a pattern: People kill people. For a lot of reasons. Okay, maybe that wasn't a pattern, but it was the truth. And it's not like the past murders were the only murders in Massachusetts. They weren't even the only unsolved murders. There were many. She'd seen that website, and even that wasn't complete.

She needed to learn why Roux was concentrating on these ten particular past murders. But maybe she wouldn't have to ask. Maybe he'd spit it out. The man did love to talk.

"We have talked about these murders, Mr. Roux. Terrible, as you know, and particularly painful for me. I'm not sure that this exercise is going anywhere."

"The fourth," he said, running over her response, "was in Plymouth. Just a day ago, a mother of two was poisoned. Found outside her home. No suspects. And twenty years before that, a Plymouth man was poisoned. His name was—"

~

PETER COLLINS.

Peter had insisted that people call him by his nickname — "Pete." What was it with douchebags and their stupid nicknames? Richard "Richie" Eidenberg. Peter "Pete" Collins.

Pete had owned a liquor store, near where Donald worked off-Cape, in Plymouth. The place was a dump. "Pete's Package Store." A Massachusetts thing, calling a place that sells booze a package store — a packie, as the locals called them — so everyone called it Pete's Packie.

Pete had grabbed Jane's package the few times she'd ventured into the dump with Donald. What had passed between Pete and Donald to make her husband think it was okay for Pete do that, she'd never found out. Donald hadn't intervened. Had instead laughed, egging the guy on. "Jane, looks like Pete wants a piece. Maybe I can get some free beer out of it."

The second and last time it had happened, she'd snapped, grabbed a bottle of five-dollar vodka, and swung it at Pete's head, but Pete was strong and he'd caught her arm. "Feisty," he'd said. "I like that." Nothing more had happened, but she knew that one day, probably the next time she came here, Pete would pounce on her and not let go.

After she'd killed Donald, she'd spiraled. It wasn't from being suddenly alone. She'd relished the solitude. It was that something was missing, besides her abusive husband. She didn't realize until much later, when she stepped back and looked at who she'd become and finally stopped, what it was that she'd been missing.

Feeling. She'd missed *feeling*. And the only way she could *feel* was to *kill*. Nothing else touched her emotionally like that. Drugs and alcohol affected her, but not emotionally.

She tried putting herself in situations where she'd feel. It was one of the reasons she originally spent time at the dog shelter, because dogs had always made her happy, as had volunteering with the seniors. But when even puppies didn't bring her joy, she knew how broken she really was.

She'd even tried making herself scared, barreling down the Mid-Cape Highway in the middle of the night with her headlights off. That should have made her petrified, but instead, she felt nothing.

So in her broken state, like a computer with really bad programming, her solution had made sense. You want to feel. The only way you can feel is to kill. So kill.

That sense of power, coupled with not getting caught even though she was ready to be caught ... there was nothing like it. *That* had been what led her to keep killing after Donald.

Pete had been so painfully easy to kill.

Besides the front of the store, where he carried only the lowest-grade crap plus a dizzying area of cigarettes, lottery tickets, and nip bottles, there was a back room, where something unseen and unseemly was always going on, she suspected

There were no security cameras in Pete's Packie, of course. An upstanding liquor store would have the entire sales floor blanketed with cameras, even back then, because you couldn't trust people, especially people who loved booze. But Pete's Packie was shady, and Pete had no need to capture any shenanigans on camera.

She came in right before closing and leaned over the counter, giving him a big smile, her a new widow, him not giving a shit about how much time should pass, propriety-wise.

"Hey, Pete," she'd said, keeping her smile broad and easy, even as he leered. "I'm wondering if there's any place to party in this one-horse town."

He'd nearly jumped over the counter to lock the door and flip the sign to Closed, then he slid over and put his hands on her hips. She closed her eyes as if in heaven at his touch, then drove a vial of death into his neck, jamming the plunger down so hard that it bruised her thumb and the syringe's needle broke off.

When he hit the ground, she kicked him in the groin, stuffed a wad of cash from the register into her bra, then walked toward the back room, ignoring his moans and spasms. She eased the door open. Inside were a six-person round table, chipped and scarred, folding chairs, ashtrays, and a stained mattress on the floor. On the mattress sat a strung-out waif of a woman who looked fifty but was probably thirty, her stringy brown hair down to her shoulders, swaying, a cache of needles and, oddly, several boxes of Cheez-Its at her feet. She hadn't been trapped in the room, which had a separate door leading to the alley running in back of the store. She was free to come and go. Maybe she lived there. Maybe she crashed there. Jane guessed her mind was somewhere far off Neptune, so she'd never get a solid answer from her. Also, in the woman's state, Jane could have admitted to killing anyone and no one would believe the waif.

The woman startled at Jane scuffing her shoes on the floor. "Oh," she mumbled. "Time to feed the cat, I guess."

Jane was about to tell the woman "Go" or "He's not coming back" or something equally dramatic, something that Belle would say (and who was she kidding; Belle would adopt the woman, get her clean in twenty-four hours, and pay for her college tuition; Belle was a do-gooder), but instead, she left the door open an inch, then walked toward the front door. There wasn't even a decent bottle of bourbon in the place to celebrate with, so she'd kicked Pete in his dead neck before leaving.

ROUX BROUGHT her back to the present. "So, Jane, four current murders, all unsolved, copying four past murders, all unsolved. What do you think?"

Who cares what she thought? "I'm no expert on murder, Mr. Roux. I sometimes write about them for my fiction, and I've had murder upend my life, but it doesn't matter what I think, does it?"

He seemed stymied. "Let me rephrase that. Why would someone copy four old murders? Including that of your husband?"

She let out a long sigh. "I don't know. I've told you this before, but I'll repeat: I don't know. I'm tired. This has been a lot for me. I'm done talking with you today."

AFTER PAYING FOR PARKING, taking a wrong turn out of the garage, and spending twenty minutes navigating (and swearing) through one-way streets designed for cows in the 1700s, she found her way out of the city and headed back to the Cape.

She hadn't said anything she shouldn't have to Roux. Perhaps she had talked too much. But he'd helped solidify that someone really was copying old murders. Her murders.

Was Roux behind this? Could he be the murderer? It might explain his enthusiasm for talking about the new murders — he did come across as boastful. Plus it would give him plenty of story fodder. But she'd watched him discreetly as he talked and walked. He had no scabs or contusions. He didn't walk differently to hide a limp or injury. She knew from experience that people fought when they were being murdered, Pete and Donald being exceptions. Much of it was uncontrolled, just the drive for survival when death was literally staring you in the face. One time, she thought her victim, this was number seven, was dead. Turned out he was only almost dead. He bolted upright and smashed his forehead into her nose. He hadn't done it on purpose. Just the body dealing with last instructions. Try to escape, even when you can no longer escape. The fight to keep living was strong.

Roux did know too much, however. He'd implied that he had a police "source." Massachusetts police had two main levels — local police attached to each town or city, and state police. The staties got involved with most murders, but they weren't usually the first responders. Nothing was particularly centralized.

So where was Roux getting his information? A single source would have a lot of information on some cases and none on others. Although the way everything was computerized now, who knew? In her books, Beachcomber Belle dealt with just the locals. Small setting. Keep it in town. She'd invented a Cape town called Yardley and had placed it right where Port Fletcher was. The Yardley cops were bumbling, and Belle was usually two steps ahead of them.

Should she call Perez? The detective didn't want Roux bothering Jane. But Perez didn't know that Jane needed to talk to Roux, or at least glean whatever information he held. Perez, and probably most of the police, probably still thought the ties between old and new murders were theoretical and that the old kills were not linked to each other. Jane knew the truth about that.

Another question: who would benefit from copycatting old murders? And why hers? Sure, it gave Roux a good story. And he had found the link. How, she didn't know. He was the classic dog not letting go of the bone. But someone else had to have given him the bone, and for reasons she hadn't figured out yet.

She drove to Hyannis and found an open thrift store. She pawed through the racks until she found a summery dress, blue with big orange flowers. It was hideous. And perfect.

The next stop was a boutique electronics store. The woman running the store — bored, middle-aged, looking like her name should be Debbie Downer — was shuffling about, tidying, ready to close up shop for the day.

"Hi!" Jane said when she entered. Faking excitement was taxing. She'd need a nap after all this was over. "I know you're about to close, but I need help." The woman perked up.

May as well push it. Jane looked over her shoulder before whispering, "It's my husband. He said he's going to leave me. I think he's seeing someone else. Of course he denied it. You know how men are."

Debbie Downer leaned in. "Men are bastards."

She had an ally. "I want proof. I've heard about, what are they called? Trackers. You can see where a car is? Does that make sense?"

"One hundred percent," Downer replied. "Let me show you what I've got." She hurried, well, hurrying for her, off. Jane turned, saw a rack of prepaid phones, and tossed two on the counter. Be prepared.

JANE STUCK the trackers into the hidey-hole. It was getting crowded in there. She changed into the garish dress, found the red wig from the other day, then hauled her stolen garbage bag out of the basement and stuffed it in the car's trunk. Back inside, she pocketed a few syringes, filling one with a dose of the expired doggie death and the second with another concoction, then put those and the stun gun into a shopping bag, along with a change of much better clothes and some surgical gloves.

One more thing. Lipstick. And lots of it.

And another one more thing: a burner phone.

She caught sight of the dead computer tower, the one filled with spyware. Flounder. *Why did you have to do this? We had a nice arrangement, until you decided to go full perv on me and half the people on the Cape.* She'd kept the computer because she'd had half a plan to lure Flounder with it. She wouldn't know if he was looking at her through the camera, of course, but if he was, she could act all horny, maybe whisper his name as she pretended to browse pornography. But she'd never browsed pornography, she wouldn't know if he was online, and she'd rather stick the doggie death in her *own* neck than fake fantasizing for Flounder. The plan she'd come up with was more direct. The computer could stay sitting in the corner and gather dust. Maybe it would serve as inspiration. More likely, it would eventually serve as trash. Just another body to discard.

She drove toward Byte Junction, then past it. The Cape being the Cape, so dependent on seasonal tourists to survive, there were some great hotels. And many not-so-great motels. She chose one of the latter, The Gull's Wing. She parked in back, out of sight, and walked around to the front.

The Gull's Wing looked to be permanently broken. The single-story roof was bowed, the hedges planted way too close to the foundation looked unhealthy, and the place, even from the outside, smelled like desperation. The only way she'd be remembered here is if she tried to pay with a valid credit card. It was perfect. There were only two cars out front, one at the entrance, one all the way to the left. She assumed that was the first room.

Wig adjusted, lipstick painted on, she strode into the "lobby."

"Hey, precious," she said to the scarecrow-like guy browsing his phone at the front desk, which was actually a card table. "I need a room for an hour."

He looked her up and down, but without surprise or lust. Guess he'd seen enough clandestine hourly meetings to no longer be affected. Although she felt a little hurt — she did look lusty. "Forty. Cash."

"Here you go." She laid two twenties on the desk.

"Room seven. Lock's busted, so shove a chair up against the door when you're inside if you want some privacy."

"Oh, he'll want privacy," she chirped, adding a Southern drawl for no other reason than it was fun.

She walked back to her car, retrieved the shopping bag and garbage bag, and went past Room Seven, trying all the doors until she found another busted one at Room Eleven and went inside.

If you asked rabid raccoons to live in a no-tell motel, even they would shake their foamy-mouthed heads "no" once they saw this room. There had to be enough DNA here to seed life on a new planet. Again, it was perfect.

Not daring to sit, she leaned against the wall and made a call.

"Harley, it's Jane Hawkins."

She could almost hear him sitting up. "Jane. Didn't recognize the number. You looking for more party for your 'friend'?"

She forced a laugh, then forced cheer into her response. "No, not that. I'm on a tight writing deadline. A pipe in my upstairs bathroom burst, so I moved into a motel for a few nights. Dragged my computer along, and wouldn't you know it, it's not working. Neither is my cell phone — it got so wet, so I just bought this new one. I need emergency help."

"Well," he started, "I don't make emergency calls. But you're such a good client … and since you're already wet to boot, sure. Going to cost you."

"I've got cash."

"Not what I was thinking, but that's a start." She could feel the oil oozing through the phone. His voice turned to distracted. "Been here cleaning up. Someone broke in and tossed a few things around, plus my office computer is all fucked up. I don't know what happened, but it's a pain in my scrotum, pardon the French."

She gulped before saying sweetly, "I'm at The Gull's Wing. You know the place?" She had no doubt that he did. Places like The Gull's Wing were made for men like Flounder.

That perked him up. "I can be there in fifteen minutes."

"I'll be waiting for you, Harley." She added a little drawl to his first name. "Room Eleven. See you soon."

She went back to Room Seven, mussed up the bed, which was fairly pre-mussed anyway, then went back to Room Eleven to wait.

Flounder's loud knock caused her to exhale sharply. She'd been leaning against the wall, seeing how long she could hold her breath before she passed out. She didn't want to breathe too much in this room, plus holding her breath was a way to kill time. She'd gotten close to two minutes. Her record was two minutes, twenty-three seconds. And that was back when she'd smoked more frequently. Maybe she was in better shape than she thought and didn't need to exercise after all. Win win.

"Come in," she said, sitting for the first time on the bed, her legs crossed. Ready and waiting.

Flounder opened the door, and immediately, his jaw dropped like he was in a cartoon. With the wig, the garish dress, and the brightest red lipstick on the planet, she'd been going for overwhelming shock. Guess it worked.

"Better close the door, Harley," she purred. He did, reaching for the lock.

He took a few hurried steps forward, then stopped. Confusion draped his face. "I've … you never look like this. Or act like this."

"A flood can do that to a girl. Messes with your senses. Gets you all worked up, all that wetness. Have a seat." She patted the bed next to her. As he sat, she got up. "Let me get the computer. You are *such* a doll for coming over."

He turned to gaze at her ass as she walked around the bed toward her bag. He was so predictable. They all were. May as well play it up. "You know," she added, "why not try that lock again?"

He bolted out of the bed to the door. As he fumbled to lock them in, Jane hit him with the stun gun.

"Gleech!" he yelped, falling to the floor and twitching like a beached, well, flounder.

Stun gun stowed, she kneeled on his chest and brought out the first syringe. "You put spyware on my computer, you fucker." She jammed the syringe into his neck, forcing the plunger down.

He clawed at her arm, flailed, bucked. More gleech sounds. And it went on for far too long. The doggie drugs weren't working as fast as she'd remembered. Guess being in a freezer for twenty years hadn't done them any favors.

She kept a knee on his chest and brought out the second syringe.

"Jane!" he oozed. His voice sounded weird. Or maybe just weirder. "I didn't … you don't … videos … I gotta…" He made to rise, but she pushed down.

"It's not nice to invade someone's privacy, Flounder. *And you invaded my privacy*." She steadied the syringe.

"You have to believe me. I would never … I'll do any…" His kicking slowed and his eyes dimmed.

"Fuck. You. Harley. Hawley." She jammed the second syringe, this one full of bleach and ammonia, into his neck. She wasn't sure what it would do, but it couldn't be beneficial. "Now you're vaxxed. Remember, we're all in this together."

She clamped a hand over his mouth as he screamed. Then he kept on screaming. This was taking quite a long time. Was bleach the right backup? Wouldn't ammonia do something? What would have been better? She'd have to research that.

He was done flailing, instead balling his hands into fists and then relaxing. She smelled urine. Fresh urine, she corrected. The room had come with a urine pre-smell. Since this was getting boring, she drew the plunger back, filling the syringe with air, then jabbed that into his neck and pressed hard. Then she stood, smoothed her dress, and reached for the stun gun.

Flounder wasn't going anywhere, but what if someone had heard his screams? Maybe nothing to worry about. This was The Gull's Wing, after all. People probably heard all sorts of noises coming from these rooms. But still, better to end this. She forced the gun's probes up against his skull and pushed, pushed, pushed. Boss had said you only need short bursts of half a second or so — much longer, and you can damage the device. Didn't want to do that.

Flounder lay unmoving. She felt for a pulse, unsure if she'd feel a faint one through the gloves. Nothing. She gave him a kick. Nothing. She took his phone.

His car was here, his body was here, his ID was here. Should she move the car, take his ID? Ah, screw it. He'd be

ID'ed soon enough. Flounder stuck out, even in a sea of Flounders.

She gathered her things and placed them near the door. She decided to take no trophy — a first for her. Then she grabbed the garbage bag and dumped the load of barber hair all over Flounder and the thin, cigarette-scarred rug. If this place had a fan, that would be even better, as it would drive any crime scene techs to drink, but she didn't want hair all over her, and this was probably overkill anyway. With luck, Flounder wouldn't be discovered for a while.

Then she placed the baggie of cocaine she'd bought on Flounder's dead chest.

She eased the door shut as she left, then headed back around the building and to her car.

Besides the spyware, Flounder hadn't been that awful of a guy, at least to her. But the way his eyes had popped with lust when he'd seen her all dolled up ... he'd have eventually crossed a line.

She giggled as she drove away. On to the Roux problem.

As she drove, she took off the wig and put that in another shopping bag. She headed for a strip mall, where the only two open places were a crappy Chinese place and a crappy Indian place, and parked. She got out, shimmied out of her dress, and changed into her spare clothes, then wiped away the lipstick with a wet wipe from her glove box. She bagged the clothes and the trash, dumped in the syringes and surgical gloves, and swung around the back of the plaza, where she lobbed the bag in a dumpster.

If she were more research-driven, she'd learn dumpster pickup routes. Hopefully this one would be emptied in the morning after a busy weekend. Whatever. In a few days, the bag would go to a landfill or be incinerated. She'd heard that most of the Cape's trash was shipped via train to someplace on the mainland, but who knows.

She stopped at a public beach in Chatham and whipped Flounder's phone into the Atlantic. Hopefully by the morning, his phone would be buried in sand, just another artifact to be found by future archaeologists.

At home, she started the shower, then stepped in with a lit cigarette, a victory smoke. She washed away all traces of Flounder while she smoked and soaked. Long day. Her arms and wrists ached from her time at the gun range, her ass and legs were sore from the driving to and from Boston, and she was generally sore from holding down Flounder while she killed him. She was feeling her age, she knew, and playing a game better suited for Younger Jane. Unfortunately, Younger Jane was not walking through that door anytime soon.

After, she poured a victory bourbon, then started a small fire in the pit out back. It was chilly, so she went back in while the fire took hold and put on a hoodie, then had a thought and took a spray can of Lysol out with her, along with the bourbon.

She dragged a chair close to the pit. Too much ambient light to see a ton of stars, but there were some. The bourbon hit harder than she thought — it was probably mixing with the adrenaline. A nice combination.

She checked her phone. Just about T minus zero. She pulled up her mail, refreshing her inbox. There. An email from Flounder to his customer base, a newsletter with an odd subject line and some *very* large attachments. She deleted it.

Nice to have victories. She made it nicer by spraying some Lysol over the fire pit to make the flames erupt. As long as the can didn't explode, this was fun.

"Ms. Hawkins?" came a voice from over the fence.

"Ryan! Come on over."

There was no gate between their houses, so he put a hand on the post of the post-and-rail fence and swung himself over. Very athletic.

"Pull up a chair," she told him. He did, sitting about four feet from her. He seemed more glum than usual.

"You want a drink?" She waved her bourbon glass. "I won't tell."

He shot a nervous look over his shoulder at his house. "My mom, she's asleep … I don't know."

She sighed. "Ryan. The only time I've seen you happy since you were ten was when you were fixing my computer. Talk to me."

"I dunno, I mean…"

Kids these days. Too busy with their noses in their phones to have adult conversations. And "I dunno" was a teen boy's standard response to any question or demand. "Stay here," she told him. "I'm getting me another drink. I'm bringing you one, too."

He was old enough to drink, right? Legally? She did some quick math. Nope, he was 19 or 20. She'd started well before eighteen and had looked forward to her eighteenth birthday, as that was the drinking age back then, but then Massachusetts had gone all nanny-state and raised it to 20. Fake IDs had never been a problem back then. Now, do kids even want fake IDs? Do they even go to bars unless there's dependable wifi or something Instagrammable?

She brought out two glasses, handing him one. He muttered thanks and swirled the drink without sipping.

"It's bourbon," Jane said. "Don't let it go to waste. It won't drink itself."

He leaned back. "You know, why not." He took a big gulp, grimacing.

"Easy. I said it's bourbon, not Gatorade. Sip, don't gulp."

He set the glass down. "Thanks, I mean for inviting me over. I saw the fire, then saw it get big. I wanted to be sure nothing bad was happening."

Nothing bad was happening right now. But you should have seen things earlier. She handed him the Lysol. "Give it a spray. It's fun."

He did, then let out a big whoop. There we go. Drinking, flaming, her corrupting her sweet neighbor. No matter. It's a nasty world out there. Everyone gets corrupted sooner or later.

The bourbon loosened Ryan. He talked about school, how he wasn't sure what he wanted to do, let on that his mom drove him apeshit with her hovering and his dad, when Ryan stayed with him, drove him apeshit with his apathy. Jane let him speak, telling him only to follow his heart.

"You're a good kid, and it's time you found yourself," she said when he fell silent. "Your parents are very nice people, your mom especially." Ellen was nice. Ben had been a doofus. She didn't care if she never saw him again. Whatever. Ryan needed to find his own path, hopefully walking the non-doofus, non-helicopter route. "They mean well."

"It's just been a weird week," he said, slurring a little. He'd nearly finished the bourbon and was cradling the Lysol like it was a newborn. "Some kids from school, I mean high school, younger than me, skipped school the other day and one of them got hit by a car on his bike. You know Woodman Road, that hill? He couldn't stop. His bike brakes failed. He's in the hospital, really banged up."

Poor Doritos Boy. Maybe don't tease dogs next time. "Such a shame."

"Yeah…" He trailed off. "And then with everything that happened to you … I hope the computer is working out."

"So far, so good. You know that stuff way better than I do. I'll need your help again, I'm sure."

He grinned. Money was also a great motivator.

"Is it all right if I … I mean…" He held up the glass.

"Another splash? You got it. Our secret."

She refilled him, and they talked some more about this and that.

Her phone pinged. A text from a number she didn't recognize. She opened the message.

No words. Just a picture of her. All dolled up in that garish orange dress, walking into Room Eleven earlier this evening.

She nearly dropped the phone, then steadied herself, her bourbon buzz gone. Looked like someone had used a telephoto lens — the stuff in front of her was all blurry. This wasn't taken on a phone. This was from a camera.

Shit shit shit. Someone knew she was there.

"Ms. Hawkins?"

"Just a sec."

She texted back: *Who is this?* No reply.

She texted again: *Who is this in the photo?* No reply.

She texted a third time: *Why are you texting me?*

A reply: *Oh, Jane…*

Oh, shit.

"Ms. Hawkins," Ryan repeated, "are you okay?"

She blinked, cleared her throat. "What?"

"Are you okay? You look like you got bad news or something."

"No, it's just…" Right. Like you can tell him anything. But better tell him something. "I've been … dealing with someone. A podcaster who's doing stories about unsolved murders and new murders, and he keeps asking me to tell him about my husband's murder. I've talked to him, but I'm done. Now he's bothering me. And someone just sent me some very … X-rated videos. Which I will not show you."

Best to merge the stories. Not a total lie. Roux *was* bothering her. But whoever sent the picture wasn't Roux. Unless he had another phone. No, this didn't *feel* like Roux. It didn't feel like anyone she knew.

The "Oh, Jane…" were the only words. Had Roux ever used an ellipsis? She pulled up his texts, scanned through the thread. No. He was more direct. He would have used a period, or nothing at all.

Right. Like everything could be solved through punctuation.

She caught herself. She didn't know Roux at all, really. This could be anyone. Well, not anyone. Someone who knew her name, who'd followed her to the motel, and who had her cell number. Who?

"This podcaster … he's stressing me out. Maybe I better turn in, Ryan. But thank you for coming over. Are you in good enough shape to drive home?"

He'd been gazing at the fire while she'd been texting and mulling. He looked up. "What?" Then he got it and laughed too hysterically.

After Ryan settled down, they tamped out the fire, putting a cover over the pit, and called it a night. Ryan hopped back over the fence and disappeared into his house, his drive home over. Another athletic move. If she'd tried that, she'd be face down on the grass and not moving.

Jane hurried inside, glasses and Lysol in hand. She locked all the doors, then pulled up the security cameras. She hadn't gotten any alerts, although she'd been home.

She guessed the camera app knew it was her in the back yard and hadn't notified her.

She scanned through the footage. Nothing unusual.

She checked all the windows and doors. All normal.

She sat on the couch, drawing her knees up and hugging them. This was not good. Not good at all. And she was acting like a coward.

It became hard to catch her breath.

Someone knew something.

She hopped onto Facebook, a platform she hated, and pulled up some local town sites. If Flounder had already been found, someone would be shouting it to their followers. Most everyone wanted to be the first to share news in this cannot-wait world. But there was nothing.

She checked a few police sites. Nothing.

Who had sent her the photo? She'd ask why, but she knew the answer. Because she was a bad person, and someone knew that. But who?

Once in bed, she stared at the ceiling, talking to Kate. "I have to stay focused, honey. I'm caught up in something I'm not controlling. And I'm falling back into bad habits. I can't stop myself. I'm being hunted. I don't like it. I don't know how I'm going to get out of this."

Day 9 (Monday)

THE NEXT MORNING, Jane thought for half a minute about attending an AA meeting, but that felt non-productive, plus she didn't want to start off the day by lying to innocent drunks. She drank like a fish, and lying to real people having real problems wouldn't make her feel better. Before the last week, threats to her past had seemed theoretical. Now they were real. It was time for action, not pretending to not drink.

She headed off to the bank. She needed two things, one being cash. Once inside, she withdrew another thousand in fifties and twenties, then settled into the private room with her safe deposit box.

She put on the gloves she kept there, then thumbed through the binder, stopping at the last of her ten kills. The Harley-Davidson chain. She'd been careful to not get fingerprints on it, or smudge whatever was on it. She sighed, then pulled it out of the binder, dropped it into a plastic bag, and sealed it.

Dammit. She realized that it would have been very literary of her to drop the Harley-Davidson necklace on

Harley "Flounder" Hawley's body. Think of the tabloid headlines — "Harley on Harley," or "Live to Spy, Spy to Die." Some newspaper copy editor would have had fun with that.

Whatever. The binder would never be the same. She hadn't wanted to break up the band — the binder told her story. But better to be prepared and lose her story than lose her life — or her freedom.

Life or freedom: which mattered more? If she was caught, if she went to prison, she'd kill herself. She'd researched a dozen ways to do so, no hackneyed bedsheet noose needed. What stopped people from killing themselves in novel ways was, she thought, worrying about the pain. She'd been prepared to stab herself through the heart, and that would hurt a lot. But what would pain matter if you were dead a minute later? Before you stopped feeling anything, you felt everything in those last moments. You'd feel as alive as you ever did while your body fought fruitlessly to stay alive. She bet that would be the biggest rush a human could feel.

She got a text from Ellen next door: *Can we talk? About Ryan? Last night?*

Was this about the bourbon? The kid needed to drink if he was going to live under the thumb of a doofus dad and a helicopter mom. He was an adult, for chrissakes. And a college kid. All college kids drank. It was part of growing up. Plus he'd had fun. Lord knows he seemed to need fun in his life.

She decided to answer, but later. She had another twenty-five pounds of puppy chow in her car's trunk to deliver to Take A Paws. After sealing up her safe deposit box, she walked out of the bank, then sat on the curb.

She'd thought about stopping her shelter donations, seeing as how she was still upset about Rigsby getting adopted. Sure, she'd had her chance and hadn't done anything about it, but it had been a ritual for the last several weeks, donating food, then seeing Rigsby.

What had stopped her from adopting the dog? Commitment? Not knowing if she could keep a mammal alive? Kate had been different, of course, being human instead of dog, but more importantly, Jane knew she hadn't been ready to raise a daughter. Especially being with Donald. And especially since Kate wasn't his daughter.

Maybe once this was over — "this" being finding who'd taken her picture and cutting their heart out, "this" being no more need to talk to Esmir Roux, "this" being sure that no one else was going dredge up her past — she'd think about … what? Adopting a dog? Patching things up with Kate? What was there to patch up? They'd never had a relationship, barely knew each other. Kate's choice, but Jane hadn't tried, either. They drove each other away mercilessly and without much looking back.

Kate really was her daughter.

She wheeled into the shelter parking lot and lugged the puppy chow inside. "Hey there, Kendall," she said after placing the food on the counter.

A loud braying came from deep in the shelter. Like a moose, Jane thought. A pissed-off moose.

Kendall cut in. "We took in some dogs from another shelter this weekend. I think they're going to be here for a while." She sounded disappointed. You run a no-kill shelter, you keep the dogs until they find homes. That's the bargain. However, she could see Kendall's point. After ten seconds of that braying, maybe she'd be reading the fine print, too.

"You want to see what's making that noise?" Kendall added.

Not really. "Of course."

Kendall walked her back, then pointed to a far pen. Jane peered inside.

A basset hound, sitting on its haunches and howling like it was warning the Earth about an impending asteroid strike. One long ear was ragged, pieces missing. It had rheumy eyes — like Donald's, but his eyes had been mean. This dog's eyes were kind, but it was also clearly annoyed about something.

Kendall said, "He just hasn't stopped howling since he got here. He's otherwise healthy, though. Just really unhappy about being here. Or maybe about life in general. The shelter we got him from said the same thing. He's not adoptable, but we didn't know that until he got here. Who'd want to put up with that racket?"

Kendall crouched in front of the pen and motioned the dog over, but it kept haunching and braying. Jane swore it shook its head at Kendall.

Jane crouched to get a better look at this loud monster. The dog caught the motion, stopped braying, and shuffled over to her, giving her hand a lick through the bars and wagging its tail.

"Huh," Kendall said. "Maybe I should pay you to sit here all day, Jane."

Jane barely heard her. She looked deep into the dog's eyes, and the dog did the same. Instant bonding.

"What's his name?" she asked.

"That's the worst part," Kendall said, standing up. "He's named after a TV serial killer. Meet Dexter."

"I'll take him."

KENDALL COULDN'T FILL out the paperwork fast enough, and gave Jane her bag of food back, along with some blankets and leashes and whatever else she could ply her with to take the braying monster away. Jane got it — Kendall loved dogs, but Dexter was not a good advertisement for a shelter.

Kendall let her know that Jane would have to get Dexter a license at the Port Fletcher town hall, then shoved all of Dexter's paperwork and medical records into a folder. The dog sat at Jane's feet, not making a peep, like they'd been together forever.

Jane was smitten.

She whistled as she led Dexter to the car. He hopped into the front seat like he owned the car, and they headed to a pet store to load up on supplies — two dog beds, a fresh collar, snacks, toys. On the drive home, she fired up the podcast app to listen to Roux's latest episode. He was releasing them frequently. Eager to get his story out.

This episode, he said at the start, was a short bonus episode, a lead-up to the regular episode dropping in a few days. She made a mental list of what he'd gotten right and what he'd gotten wrong about the old kills. He rehashed the first two, Richard Eidenberg and Sal Lomasio. She knew all about those. Weird hearing him talk about them. What he said was fairly accurate, but most of what he'd said, he'd gotten off the police reports, it sounded. He hadn't talked to other family members. Had he said he had? Or maybe he'd said he would? She couldn't remember. Maybe it had all been background and color, like her interview. She'd have to see when he released the episode focusing on Donald.

"For our next episode," Roux said near the short episode's end, "I have a special guest. The widow of Donald Hawkins, whose murder I've discussed, met with me in studio. This is my goal, listeners: to show how the monster who killed these people affected so many lives.

Noted author and widow of twenty years, Jane Hawkins, on the next episode of Mass*Murderers."

Jane pulled over on a side road and parked, cracked a window so Dexter could get some air, then got out of the car and kicked the rear tire, over and over. The world went blue. Once her foot was too sore for more kicking and a neighbor came out holding a cell phone and demanding she stop the commotion, she got back in the car and peeled away.

She concentrated on driving, barely. That man … how dare he record her without her knowledge. Another invasion of privacy.

She needed to settle down before she called him. Back in her driveway, she leashed Dexter and walked him around the yard so he could get acquainted with all the places where he'd poop and pee in the future. No braying, so maybe he'd gotten it out of his system. She knew the feeling. She had a lot to get out of *her* system. And it wasn't going to be pretty.

Ellen from next door hurried over. Jane tried to wave her away — now was not the time. But Ellen could not be stopped.

"Jane?" she asked. "You got my text? About Ryan? About last night?"

If everyone in the world were allotted a finite number of questions to ask before they died, Ellen never would have made it out of year one.

"I did." She indicated the dog. "But first: this is Dexter. I adopted him."

"Ooh!" Ellen bent down to pat the dog, who let her, then he let out a huge bray, causing Ellen to stumble backward and fall on her butt.

"She's okay," Jane said to Dexter, who then stopped howling. This was too easy.

"He's so … he looks like he's been through a lot," Ellen murmured, standing.

"Haven't we all."

Ellen shook her head to clear it. "So, my text. I wanted to say thank you for talking to Ryan last night. He said he couldn't sleep, saw you outside, and you talked to him really nicely. That was so sweet, Jane!"

Nothing about the bourbon. Ryan had hidden his drinking. Or maybe Ellen didn't care. Jane certainly didn't care.

"Any time, Ellen. He's a good kid. Really smart. It was nice to see him laugh for once and let loose."

Concern crossed Ellen's face. "Let loose?"

"You know what I mean. Nothing against Ryan. He's a teen boy. They're all like that. And a great kid. I mean let loose meaning not act like he's got a stick up his rectum, is what I meant. He had fun last night. He can come over any time."

"Oh."

Jane figured that Ben had never talked to Ellen directly, Ellen had probably always talked to Ben directly, and neither of them talked to Ryan like he needed, so the kid was fumbling through learning how to talk to adults. Ellen was too confrontational, and Ben had been as passive as a bad writer's sentences.

"Let him live, Ellen. Give him space." Not that Jane should be giving anyone parenting advice. She turned away and led Dexter inside the house, not looking back at what she was sure was Ellen with mouth agape. She'd bring in her purchases in a bit. Let the dog sniff around and get to know the place.

Dexter became fascinated with licking the kitchen floor, so she let him as she called Roux. He didn't pick up, so she left him a message.

"Mr. Roux. You recorded me. You had no right."

She toted the phone around for an hour, settling Dexter in — he liked his new beds — and walking him around the yard again. Roux didn't call back. She felt like someone was squeezing her heart, sticking their fingers in her ventricles, probing, laughing.

Esmir Roux.

LATER, she walked Dexter up and down the street. No barking, braying, growling, or howling. He did his business, then he curled up for a nap once they were back inside, giving her time for a little research.

First, she looked over that texted photo again. It did look like it had been taken from a distance. And it seemed that whoever took it was at the same level as her, so he or she hadn't been perched in a tree or slithering on the ground. What was across the street from The Gull's Wing? She tried hard to remember. Nothing. Nothing of note, anyway.

So how had they found her? She'd have to ask Ryan about tracking software on her phone. But how would someone have put that on there? She scrolled through her phone's screens. None of the apps seemed weird or new.

Tracking. Like the trackers she bought yesterday. Could someone have put a tracker on her car? In her car? In her purse?

She dumped out her purse. Lots of junk. It could use a good going-through, but there was no time for that today, and nothing in there looked anything like the trackers she'd bought.

"Dexter, watch the house. Mommy's going outside."

She changed into grubby clothes, then went outside

and crawled under her car as best she could, shining a flashlight here and there. Nothing. Although she'd rarely looked under a car, so a tracker could have been two feet from her nose and she wouldn't recognize it.

She lifted the hood. The insides looked like something aliens had built. She didn't know what any of it was besides where you put the wiper fluid.

Inside the car? She opened all the doors, looked under the seats, checked everywhere. Nothing.

Her head was deep in the trunk when she heard, "Jane?" from behind her, startling her. She smashed her head on the trunk and swore. She started to see blue but tamped it down. It was Ellen, who was just being Ellen.

She climbed out of the trunk and turned to her neighbor. "I'm looking for a lost ... something."

Ellen gulped. "I hope you find it."

Ellen, despite the many Ellen things that Jane found annoying, was nice. She didn't deserve Jane being instructive about her son. Lord knows Jane would never win parent of the year. You don't get a certificate for giving your own kid up for adoption.

"About earlier," Jane said. Ellen made to reply, but Jane shushed her. "I liked having Ryan come over. I shouldn't have said the thing about the stick up the butt. Uncalled for. You have done an amazing job raising him. He just seems, well, sullen all the time, and last night he wasn't. He was a pleasure to be around."

"Oh!" Ellen started. "Thank you! Ryan has always been so..." And then she talked for five minutes about raising Ryan, while Jane nodded and remembered to smile and thought about the bastard who sent her the picture and what she'd do to them when she found them.

~

AFTER ELLEN GOT everything out of her system — or something out of her system; the woman had an unlimited capacity for oversharing once she got going — Jane and Dexter stretched out on the couch. She eyed the mutt. He was acting like he'd lived here his whole life, snoring away like a pro.

"Mommy needs to think," she told the dog.

She was spiraling. She knew that. No need to pretend it was anything else. Old murders. New murders. Her murders — the carjacker, Flounder. Add in Roux, add in whoever texted her that picture. Too much to take. Her body ached to vomit, but she'd feel worse if she let it out.

She closed her eyes while she stroked Dexter's head. Every problem has a solution. Even the big ones. But there were too many problems right now.

She needed to clear a path, clear her head. Before this last week, back when she'd been simply Jane Hawkins, Cozy Mystery Author, she'd write, have some coffee, and that was it, because the past had been buried and no one was digging it up. Now, she wanted to drink, smoke, and destroy everything in sight except Dexter, and none of that would help.

Talking to Kate helped, but only because Jane was talking to Imaginary Kate, the daughter who'd forgiven her and was patient and kind and supportive. Real Kate? The wedge between them wasn't budging. Talking to Dexter would help, she'd already realized, but that was one-way.

Exercise cleared many a person's head, she'd heard, but she sucked at exercise and had no desire for it. A walk? Walks kept leading her to trouble (hello, chip-tossing bike teens).

There was only thing she was good at, only one thing *guaranteed* to clear her head and bring her back.

She'd lucked out with that. Nothing on the news about Flounder yet. She'd gotten away clean so far. And nothing more from Perez, or any police, about the carjacker. Weird. You kill someone in a parking lot in self-defense, get interviewed about it for an hour, and no one asks again? Case closed? That was fine with her.

She mulled that over for a bit, then gave Dexter his first meal in his new home. When she took him out, she said, "Dexter, you have the run of the house tonight. Mommy needs to go out."

She locked up, checked the windows and the red thread, then sat in her car and pulled out her phone.

Finding out where Bettina Yothers lived was easy. The woman shared her entire life on Facebook (where you'd think her marriage was perfect). Bettina had taken enough pictures of her house, inside and out, that Jane could see there were no security cameras or video doorbells or other gadgetry she'd have to avoid. She also got a good look at Yip's pickup truck, the license plate clear as day. He was proud of that truck.

If she had her way, he'd die in that truck.

She parked across the street from the Yothers, nestled between two other cars. Blending in. Dusk had arrived, and even from across the street, she could make out the raised voices of Bettina and Yip. Close your windows — the world doesn't need to hear your business.

She walked across the street and around to the side of their house. Whatever they were arguing about seemed trivial, but Jane knew that underneath every rippled surface were huge waves of anger. She'd lived it through that. She knew these sounds well.

"Then go!" Yip yapped, close to the window. Guess he'd been pacing. Jane ducked.

"Fine, I'll be back at ten," Bettina said.

"Don't care. I'm heading out. Don't wait up."

Success here would depend on who left first. Jane got lucky — Bettina headed to her car and drove away. Jane hurried to her own car as Yip climbed into his pickup.

It'd be easy to tail Yip. Problem was, Jane might have a tail of her own.

She'd started her car and watched for action other than Yip. Nothing. She gave him a five-second start before pulling out behind him.

Checking her rear-view mirror this often was annoying. At a four-way stop, a white Chevy Tahoe nestled in behind her. Yip seemed oblivious to what was happening behind him. Jane was not. It seemed like every time she caught the driver's face behind her, he or she looked down or to the side. And they were following too closely. Or were they?

Yip took a right. Jane took a right. The Tahoe took a right.

Yip took a left at the fork. So did Jane. So did the Tahoe.

Yip wouldn't look for a tail unless it was Bettina's car, but Bettina drove a red Hyundai, a very obvious car. Yip must love that, as he could easily spot her. The Tahoe ... if it was tailing Jane, it was doing a lousy job of hiding it. Granted, so was she.

Her palms started sweating. She didn't like being boxed in, even theoretically.

Near a warren of side streets, the Tahoe took a sudden left and sped away. Yip and Jane stopped at a red blinker — there were four cars ahead of them, and they didn't have the right of way. Yip eventually sailed through the intersection, and when Jane braked before it was her turn, the Tahoe appeared to her left, its signal on, indicating it would be going the same direction as Jane would.

She plowed through the intersection before her turn,

dodging two cars, one of which blared its horn. The Tahoe soon reappeared behind her. Was it the same Tahoe? This time, the driver was looking straight ahead and had put on sunglasses and was tapping the steering wheel, maybe to some tune. Was it even the same driver? The same Tahoe?

Yip pulled into … The Gull's Wing. Of course. He was definitely not running out for a beer with the boys. The Tahoe behind her slowed as Jane slowed. At the last moment, she swung a hard right into the lot, fishtailing a little on the gravel, Yip pulling in near what she guessed was Room Six. The Tahoe drove past the motel and into the night as Jane parked outside Room One at the far end.

It was hard to tell from here, but it looked like there was crime scene tape crisscrossing the door to one of the rooms way down on the right.

Things stilled. Yip eventually climbed out of the truck and leaned against the hood, firing up a cigarette and checking his phone. Jane got out, eased the door shut, and walked toward the far end of the lot so she could then walk straight toward Yip's truck from the rear.

Jane crept forward, then jammed the stun gun into Yip's side and fired. He let out an "ugh" and clamped down on the cigarette before falling to the ground on his back, twitching. The cigarette, still lit, sprung loose from his lips and nestled on his white tee.

He looked up at Jane through heavy-lidded, dull eyes and said something that sounded like "Canada." Not having time for a geography lesson, Jane injected him with her bleach and ammonia cocktail — she could no longer trust those expired meds — then shoved the stun gun next to his eye and fired.

A cavalcade of smells — urine, shit, burnt flesh, cigarette smoke. She crouched and felt for a pulse. None, but she was wearing gloves. Good enough. If he lived, he lived, but she'd rather he died.

She dropped the Harley necklace onto the front seat of Yip's truck through the open window, then jogged to her car, got in, and looked intently at the scene.

No movement from Yip or the motel. No other cars. No Tahoe.

She started up the car and kept her lights off, then headed back for the exit. A car pulled in, passing her, a Subaru something, and Jane caught the profile of a bushy-haired woman as the Subaru headed toward Yip's truck. Ready for your quickie?

Two bodies in two days would not help The Gull's Wing's Yelp rating. She headed home, cranking up the radio, enjoying the cool night air.

SHE ARRIVED HOME, checked the thread, went inside, and greeted Dexter. Nice to have someone in the house when she came home. They went outside and sat on the grass, looking at the stars, for half an hour.

Once inside, she pulled up a local news site. A body had been found at The Gull's Wing, the second in as many days. A local man was found unresponsive and had died on the way to the hospital. This followed the discovery yesterday of local resident Harley Hawley in one of the rooms. Crime scene technicians were still cataloguing the scene, which was not described, and said the scene would not be released for at least a few more days.

A shiver of glee. She clapped her hands, startling the dog. "I'm sorry, baby. Mommy got good news, is all."

She brought her laptop down to the couch and worked — half the screen her word processing program to type out some Belle words, the other half a grid of squares showing her security camera feeds. She figured out how to stop the views of the inside — she had no need to watch herself type. The cameras showed a static, peaceful scene, mostly dark because it was night, but no movement.

Eventually, after a few hours of furious writing and camera-watching, she made sure the house was secure, then settled in for the night, Dexter sleeping next to her on the bed like he'd lived there forever.

Day 10 (Tuesday)

JANE WASN'T USED to waking up to whining, except from herself. But she had a dog now. Dexter was apparently an early bird, so she fed him and took him outside, where he sniffed every piece of vegetation, then she zombied back inside to make coffee.

Her phone flashed a string of missed calls. All from Roux. Before seven in the morning? Maybe he'd stayed up all night perfecting his sly recordings of her and wanted some more "background."

He called again and cut in as soon as she picked up. "Did you hear the news?"

She answered with silence, then, "No." She hung up.

He called back. "Jane, stop. The news. There's been another murder. At The Gull's Wing hotel on the Cape."

Motel, she silently corrected. Or *shithole*. Was there a Yelp category for shitholes? Also, there had been two murders there, so which one was he talking about?

She sighed, trying to make it sound dramatic. "Tell me what you heard, Mr. Roux."

He gushed, "A body was found late last night in the

parking lot. A man was poisoned. And something was left behind linking it to one of the past murders. But…"

She really didn't want to indulge his need for her to show interest. But … "But what?"

"It's impossible."

Oh, it's very possible. "Why is it not possible?"

"I'll get to that. This man, Jane. You knew him. I did some digging. Frank Yothers. He lives in Port Fletcher. His wife Bettina volunteers with you at the senior center. I saw your names on a newsletter archived on the town site."

Stupid podcasters, always digging around. "Poor Bettina. She's such a gentle soul."

"And," Roux continued, "another body was found at the same location the night before. A business owner, Hawley Hawley."

"I'm sorry, Mr. Roux, I'm not familiar with anyone named Hawley Hawley."

"But you are. I know you are."

A hand squeezing her heart again. "Come again?"

"You knew him, Jane."

"How?"

He didn't speak for about fifteen seconds, which to Jane felt like fifteen hours, then his voice took on a sharp edge. "Of course. It's you."

Squeeze. "I don't know what you mean."

"You. You killed Hawley. You killed Yothers. You killed the other ten people. It's the only way to make the impossible the possible."

And there it was. Someone had cracked her past. But … something was off.

She took a deep breath, held it, let it out slowly, gathering her thoughts. "Mr. Roux. You call me, accuse me of murdering … how many people? And talking about impossibilities? I'm calling the police. Your harassment has gone on for far too long."

"I knew all along, Jane Hawkins. I was pretty sure it was you from the start. And I won't tell you how. But the world will find out. By next week, I'll unveil a killer hiding in plain sight to the world, and you'll rot in prison for the rest of your hopefully short life."

A calm settled over her. It was not unwelcome, more like meeting up with an old friend you haven't seen since elementary school — two minutes of formalities, then you were deep friends again like you had been years ago. It had far too long since she'd felt peaceful. These last twenty years, she'd been metaphorically looking over her shoulder all the time. Before that, her marriage, and getting pregnant with Kate and giving her up. Before that, dealing with being different, not laughing when everyone else was laughing, not crying when everyone else was crying.

"Mr. Roux. This is very entertaining. But now it's my turn. Why did you send me that picture?"

A beat. "I didn't send you a picture. What picture?"

He was telling the truth. She could tell. He wasn't lying. Unfortunately, he wasn't lying about knowing that she was a killer all along.

She went down a different path. "What did you mean about impossible?"

"I mean," he said, sounding like he was talking to a toddler, another reason to make him pay, "that what was left at the scene is impossible. There's only one possibility. And I'll reveal that on my podcast."

Enough. "I'm calling the police, Mr. Roux."

"I could, too. But I'm not. I don't need to. I have everything I need."

She ended the call just as he ended the call, then took a minute. So many moving pieces. How would this play out?

She could only control what she could control. Roux said something about next week, so she had the weekend at the most to clean up this mess.

She sat on the couch. "Up, Dexter." The dog obeyed, jumping up and putting his head on her lap. She scritched his neck while she thought about the pieces, the timing.

Roux. Weekend. The necklace. Flounder. Yip Yothers.

Yip. She'd given in to her darkest dark side by killing Yip Yothers. It had been impulsive. Too impulsive. But she'd needed it. If she hadn't, her head would be too muddy to deal with Roux. Killing Yip had given her some clarity. And if Yip had been a better person, he'd be alive. This was clearly his fault.

She needed help. She called Ryan.

"Ryan, it's Jane Hawkins. Are you at school today?"

"Uh..." Why the pause? You're either at school or you're not. "I am. Is everything okay?"

"I need some help. It has to be today."

"I'm between classes, Ms. Hawkins. I'm about to go into my next one."

"I'll give you five hundred dollars in cash if you cut class and drive to my house."

"I'll be right there."

He didn't want his mom to see his car in her driveway, so they agreed that he'd park down the street and cut through some back yards to her house. She checked her cash stash. The thousand from yesterday was mostly still there, plus a few hundred more, along with the stun gun. And the ring she'd taken from the carjacker.

She hadn't taken anything from Yip Yothers. Well, that's not true. She'd taken his life. Except you couldn't put that in a safe deposit box.

Coffee. That would help. And a cigarette. She went outside, smoking furiously while the coffee brewed, then took a quick shower and gulped coffee until Ryan appeared at her open door. She waved him in.

"This is Dexter," she said as the dog shuffled over. Still no barking. She'd adopted him for companionship, not as a guard dog, but still, he didn't know Ryan.

She poured Ryan a coffee as she handed him a stack of cash and explained what she needed.

"There's this podcaster, name of Esmir Roux. I told you about him the other night. He's stalking me, bringing up my late husband's murder and accusing me of murder."

Shock crossed his face. "Murder? You? That's impossible, Ms. Hawkins."

"Right?" There'd come a day, hopefully far down the road, where Ryan would be on TV, or maybe on some holographic device, being interviewed about his elderly neighbor. "She was a quiet woman. Kept to herself. We had no idea." They never said, "Oh, we knew she was a killer. She talked about it all the time. She had bodies stacked in her yard like firewood." Until then, let him believe she was simply an elderly neighbor who needed computer help.

She continued. "Together, let's find out everything we can about this man. And some other things. I'll warn you, though." She lowered her voice. "This is between you and me. We aren't doing anything wrong, but I want this kept secret for now."

He grinned. "I don't tell anyone anything. Especially my parents."

She patted his hand. "Good. Finish your coffee, then let's get started."

After coffee, Ryan brought out his laptop. Jane told him, "You can set up in my office upstairs. I'll be right there."

He hurried out of the room and up the stairs, Dexter

shuffling along behind him, while Jane added a healthy dose of whiskey to her coffee.

Upstairs, they got to work. Ryan's fingers flew over his keyboard as he pulled up genealogy sites, public records, and other places Jane hadn't thought of. She pulled out a notebook to take some notes. Beachcomber Belle needed to up her research game.

Jane mined through the transcriptions of Esmir Roux's Mass*Murderers podcast. It was faster than listening to Roux crow through each episode, plus easier to save if she needed to refer back.

"I can't find anything on this man," Ryan said, "before, let's see, eleven years ago."

"That's odd. It's such an uncommon name. Keep going." She looked through the other pages on his podcast's website. His bio noted where he'd gone to college, where he'd been born, but she'd already looked at that page. She typed in his name and the college but got nothing of note. Same for his purported hometown.

"He's not an alien who got stranded on Earth eleven years ago," she muttered. "Aliens would have nicer personalities."

"What?" Ryan asked, absorbed in his search.

"Nothing." Dexter was on his back, his ragged ear jammed under his head, and snoring. No help there.

"How old is he?" Ryan asked.

"Let's see. His Wikipedia page says he's 45."

"Hmm." Ryan leaned back. "Ms. Hawkins, you said to keep this secret. And I will. But … can I text a friend?"

"A friend."

"A friend. She's really good at pulling up information on people, information that, well, you know…"

She did not. "Your friend, can she keep a secret?"

He lit up. And blushed. "Sure, she's really good at this

stuff. I just want to see if she can get me into a few sites that I'd have to pay for."

It might be worth the money to pay for access to research sites, although someone could track her activity. But if using Ryan's friend kept him engaged … time better spent.

"What's her name?"

He looked away. More blushing. "Cecelia. She goes by Cease."

He wasn't going to offer up information without her asking. Boys. "Tell me why you think she'd do this and would be good at it."

"Oh, she's great. She can get into any system and leave no trace. I've seen her force her way into the school's admin system, find out stuff about anyone." He then used terms she didn't understand, complimenting Cease with terms like "slay" and "slaps," but Jane got the picture. Cease was a hacker, or whatever hackers were called now. Got it.

"Have her come over."

He blanched. "Like in person?"

This generation. "Sure. If she wants. I'll keep her secrets if she keeps mine."

"I'll, umm, ask?" Again with the questions that aren't questions.

Ryan texted. Cease replied that she was busy with "something" but sent him a string of sites and passwords. He looked proud as he told Jane about the reply and dove into the sites.

Something about Roux's college rang true. Maybe he'd changed his name. But if he went to a big enough school, it wouldn't be unusual if no one remembered him and if he cherrypicked details about his time there.

Using one of Ryan's cracked genealogy sites, she

started browsing through archived copies of old yearbooks. Back in the 1990s, before digital everything took over, yearbooks were a physical representation of a school's year. There had to be photos of him someplace.

Ryan plowed through data as she pulled up yearbooks. She'd have to target her search, so she started with anything about certain liberal arts majors — English, journalism, communication studies. A ragged search for the name "Esmir Roux" pulled up zero results, so either he hadn't attended Lafayette, had never been mentioned in the yearbooks, or was hiding in plain sight in a photo. Or maybe he'd changed his name.

Nothing in the first yearbook. She skipped back two years. Still nothing.

Maybe Roux had put the wrong age on the Wikipedia page. She certainly couldn't ask him. Was he older than he looked, or younger than he looked? She'd just tried older, so she went with younger, pulling up a yearbook for the class two years later than the first one.

Scan, scan, scan.

Bingo. Maybe.

"Ryan, take a look at this picture." She zoomed in on a photo of two students laying out the college newspaper. The guy in the picture had turned to look directly at the camera.

Ryan looked. "Okay."

"Now look at this picture." She brought up another web browser tab, this one touting Esmir Roux's bio on his podcast page. "Does this look like the same person?"

"Huh. Maybe." Ryan looked at the caption on the yearbook photo. "This says that his name is Jeff Parker." He went back to his computer for more furious typing.

She searched the yearbook for the word "Parker" and found several hits. She eliminated all but one of them — a blurry photo of the college archery club, under which was a listing of all the students, one of whom was a "J. Parker." She couldn't tell if it was Roux in the picture, however.

"If it's him," she said, "then why would he change his name?" Esmir Roux sounded much more exotic than Jeff Parker. That would fit with Roux's personality. Appearing smart, unique. A new public persona. Or maybe he was trying to hide from his Jeff Parker days.

She googled "Jeff Parker" but that was a very common name. Coupling it with "Massachusetts" didn't help. Still too many hits. If only there were a way to get deeper. Roux owned or rented that recording studio in Boston. Could she find out his real name through a lease agreement? Some paperwork someplace had to have his real name.

No, not paperwork. The murders. The new ones, the ones copying hers. If Roux was involved with the new murders somehow, were the victims random? Or were they chosen?

"Ryan, you're better at searching than I am. What about this?" She wrote down the names of the newest murder victims — leaving off Yip Yothers and the carjacker and Flounder, of course. "What if you searched for 'Jeff Parker' and each of these names?"

"Hmm. Cease gave me sign-ins to some newspaper archives. I could start there."

A few minutes later, he whooped, startling Dexter, who brayed. "Sorry. I think I found something." He rotated his laptop and showed her a text-only version of an old, archived newspaper article. "It says here that a Rosie Parker died after a botched surgery, and her estate filed suit against the doctor, Douglas MacGonagle. It says she left behind two children. One was named Jeffrey."

MacGonagle was the doctor killed right here in town.

A shiver of pleasure, and it felt terrific. "Okay, that's a start. If we can find something else to corroborate that, we might have something."

A good lead. It didn't prove that Roux had killed anyone, but there was a connection. But what of the other murders? He could have known them a million different ways that wouldn't show up in a web search. Or … maybe they were practice kills. Not unheard of. She'd done it herself.

No matter what happened, it felt good to be the hunter.

RYAN HAD EARNED HIS MONEY. He promised to dig into a few things, then headed back to school. He said he'd split the cash with the mysterious Cease, who Jane wanted to meet someday. It couldn't hurt to have a hacker type on her side.

Roux, Roux, Roux. She had to go on the offensive. Killing was one thing; scheming was another. Scheming was fun, but harder. She was in the mood to be direct, dropping nuclear weapons instead of performing spy craft.

She sat with Dexter and a notebook. If Belle were going on the offensive, what would she do? Not kill, obviously. Belle was a bit of a pacifist, but that's what her readers liked and the market demanded. That reminded her — she pulled up her texts. Her agent Margo had texted shortly after the carjacking. She'd "heard" about it — how? — and wanted to be sure that Jane was okay. Jane knew that her agent had probably salivated over the publicity — a mystery writer with a new book getting attacked in a parking lot and killing a man to save her life?

All publicity is good publicity. She'd table getting back to Margo.

What Jane needed was to tie Roux to a new murder. Any new murder. Then she could go straight to Perez. Roux could do the same, but Jane didn't think he had proof, more like an aligning of facts that, if you looked at them the right way — or wrong way from her point of view — showed a possible answer. She had to do two things: get solid proof about him before he got solid proof about her, and make sure that his facts never aligned.

"Dexter," she said to the dog, "we are going on an adventure."

For this, she'd need just a few things: her purse, some doggie waste bags and water for Dexter, and the two track-ers. She took along a few copies of her latest book, just in case. She gathered it all, then cracked open the two tracker packages. Different manufacturers, so two more apps for her phone, but they worked pretty much the same way — activate the trackers, see your target on a little map. She spent thirty minutes figuring them out, but in the end, they worked. Each app's map showed a blue circle where the tracker was. Both were pretty close, and good enough for what she needed.

She took Dexter out in the back yard. She shook her head at the landscaping nightmare that was Leaf Guy's lawn. Your house, your yard, but still, she was sick of his shit blowing onto her yard.

She had an idea, something that would give her some joy. She left Dexter to poke around and grabbed a shovel. When Dexter was finished squatting, Jane shoveled up his poop and catapulted it up and onto Leaf Guy's roof. Good luck getting *that* shit to blow onto her lawn.

With Dexter safely in the back seat — he'd been a little nosy being up front with her while she was driving the other day, plus he could better stretch out back there — she headed for Boston. While she battled traffic up Route 3 towards the city, Perez called. Jane let it go to voicemail.

Two hours later, she'd parked at the same garage as before, only this time with bonus higher prices since it was a weekday. She desperately had to pee. So did Dexter, but he was able to go on grass. She stepped quickly to Roux's building.

She'd been riding a lucky streak, and today was no exception — she saw the same security guard as on the weekend.

"Hey," she said brightly to the guard when she walked in. "I was in town walking the dog, and I thought I'd see if you were here so I could drop off your book. Who do you want it made out to?"

The guard beamed. "Lester," he said, coming around from the back of the desk and crouching before Dexter. "This old guy looks like he's seen some action. What's his name?"

"Dexter."

"Like the serial killer on TV?"

"Isn't he great?" She meant both Dexters.

They chatted for a bit, and Jane inscribed his book. "Lester, is there a bathroom here? The dog has it lucky. He can go anywhere. Me, I need some privacy."

Lester chuckled. "Sure. Take a right over there" — he pointed to his right, her left — "and head down the hall. The women's room is on the left just before the door to the dock. I'll watch Dexter."

Jane handed him the leash, hit the women's room, then examined the door to the dock. It was locked. She wanted to find a way into the building on her own terms, with no Lester required. She firmly believed that there was always a way inside any building. You just had to think out of the box.

She walked back to the desk. "Thanks for watching Dexter. Let me know how you like the book."

"I already subscribed to your newsletter," he said, holding up his phone. "This job gives me plenty of time to read."

"I bet. Got weekend plans?"

"Work. Every Friday, Saturday, Sunday. Just filling in today. The other folks hate working the weekend, but me, I have a four-day weekend every week, except my weekend starts on Mondays."

"I like it, Lester!" She thanked him again, then made to leave but turned back. "Oh, one more thing. Where do people park around here? I get so turned around with these side streets. I parked over at the Common. Not a bad walk, but there's gotta be something closer."

"I park with the occupants," he said. "There's a private lot, maybe 30 spaces, one block over." He drew her a map on a napkin. "Not saying you can park there legally, but not saying you can't try. Other than that, people take the T."

She couldn't take the subway here from the Cape. Hopefully Roux would be too proud to take the T as well. And hopefully he was here but *not* peering through his studio window.

She bid goodbye to Lester, then left the building, taking a moment to get her bearings. Let's see. To the right, another building butted up against this one, so no access door there. She walked to the left. Windows to the lobby, nothing, nothing. Around to the back, she spotted a small, enclosed loading dock with an adjoining door, maybe the one she had tried. She walked over and tried the door and found it locked.

So, no unobtrusive way in except through the lobby. She'd think about it. There was always a way in.

She and Dexter walked down the street to the lot, following the map, but not needing it — the lot really was one short block away. She spotted Roux's black Acura parked diagonally, taking up two spaces. Jerk.

From here, she couldn't see what she thought had to be the window to Roux's studio; hopefully, he couldn't see her. She tied Dexter's leash to the Acura's rear door handle, put on gloves, got the trackers out of her purse, and dropped to the dirty pavement. Where to put them? They were magnetic, but newer cars had more plastic, plus she didn't know anything about the underside of cars or what they were made of. Something more to research in case Belle got into trackers in the future (she should — trackers were cool).

She stuck one near the tailpipe, then shimmied under the car as best she could and jammed the second under a fold of metal. Best she could do without getting in the car, but besides the sand she'd dumped in there the other day, Roux kept his Acura immaculate inside, so he'd spot them in there anyway. Under a seat would be best, but she had no plans to get into his car again.

She stood, wiping off grit, unhooked Dexter's leash, and discarded the gloves in a dumpster in the corner of the lot. "You make a good partner," she told the dog, tousling his head. He looked up in appreciation with those rheumy eyes. Yup, she was totally smitten.

Her phone rang. An unknown number from East Bridgewater, a town in southeast Massachusetts. Did she know anyone in East Bridgewater? The timing was too coincidental — this had to be Roux. Or the person who texted her that picture.

In for a penny. She answered. "Hello."

"Jane?"

Shit. "Yes."

"Jane, this is Stephanie from Vision America. I can save you money on your electric bill. I just need—"

She ended the call. Half the calls she ever got were unsolicited calls from roofers, solar providers, and shady nonprofits. The "phone" part of phones was the worst part about owning one.

She pocketed her "phone," then caught a figure walking around the corner of the building. Roux.

She crouched behind the dumpster, with just enough of a site line to keep an eye on Roux. née Jeff Parker. He walked to his car, circled, didn't see her, put his hands on his hips, and checked something on his phone. There had been no alarm, but maybe he had some app that let him know if someone touched his car. Too many apps in the connected world.

Eventually, he gave up and walked back to the building.

"Close one, boyo," she said to Dexter once Roux had gone. She was jittery from the adrenaline, but it was a good feeling.

The cat and the mouse.

JANE AND DEXTER headed back to the Cape. The dog seemed to like car rides. He'd settled in so nicely. Jane spent the last part of the drive daydreaming where she could take him, but those dreams fell apart when she arrived home.

Perez leaned against a police car parked in Jane's drive-way, smoking, talking to Ryan. Jane waved as she pulled onto the grass next to Perez's car. Five seconds to come up with a story, five seconds to decide who she'd be.

Talk less, shut up more. Follow Perez's lead, and give her no leads.

She extended the thinking time by fake-fumbling to get Dexter out of the car. The dog looked at her like she was an idiot. He knew how to jump out of a car.

"This is Dexter," she said to Perez, who stubbed out her cigarette and then crouched, along with Ryan, to pet the dog. "Just adopted him yesterday."

"He looks like he's been through hell and back," Perez said. "And he's adorable. Even if he is named after a killer."

The conversation to come — why Perez was even here and talking to Ryan — was Jane's version of Hell. Might as well dive into the deep end. "So, what brings you here, Detective?"

"Talk. About a few things." She indicated Ryan. "This kid came over, wanted to be sure you were okay when he saw me pull in."

"Ryan's been helping me with computer stuff." Jane patted his shoulder, hoping he'd shut up about the search earlier. "You know how it is. Technology is always changing."

"That it is," Perez said. "It's a new world out there."

No one said anything for a bit. Perez looked determined. She was wearing the same brush jacket, same boots, her jeans now blue instead of black. Her detective uniform.

"We can go inside to talk," Jane said. "Mind if Ryan joins us? He can keep an eye on the dog. Dexter's still getting used to his new home."

Perez shrugged. "Fine with me. Just want to run a few things past you."

They walked to the house. Jane caught Ellen peering through the window. "Hold on." She got out her phone and texted Ellen: *All good, just some ?s about last week, Ryan helping w Dexter.*

Once inside, they settled in the living room, Dexter sniffing about. "You can talk in front of Ryan," Jane told Perez. "He knows about the carjacking."

"Not here to talk about the carjacking," Perez said. Jane caught a whiff of annoyance in her response.

Oh. "Then whatever you need to ask, go ahead."

"Okay." She withdrew a small notebook. "Do you know a Harley Hawley?"

Ah. "Harley … that is an odd name, isn't it?"

Perez gave her cold look. Right. Her answer wasn't an answer, but a dodge. Perez obviously could spot a dodge a mile away.

"Sorry. I don't know a Harley." If pressed, she could logic her way out of that sentence. For instance: does anyone *really* know anyone?

Perez looked at her notebook. "Went by Flounder. For some reason I don't know."

"Oh, Flounder. Yes, Harley Hawley. Flounder used to fix my computer. I heard about what happened to him." She eyed Ryan, gave a slight head shake when Perez looked down again.

"I see. Harley Hawley was murdered at The Gull's Wing motel on Sunday night. Before that, though, he sent a group message to all of his customers. This email contained … videos. You were in one of them."

Jane gasped. "That. I saw that message. I didn't make the connection with the name Harley." Talk less, shut up more. But not now. "I saw the message and deleted it right away." She turned to Ryan. "Ryan came over the other night when I was out at my fire pit. Ryan, remember I told you I got a message like that?"

Ryan nodded. "That's right, Detective. I could tell that something was wrong. Then Ms. Hawkins said, umm, that someone sent her something X-rated."

Perez nodded. "Did you talk to Mr. Hawley — Flounder — after that message?"

Jane nodded back. "I did. I saw my video, which was disturbing but harmless, then one more, not of me, that was … explicit. I let him know that under no circumstances would I do business with him again."

"And you waited almost a day to do so."

"I did. It felt too late to call that night, plus I was distraught. The next day, I was dealing with that podcaster, Esmir Roux." A quick glance to Ryan, who gave the smallest of nods.

"Is he still bothering you?" Perez asked.

If you haven't heard anything from him, then he's not a bother at all. "He is, and I'm dealing with him the best I can."

"Okay." Perez scribbled a few things in her notebook. "This Mr. Hawley, those videos, he installed spyware on some of his clients' computers. That's how he got the videos."

Ryan started, but Jane cut him off. "Thank you for reminding me, Ryan. Ryan helped me get a new computer just the other day. My old one died. Ryan, is there any spyware on my new computer."

Ryan, wide-eyed, shook his head. "No. I set it up myself. It's clean."

"And," Jane added quickly, "that old computer is set to be recycled. I'm sad about Mr. Hawley, but to be honest, Detective, he crossed a line with those videos. I don't know what to make of it."

"Someone knew what to make of it," Perez said. "His

business, Byte Junction, appears to have been broken into. What Mr. Hawley was doing at that motel, I don't know. His phone hasn't been found, but we are getting his call history from his cell provider."

"The poor man," Jane said. "No one deserves to be murdered."

"Can't say I disagree." Perez set down the notebook, then rubbed her eyes with her palms. "This has been quite a week. Especially at The Gull's Wing. Two bodies in two days. It's turned into a murder motel."

Jane was about to say, "I heard," but would she have heard? She knew, of course, as did Roux.

Ryan saved her. "Two bodies? You mean, one besides this Flounder?"

"Yeah," Perez said, "a local man was there for an hour of pleasure with a woman he was having an affair with. We're talking to her husband."

"My goodness," Jane said, a hand to her throat. "What is the Cape coming to?"

"I dunno," Perez said. "Sucky week." She ran a palm over her jeans to smooth them. They did not need smoothing. "Thank you, Jane. I know that you've had a hard week after the attack at the beach. And if that podcaster is bothering you, please call me. We've got to protect our own."

Was there a sharpness to that last bit? She was probably reading too much into things. "I will let you know, Detective. And thank you for coming over."

She walked Ryan and Perez out, then watched the detective drive away. "Ryan, thank you," she said when they were alone.

"No problem," he said. "There's a lot going on with you, Ms. Hawkins."

She sighed. "That there is."

Ryan headed home. Jane made dinner for her and Dexter, then she spent the night watching her tracking app and her security cameras. Nothing happening at her house. But Jeff Parker was on the move.

Day 11 (Wednesday)

EARLY BIRD Dexter woke her up before six, making noises like he had to go out, but when she stumbled downstairs and led him to the yard, he stood there, growling at her car. She dragged him to the back yard, where he eventually did his business, then she fed him, made coffee, and went back upstairs to see five missed calls from Roux.

This was getting to be a bad habit, Roux calling her this early. She couldn't deal with him without coffee, so she poured a cup, then sat on the couch and returned his call.

"Think I wouldn't find the tracker?" he snapped upon answering.

"Good morning."

"You bitch."

"I certainly can be."

"Goddam — Jane, I found the tracker you put on my car. I destroyed it."

"Tracker?"

"The tracker. The one you put on my car."

"Mr. Roux, it's too early for games. I don't know what you're talking about."

"I know you were here."

"Where is here?"

"In Boston. You put a tracker on my car. I got an alert that someone was messing with my car. It was you."

"Boston? Roux, I wouldn't cross the street to douse the flames if you spontaneously combusted. I certainly wouldn't drive to Boston to mess, as you say, with your car."

"I found it, Jane. And you know what? I'm going to the police."

"Go ahead."

"What?"

"Call the police. Do whatever you think you need to do. In fact, maybe I'll call them myself. Whatever you think I've done, I know what you've done. I have proof. You only have a fist of warm dog shit. And who do you think the police will go after? The widowed writer who's being hounded by a deranged podcaster, or a deranged podcaster who's accusing a widow of murder?"

Silence, then, "I do have proof."

"Tell it to me. Let's see how far you're willing to take this farce."

More silence. "You won't get away with what you did."

"Tell that to the mirror, Jeff Parker." She hung up.

That last bit might have been too much. But it felt good.

She lit a cigarette. Smoking and drinking coffee was the perfect way to start a day. She'd cut back in the last year, down to four or five a day (both coffees and cigarettes) and figured that at sixty, who cared. She'd carved her destiny twenty years ago. Smoking, drinking, pot, none of that compared to what she'd done. And what she'd been forced to start doing again. If anything was going to kill her, it was killing.

She pulled up her tracking app. The first one showed nothing. Roux had told the truth — he'd found the tracker. The second app … was still active. Perfect. He hadn't found that one.

And he'd been very active.

Roux had been in Boston, then just outside of Boston, then he drove to the Cape. Port Brewster. Her street. He'd parked in front of her house. He'd stayed for only a few minutes, then left again for Boston.

Dexter's weird staring this morning. She gave the dog a whole muffin. "Good guard dog, Dexter."

She put on jeans and sweatshirt. It was spitting rain, just enough to make things slick, and the forecast called for showers and chilly temperatures all day.

She got a flashlight and went outside, then got under the car and shined the light around. The underside looked kind of like Roux's car, but also kind of not, with every piece unrecognizable to her. So where to look? The tracker he'd found had been the one she put near the tailpipe. He wouldn't put it there. Her car was locked, the windows rolled up, so it most likely wasn't inside the car. She started with the tailpipe anyway. Nope. The wheel wells? No. She probed around the front grill, under the engine block, under the trunk. Nothing. It had to be somewhere. There were few reasons for him to drive down to her house if he wasn't placing a tracker.

She unlocked the car, climbed in, and pulled up the security camera footage on her phone. Hmm. Nothing from the cameras inside the house. Nothing in the back yard. And … nothing in the front. But she was still parked on the grass because Perez had been in the driveway yesterday, and her car had blocked some of the camera's view.

She scrubbed through the footage and tried to match it

up with what the tracking app had recorded and when. She thought she caught a flash of movement near her car, on the passenger side, close to the front. Maybe it wasn't enough to set the app off.

She got out and examined the outside of the door, but that was a waste of time. It was a door. She felt along the bottom. Nothing. What had he been doing?

She got back in the driver's seat. She was missing something. Roux would have had to be quick, purposeful. And sneaky. He'd want to drive away from her house patting himself on the back for how clever he'd been.

If she were placing a tracker and wanted to be clever, what would she do? A door is just a door.

What about the mirror? Placing it there would be clever, and quick if one knew what they were doing. She got out and examined the mirror, pushing on the glass delicately. Nothing. Fuck it. She pushed harder on the glass, wedged a finger in the gap, pried around — and a thin black rectangle plopped to the ground.

She clenched the tracker and twirled around in victory. Now what to do with it? Her first impulse was to smash it, letting Roux know she'd found it. But maybe there was a better choice.

She went inside and rummaged around in the basement until she found an old tennis ball. Then she brought Dexter outside and sat him on the grass separating her driveway and Leaf Guy's driveway. She rolled the tennis ball to Dexter, who stared at it, then at her, as if to say, "I do not play with tennis balls."

After a few more test rolls to make sure the dog had no interest in the ball, she bounced the ball past the dog, and it rolled to a stop next to Leaf Guy's car, parked in his driveway.

"I'll get it, Dexter!" she said loudly in case anyone was

listening. She walked over, bent down to pick up the ball, and stuck the tracker underneath the car.

She could track Roux. Roux would think he was tracking her. How to best use that advantage, she didn't know yet. But she would.

~

SHE REFILLED DEXTER'S WATER, then headed to the bank. Was it suspicious that she kept opening her safe deposit box? The bank must keep logs, but part of having such a box was the element of privacy. She could do whatever she wanted in there. She hoped.

What she was doing today was taking her binder home. She dropped it into an oversized clear plastic bag, sealed it, dropped that into another bag, sealed it, then pocketed the gloves.

She'd been of two minds about the binder. She wanted to keep it safe, hence the safe deposit box. But she also might need it close. Breaking up the band by removing that Harley-Davidson necklace and dropping it into Yip Yothers' truck had not felt good. She'd assumed she'd take her souvenirs to her grave, that once she was gone, they'd indict her, and then her real story would be shouted out to the world. She wasn't worried about her legacy after she died. She'd be dead. But still, the binder felt incomplete.

And that was what she needed it to be. Incomplete.

Once home, she wiped the binder down until there was no way it contained a speck of her DNA. Maybe she didn't need to take this step. She'd been so careful through the years. But careful wouldn't be enough. She needed to be perfect.

~

SHE TOOK DEXTER OUT. Mercifully, he did his business quickly. Not a fan of the rain. She dried him off, then wrote some Belle pages for a few hours, then napped, waking up only when her growling stomach made its presence known. Not good to eat nothing all day. She made a quick early lunch out of leftovers, then sat on the couch and checked the tracking app.

Roux was headed for the Cape.

It was over eighty miles between Port Fletcher and Boston. He'd been here in the middle of the night, put the tracker on her car, returned to Boston … and now he was heading back? Was he getting paid by the mile?

Why would he be coming back? He knew where she was. Or thought he knew. So he was coming after her. So why leave, then come back?

What did she know about Roux? His real name was Jeff Parker — maybe. He had a grudge against the doctor who'd been killed, Douglas MacGonagle — maybe. That tied him to at least one of the new murders — maybe. He'd somehow connected her to her ten kills — she still had no idea how, but he'd done it, even if he had no proof, or proof that he was unwilling to share. He was motivated enough to make a podcast about unsolved area murders, but had waited until this season to explore *her* ten murders. So maybe he'd learned something new over the past year, or even more recently.

What else? He was neat, proud, conceited. He had a need to appear clever, to appear right. He was good with technology. He might be the person who'd sent her the picture of herself outside of Flounder's motel room, but that was still unclear to her. He didn't seem to sleep. He had a low boiling point — if she didn't answer his calls, no matter how early, he kept calling. He was sneaky.

And he was feeling some urgency, driving back here so soon after leaving. What could be urgent?

If he was headed to her, why?

To talk? No, he'd call her first. He always had back when he'd been pleasant. Now they were adversaries. So he didn't want her to know he was coming, and he didn't know about the second tracker.

He was hunting her.

Or … he was hunting someone else. The new set of murders were on or near the Cape. If someone was copying her previous kills in order — someone had to be — the next murder would be in Provincetown, at the tip of the Cape.

She could watch the tracker on his car and see if he was headed to P-town, as the locals called it. He'd have to pass by Port Fletcher.

Good plan. And one that gave her time to get ready.

She'd take the binder, the stun gun, and a few syringes. What to fill them with? She couldn't trust the expired pet meds. Bleach would work. What else did she have that she could try? And would any of it be effective?

She looked under the sink and in the basement. Maybe any liquid would be enough. In addition to the bleach, she had ammonia, paint thinner, and some other nasty stuff. She didn't like the smell of any of those, but maybe that was the point — the worse something smelled, the worse it would be in your bloodstream.

She settled on one syringe of bleach (since it seemed to work) and one of Windex (because it was blue, like her rage), then put those in a plastic bag and into a plastic left-overs container, wrapping it with a rubber band. It would be hell to get the smell of either, particularly the bleach, out of her purse if there was a leak, and she really liked that purse.

She bundled that, the stun gun, the double-bagged binder, and a few pairs of gloves, then set the bundle on the kitchen table next to her keys so she wouldn't forget anything.

Was she going on offense, or defense? She'd have to see what Roux did. If he was coming for her, offense. If he was heading to Provincetown, she'd follow him and see how things played out.

She changed her mind about the purse — she really didn't want to muck it up — and instead put everything in an old backpack.

Then she and Dexter watched the tracking app. Roux slowly, in app time, made his way toward the Sagamore Bridge, as expected. Then he did something unexpected. He started down the roadway that ran along the canal on the mainland side, turned around, went back toward the bridge, then past it, and stopped near Scusset Beach, which overlooked Cape Cod Bay. There, he stopped.

He drove all this way to go to the beach on a rainy day? Scusset was nowhere near Provincetown. Something wasn't right. After a few minutes of his car not moving, Jane pulled up an online map and zoomed in. Scusset was a beach and also a wildlife preserve. You could camp there, it had RV hookups, and you could hike around and watch ships pass through the canal. It wasn't very residential, it wasn't very commercial. It was pretty, though.

"What is Roux up to?" she asked Dexter, who had no answers. Who was hunting whom?

"Dexter, I need better shoes. Mommy needs to go hiking."

She had only a few pairs of sneakers, and she didn't want to get her good walking shoes all sandy. She found a battered pair of tennis sneakers. They'd work. She added a water bottle and a few granola bars to the backpack, thought about taking her cigarettes but decided against smoking in the rain, because that sucked, and jammed on a ball cap.

What about the gun? She'd only fired it inside, at the range. Would it really come to that? Her pleasure centers lit up. This was serious — and seriously thrilling. But she decided against it. Instead, she added binoculars.

The drive to Scusset was quick, the highway leading to the mainland clear on a mid-Wednesday pre-summer, and she eased into a parking lot about a mile from the beach to check the tracker. Roux's car hadn't moved. And given the weather, he was probably the only one there. The canal was choppy, the water dark, the top of the bridge blurred with fog and low clouds. A good day to stay inside, unless you were out hunting.

She spotted an access road, shrouded by trees, to the left and took it. Thirty yards in, the road was blocked by a rusty gate, and she parked. No other cars, and hers was hidden from the main road.

She got out, took the backpack, locked the car, and pulled her ball cap low. She hadn't felt this alive in years, killing aside. She tilted her face upward, embracing the drizzle. She wasn't scared — she had a dog to get home to, and she had no intention of orphaning Dexter after only two days, so she knew she'd be okay. Roux didn't know she was here, and he didn't know what she was capable of.

She edged around the gate and trudged down the access road. It came to her — this was an old military base, or part of one. Most of the original structures had been torn down to clear land for the preserve, but there were artifacts — a pile of cinder blocks, roads that went nowhere, cleared land slowly being reclaimed by nature.

After a few hundred yards, she stopped and checked the tracker. Roux's car hadn't moved, but Roux himself could be anywhere. What was out here, anyway? She pulled up her map again. Cell service was spotty, and once the map finally loaded, she saw some rectangles overlaid on the green. Old buildings, or maybe foundations of old buildings. The pavement she was on was cracked and broken, weed-infested in places, puddled in others. Not a bad place for a body dumping site, come to think of it.

This close to the ocean, the trees were mostly stunted, the pines here not majestic like in most of Massachusetts, but instead scrubby, to better take the abuse handed out by wind and salt. Still, between the trees and the rain, her line of sight was poor. May as well continue tromping around.

She bent down next to a tree to re-tie a sneaker, then heard a *whoosh* and a *thud* above her and she froze. Birds? Birds could whoosh, she supposed, but not thud. She stayed crouched but slowly looked up to see an arrow lodged into the tree behind her, about ten feet up, the black shaft ending in a green and white vane.

"I found the second tracker," she heard Roux call out from somewhere, startling some sparrows into flight. "That was a warning shot, Jane."

She remained frozen, staring up at the arrow, her heart pounding, her mouth dry. Stupid. She'd been stupid. This was all about him proving that she'd been tracking him. "I'm just out for a walk, Mr. Roux. Also, I don't think it's bow season."

An oily laugh. "I knew you were behind this, Jane. All of it. This is the proof I needed."

Where was he? She risked a peek. Arrows fly straight, and there was a copse of scrub pines about fifty yards ahead, the ground in between peppered with thickets and brush.

He'd come prepared, much more than she had, and she'd stepped squarely in it. He was either on the ground or in a tree. Either way, he'd shot high on purpose. You can't nail a tree dead center without a lot of skill from that distance, she decided, so you wouldn't also miss that much by accident.

The gun. If she had brought the gun, she could shoot without aiming, scare him into running, or better yet, cause him to fall out of a tree. Of course, the sound would give her away to anyone listening, then they'd report the shots, and she'd be eminently screwed. She could pass herself off as a local woman out for a hike regardless, although most people don't go out hiking with a gun or a stun gun or a binder full of murder souvenirs.

"It's so coincidental that we are both here," she said. "I'm content to sit and talk more. Come on over."

Another whoosh and thud, the arrow five feet closer this time. "I can do this all day, Jane."

The idea of the protagonist and the antagonist having a heart-to-heart conversation was so stupid, done only in bad books and bad TV shows and bad movies. It had happened with Belle a lot, though — her fictional amateur sleuth cornered the most verbose criminals.

What would Belle do here? The same thing Jane decided to do.

Run.

She took off back down the road, splashing in puddles, her backpack bouncing against her spine, her ears alert for a third whoosh, but all she heard were startled birds and Roux calling out to her, "I've got you, Jane!"

She reached her car, panting, and put two hands on the hood to catch her breath. The car didn't feel right. Ah. All four tires were flat.

Her curtain of blue rage came and went quickly. Most of the rage was directed at herself. Stupid, for walking into Roux's trap. Stupid, for giving him the upper hand. Stupid, for not thinking through the possibilities before driving here. Stupid, for not hiding the tracker better.

She slumped against a flat tire, took a drink of water, then opened a granola bar. Okay. She couldn't drive out of here. She couldn't walk back home. She'd have to call someone. And the only someone she could trust with a bullshit story was Ryan.

A horn blared for ten seconds from a car, unseen, driving slowly past the access road. Then she got a text. Roux: *Beep beep! I've got you, Jane!*

Stupid. She had to stop being so stupid.

First things first. She found a football-sized rock near the gate and smashed her driver's side window, then opened the door and gave the ignition a few whacks. Poor car. She lobbed the rock into the woods and called Ryan, explaining that she'd been for a walk at Scusset Beach and came back to find her car stolen, then she hitched up the backpack and walked toward the beach as the rain fell harder.

RYAN CUT class to drive and meet her, and she thanked him with the promise of more cash. He said no, he was just helping out, but she waved that away. She needed to pay for this morning. She filled him in as they left the beach for home.

"And it was just gone," she said. "What is it with my car? First the carjacking attempt, and now this. There's nothing special about my car. Why does everyone want it?"

Ryan shrugged as he drove over the bridge. "Lots of crime lately."

True. A one-woman crime wave was sitting in your passenger seat. "I don't know what the Cape is coming to."

Ryan let out a "dunno," not an unusual way for a teen boy to sum up a conversation. "I've been thinking, Ms. Hawkins. Can I tell you something, and don't tell my mom?"

Of course. "Of course."

"I'm, umm, thinking of transferring. Out of state. I feel like I need to get away from here."

"Here" might mean Massachusetts, or out from under the heavy thumb of Ellen. One can only stand under a helicopter for so long before they get blown away. "You should explore it," she replied. "Find your own path."

"You've lived in Massachusetts for your whole life, right? Did you ever think about moving away?"

"I have, and I have." No lies there. She'd thought about running away from Donald to anywhere. Pick a country. Except she'd never traveled abroad. Getting beaten by your husband tends to make you less worldly. You know you need to leave, and that makes leaving even harder.

Massachusetts was in her bones. The state was lovely. Mountains, well, big hills, to the west, beaches to the east, a compact state with a lot to offer. Expensive as hell, taxes through the roof, and an overreaching state government that loved regulations and commissions and bureaucracy to the point that it was nearly impossible to get anything done. But that fueled Yankee pride — stubbornness, thriftiness, and most importantly, sarcasm. She couldn't live anywhere that wasn't heavily sarcastic.

Also, she had no other place to go. She didn't know anyone anywhere. And she was picky. She knew it. Massachusetts had ferocious mosquitoes, but other places had scorpions or snakes that could swallow a whole pig. No thanks. The winters here sucked, and the summers sometimes sucked, but everywhere else was too hot or too cold or had tornadoes or dust storms. Like most New Englanders, she knew she'd die here, complaining about the place even as they lowered her coffin but also defending it with a sharp wit and a lot of swearing.

Ryan was feeling the itch to be on his own. He loved his parents but was sure he would still love them at a distance. His world was small, and he was getting mixed signals from his mom — follow your heart, do what you love, be home by five.

"I turn twenty next week," he said, sounding both proud and worried. "I'm an adult. I don't want to be treated like a little kid."

She stifled a laugh. Twenty? You might legally be almost an adult, but you are still a baby. Still, no need to be treated like a baby. Let you figure that yourself.

He asked if she'd heard any more from that podcaster.

"A little," she said. "I like to think the best of people, but he's not the straight arrow he makes himself out to be."

Halfway to home, she called the Scarborough police to report her car missing, giving them the details and that she'd already found a ride home and that they could contact the Port Fletcher police if they found the car. She had no intention of walking into a police station, where they might get curious about her backpack and her story. Don't be stupid, but sometimes play dumb.

Soon, Ryan pulled into her driveway, the wipers still going. "Uh, Ms. Hawkins?"

She was fiddling with her seatbelt. "Hmm?"

"Your front door is open."

Oh, shit. Roux. Dexter. Everything went dark for a moment as her body went cold. "Okay. Maybe I just left it open by mistake." Never.

"Should we like call the police?"

"Like" call the police? "No. But come in with me."

They got out. No cars in the street. Leaf Guy's car hadn't moved. How had Roux found her without the tracker? Maybe he'd put another one on her car. Or maybe he knew her better than she thought he did. Or maybe after trashing her car, he'd sped here and found that she'd moved the tracker and had gotten pissed off.

She and Ryan rushed to the house. Inside, the carnage was better than she'd hoped. Stuff had been moved, cushions tossed to the floor, again like a bad TV show.

"Dexter?" she called out, not knowing if the dog really knew its name, but she heard nothing. What if he'd gotten out? Or what if Roux had taken him?

"Ryan, check the basement for the dog." Ryan hurried off, probably not thinking, as she had immediately, that the killer always hid in the basement or the attic. She was sure that Roux wasn't here, and she was sure he was behind this. She wanted to check one thing without Ryan being present, so she hurried to the living room, swept the books off the shelf, and lifted the wood. Roux hadn't found her hiding place.

"Nothing down there," Ryan said from behind her.

She covered up the hole with a pile of books. "Let's go upstairs."

They walked softly up the stairs. Everything looked normal, except that the pillows on her bed were slashed and her underwear and bras were piled on the sheets. Fucker.

They heard a whine. "Dexter!" she blurted out, then swung open the closet door in her bedroom. Dexter looked up at her, then at Ryan, then jumped on the bed and put his head on the underwear. Okay, maybe Dexter was not the best guard dog. Good to know that Roux wouldn't hurt a dog. But it was not enough to save him.

Back downstairs, they picked their way through the house. Nothing else appeared stolen, or even that damaged, except that her framed picture of Kate, the one she'd hidden in the oven, had been smashed, the glass scattered across the floor.

Her blue curtain of rage came swiftly, and strongly, and she had to sit for a moment, Ryan consoling her but not knowing what was really going on.

"Okay, here's what we're going to do," she said after she forced the rage back deep inside. "Let's go out to your car. I'll take the dog, too, if that's okay. Then I'll call the police. Detective Perez."

Jane leashed Dexter, making sure he didn't step on glass, and they went out to Ryan's car. Five minutes later, Perez wheeled into the driveway, along with another cruiser. She stepped out, followed by two uniformed officers and Detective Bill Ramsford, who'd mock-interviewed Jane last week, which seemed like a year ago, back when she'd been playing the suspect instead of being a suspect.

They got out and stood in the drizzle as Perez and Ramsford walked over. Ramsford fanboyed, wanting to be sure she was okay, showing way more concern than she was worth, she knew. "I'm fine, Bill," she said. "But trouble does keep finding me."

"I was just about to call you when your call came in," Perez said, sounding like she was no fan of sympathy. "We heard from the Scarborough police. They found your car down the road from the beach, smashed window, all the tires flat. I'll have someone tow it back once they process it." She looked at Ryan. "And now this. What is going on with you, Jane Hawkins?"

"I wish I knew, Detective. Come on in."

The police took pictures and notes, and someone dusted for prints, even though they all knew that was useless. Jane had stuffed her backpack deep in the closet. No need for them to search her house — she'd already told them that nothing appeared to be missing.

"Bill, I'm fine," she said to Detective Ramsford for the third time as she got them all coffee. She'd smoothed out the picture of Kate after tossing the frame into the trash and cleaning up the glass. The uniformed officers milled about, but a break-in without anything being taken was apparently boring. Ellen Bligh from next door had seen the commotion and joined them, sitting as close to Ryan on the couch as humanly possible. Ryan looked trapped, because he was trapped.

"Tell me about these," Perez said, pointing to the security cameras.

Ryan started but Jane talked over him. "Ryan helped me get these put up," Jane said, "but I haven't had a chance to activate them. Dear me, if only I had."

Perez looked at her skeptically, then turned to Ryan. "And what were you going to say?"

Ryan blanched. "Only, umm, that I wish I had set them up for Ms. Hawkins before this," he mumbled. Ellen patted his arm.

"Tell me again what happened today, Jane," Perez said. Jane repeated the story, sticking as close to what she'd already said — she decided to hike around Scusset, her car wasn't there when she got back, she called Ryan, who was gracious enough to come get her, then they got here and found the door open and the house trashed, but not really trashed, and nothing taken.

"I can't see how these two incidents are related," Perez said slowly, "but I also can't see how they aren't. It's too coincidental."

"I am having," Jane said, "quite the week, aren't I?" Ramsford laughed, but stopped after a Perez glare.

"If you say nothing was taken," Perez said, "then I say nothing was taken. If you have no other information, then I have no other information." She shook her head as if disgusted at Jane. She should be. "I'm trying to keep you safe, Ms. Hawkins, but I feel like I'm missing something."

She looked to Ellen and Ryan, then back to Jane. "The other day, I suggested that you visit a certain place for a certain object."

Jane got it. "Yes. And I did."

Ellen piped up. "What do you mean?"

Perez and Jane ignored her. "And a certain someone who's been bothering you, is he still bothering you?"

Ellen again. "What do you mean?"

Jane said, "I think that's under control, Detective. I am sure that this break-in and the car are not related to what I told you the other day."

Perez sighed. "Look. Let's list out what the last ten days have been like for you. Car stolen. House broken into. A podcaster harassing you. A computer shop owner sending you pornographic videos, then he was murdered. You—"

"Oh my!" Ellen yelped, putting a hand to her mouth.

Perez continued. "You volunteer at the senior center with a woman whose husband was murdered. You—"

"Oh my!" Ellen yelped again.

"Ms. Bligh," Perez said. "Please." She continued when Ellen kept her silence. "Let's see. You almost get carjacked and killed a man." When no one spoke, she continued. "Am I getting it all? Is there anything else that happened?"

When you list it out like that, it really has been a busy week. "I think that's it, Detective," Jane said. "I agree, a lot has happened, but I don't think that any of it is connected to anything else. The car is just a car. A crime of opportunity. The break-in, the same. We've gone through the carjacking at length, and I'm still in shock over that." And still relishing the feeling of watching the life drain out of Jonas Ferrier's eyes. "The videos from Flounder — excuse me, Mr. Hawley — were sent to dozens of people in town. The—"

"Someone showed me those videos," Ellen said earnestly. "I've heard already that there'll be at least one divorce. Do you know the Ginthers? I always wondered why Patty Ginther wore so much leather. Now I know why."

Perez held up a hand. "I get it, Ms. Hawkins. But you've had too much trouble this week for this to all be just coincidental. In my opinion."

They talked without saying anything more for a few minutes, then the uniformed officers left, along with Perez, and Ramsford, the last to leave, hugged Jane goodbye, promising to get the bastard who did this. Jane thanked him. He must be the only real detective on the planet who talked like a TV show detective.

Then Ramsford turned to bid adieu to Ryan and Ellen Bligh, but when he got to Ellen, she and Bill froze, staring soundlessly at each other, then they both got goofy grins and blushed.

"I'll, umm, thank you for your seeing me around, I mean, for your time, Ms. Bligh," Bill mumbled to Ellen, his blush threatening to leave no blood in the rest of his body. Ryan seemed frozen as well, but with a look on his face that he'd just swallowed a cup of cayenne pepper flakes.

"Oh, yes, I hope so," Ellen said, staring up at Bill. She blinked furiously, as if snapping herself out of a trance. "Detective, do you mind walking me home? I'd feel much safer."

She could almost reach out and touch her own house from here. But Bill Ramsford, ever gallant, agreed, and the two of them left the house and walked slowly across the lawn, chatting quietly.

"Ah, young love," Jane said to Ryan once Bill and Ellen were out of earshot.

"That was kind of gross," he replied, looking like he wanted to heave. "Not, not kind of gross. Definitely gross." He shook his head, as if to clear a tawdry image from an Etch-A-Sketch. "How come you didn't tell them about the security cameras?" he asked. "It felt like you were lying."

"Oh, Ryan," Jane replied, trying and failing to come up with something sounding reassuring yet plausible. "You know."

"I, uhh…"

"It'll be fine, dear. Listen, thank you for today. Thank you for everything. I don't know what I'd do without you." She had him wait in the kitchen while she grabbed a few hundred dollars in cash for him.

"Fortunately, or unfortunately, I'll probably be calling on you again soon," she added.

"I don't want to keep taking your money, Ms. Hawkins."

"You're not taking it. You're earning it."

After Ryan left, she got tasky, stowing everything from her backpack, including the binder, which she put into the hiding place in the bookshelf, along with the stun gun. Shame she hadn't had the chance to use that on a person.

She stroked the gun safe, which she'd put under her bedside table upstairs. Roux had graduated from phone threats to projectiles. She'd keep that in mind for next time.

She fed Dexter, tidied up the mess, washed and dried her underwear and bras, and tossed the slashed pillows. She replaced them with spare pillows from the overstuffed closet in her office. They smelled musty — she'd had no overnight guests in years — so when the laundry was done, she jammed them in the dryer with a sheet of Bounce and set the tumble to low and the heat off.

Roux hadn't done much damage. Destroying the framed picture of Kate was a deal-breaker, even worse than touching her underwear. Weird. He could have taken her computer, searched for money, destroyed the security cameras—

Right. She'd forgotten about the security camera footage. And why hadn't she gotten any alerts?

She checked her phone. She *had* gotten alerts, but she hadn't told the phone to display them like she thought she'd had. Another rookie move. Too late to do anything about that now.

She pulled up the app. Roux had approached the house from the back after driving past the house and parking someplace off camera. He'd given a middle finger to the camera facing the back yard, used something to jimmy open the door, then pranced around the house. He opened all the kitchen cabinets, finding nothing of value, then found Kate's picture wrapped in the towel — why had he thought to look in the oven range drawer? — took it out, and stomped on it.

She paused the footage there. Things were things. But stomping on Kate's picture? Unforgivable.

When she continued, she saw Roux toss things, slash the pillows, and go through her underwear drawer. Over-all, he didn't seem to have a purpose, instead acting like a chimpanzee let loose in the house. Thankfully he'd kept clothed the whole time and hadn't sexually assaulted her underwear — if he'd done that, she'd have burned the house to the ground.

There'd been no sign of Dexter on the footage. Apparently, the dog had done nothing but hide in the closet and stay silent.

"Dexter," she said, "we need to have a talk about who is a good person and who is a bad person."

Roux hadn't done much else, besides shooting a middle finger at all the other cameras. So cavalier. And why not? He knew that Jane wouldn't tell the police anything. He trusted her to keep his secrets. One hangs, we both hang.

It was only just past seven at night, but Jane had a plan. She had an early dinner, showered, downed two shots of vodka, poured the nasty gin from the other night down the drain, saved the bottle, and went upstairs to bed. She set her alarm for 2 a.m.

She had work to do.

Day 12 (Thursday)

Two a.m. Preparation time.

Dexter wanted no part of middle of the night shenanigans, so he stayed on the bed while Jane got to work.

First, she called the rental car company and arranged to have a car delivered to her house by eight. The concierge delivery service was extra but totally worth it. The last she knew, her car was back at the same garage as last time. Four punctured tires, and the guy might have to replace all of them. Looked like someone shot them with an arrow, he'd said.

More money flowing out. She'd been blowing through cash over the last few weeks. She'd collected Donald's survivor benefits, and he'd had some life insurance, the one policy he hadn't cashed in to blow on booze and who knows what else. The royalties from her books kept her afloat month by month. She owned the house, but still, she was naturally frugal. She didn't regret paying Ryan a penny, though. He'd earned it.

For this plan to work, she needed to hit Home Depot early. She had everything else she needed. She booted up her computer and, using the privacy settings that Ryan had showed her, found the instructions she needed. It would be painfully easy to make what she needed to make. How did people learn this kind of stuff before computers? They went to libraries, maybe, or learned through word of mouth. Technology giveth, technology taketh away.

She ran through the plan in her head. So many "what ifs" that it made her head spin. Lots of moving pieces.

She gathered what she already had and made a short list of what she'd get at Home Depot later in the morning. Then she dusted off her sewing machine. She used to sew a lot, back in the dark Donald days, loving the hum and vibration of the machine and the chance to be busy and alone. Often, she'd simply run stitches up and down a length of fabric for no reason other than the escape, the door shut, her in her own little world. Like an escape room you don't want to leave. Right now, though, she had a mission.

From a tote full of arts and crafts supplies she'd gathered over her years of volunteering at the senior center, she pulled out some letter templates. Hmm. In her head, the letters had been smaller. Well, no time for that now. She'd improvise.

From her closet, she found a light blue long-sleeved buttoned shirt, a mix of cotton and lyocell, the label said, whatever lyocell was. It made the shirt stiffer than if it had been all cotton. Did she have something darker? No. Darker would have masked any mistakes she'd be sure to make with the sewing. But good enough. She didn't have to pass close inspection.

She got to work, smoothing the shirt, carefully tracing the letters with a red pen because she'd use red thread for the sewing and she wanted it to look professionally done from a distance. She'd be sewing only nine letters, so not difficult, but she took a coffee break after the first five, step-ping outside in the chilly night air for a smoke. Yesterday's rain had scooted, and the early morning sky showed some stars among thin clouds. Peaceful for now.

If Roux came in the next few hours, she'd be screwed. And most likely dead. But he'd made the last move, and a successful one at that. He was a game player, she'd real-ized. Now it was her turn to make a move.

She stubbed out the cigarette and went back inside, finished her sewing, napped, then woke up just past seven to see a silver Toyota 4Runner parked in her driveway, the keys in an envelope on its roof. She checked — yes, the security cameras had caught the rental place dropping it off, and no, she still hadn't set her notifications correctly. She spent a few minutes trying different settings until she fixed that.

Then it was time to call Roux.

She went to dial, but saw that she had a voicemail from Scottie, the guy from the AA meeting. He'd called while she'd been outside. Weird. People weren't supposed to call people they barely knew in the middle of the night.

She pulled up the voicemail: *"Jane ... this is Scottie, we met at the church ... I fucked up..."* She'd picked up on that from word one. He sounded drunk. *"My sponsor, had a fight with him, about, shit, not starting over, what we talked about ... I've been on a ... drinking again ... God, I missed this, but I hate the way ... I need to talk to someone, I don't know what I'm ... your sponsor, could I, or talk to you ... I need help. Shit, I'm sorry, so late ..."* Then there were some sniffling or sobbing sounds.

Not my problem, no time for this. She deleted the voicemail without listening to the rest and blocked his number, then called Roux.

He answered quickly, as if he'd been kept waiting all night.

"Jane." Only one word, yet it was soaked in glee and oil.

She'd thought carefully about how to approach this. What she wanted to do was reach through the phone and stab him in the temple with an icepick. Physics, and needing to be smart, made that a bad plan.

"Mr. Roux." She made sure to sound tired. "What is it that you want?"

"What I want?" he asked. "It should be obvious. I want two things. You come on my podcast and admit to murdering ten people — at least ten people, since I think you've gotten busy again — and then I want you to die in jail."

Nothing like your opponent putting their cards on the table. "Now why would I do that if I'm innocent?"

He snorted. "You are far from innocent. I'm still digging. Every day, I find more proof between you and those murders. You killed your husband, Jane, and you're living off his life insurance, pretending to be this sweet old lady. How can you type with all that blood on your hands?"

Melodramatic. And wrong about the life insurance. It had been a crap policy. He knew something, but he was far from knowing the whole story. "I won't go on your podcast and admit to murders I didn't commit." Not a lie, but a deep bending of the truth. "However…"

Here, she paused, and he waited for her to continue, but she didn't. Finally, he asked, "However what?"

She sighed loudly so he wouldn't miss it. "A truce. Look, I'm heading to Central Mass. later today. Worcester. I'm doing research for my next book. There are some old buildings along Hammond Street I want to accurately describe to make the story more realistic. That's where I'll be. I'll meet you there at three, when I'm done."

She had no intention of being in Worcester. She just needed Roux to not be in Boston.

"I don't know, Jane. You picking a place and time? How do I know this isn't a trap?"

Again with the cartoon antagonist response. "Mr. Roux — Esmir. I just want to be left alone. I'm tired of being scared."

"You scared?" he scoffed. "I'm the one who should be scared. You're a killer, Jane. You've been tracking me for days. I barely escaped with my life yesterday."

She was so close to breaking this facade. *He* barely escaped with his life? What did he think could have happened — strike him down with a thrown granola bar from fifty yards out? He'd shot arrows at her twice and ruined her car. The blue curtain of rage started rippling, but she brushed it aside.

"Three o'clock, Mr. Roux. We can talk about the past murders, and what I think of the new murders. I'll even talk about finding Donald. You can record all that, if you have the capability on your phone. I won't admit to anything, since I've nothing to admit to you, but I'll help you tell your story better. If you promise to leave me alone after that."

He had no intention of leaving her alone. The golden ring, for him, was her admitting to murder on his podcast. He wouldn't stop until he'd claimed it for his own. That was not going to happen.

"You said three?"

Right. Like that had slipped past him. "Yes, Mr. Roux. Three o'clock in Worcester. Call me when you get there, and we'll find a place to meet. And ... thank you."

She ended the call, wanting to take a shower after hearing his grimy voice and having to sound so submissive. "Thank you"? One of the worst things she'd ever said.

So Worcester at three. She didn't know where Roux lived, but if he was in his studio, it'd take him about an hour to drive to Worcester from Boston. He'd want to be there early to make sure it wasn't a trap, she reasoned, so he'd leave the city by 1:30 at the latest.

She pictured Roux slowly circling blocks in Worcester, scanning the tops of buildings for snipers, checking under his car for explosives, peering down alleys for Jane holding a garrote. She had to admit, she liked the sound of each of those. But he wouldn't find any of that.

Now she had to work on her timing. She'd need to be in Boston by 1, so leave here by 11:30, four hours from now, at the latest. She couldn't get there too early, because if Roux was at his studio, he'd see her.

She'd check that little lot next to the studio building for his car, but Roux being cautious, he'd probably already found a new parking space. But maybe not. If he was more confident than he was cautious, he'd flaunt parking in the same space.

Either way, it didn't matter where he parked, she decided. He'd be at the studio, or he wouldn't be, and she needed him to not be there. She'd bring the gun as a last option. But she didn't want it to come to that. She had a book to write and a dog to feed. She couldn't do either from prison. Or from a grave.

SHE LOOKED at what she'd gathered. The light blue shirt, now with new lettering. Two empty bottles, the gin one and the bourbon that she'd finished on Monday. Strips of cloth taken from the slashed pillows — thanks for making that easier, Roux. Sunglasses, a ball cap, and another old wig, this one so she'd have short, jet-black hair. A pack of gum.

Three sweatshirts. A short-handled screwdriver. Two large trash bags.

She gave Dexter breakfast, then some extra treats because he was such a good boy. He rolled on his back so she could scratch his tummy. "Dexter, you need to watch the house. I mean it. No one comes in. If they do, bite them in the balls and don't let go." The dog closed his eyes as she continued scratching. There would be no ball biting from Dexter.

She put on the wig. When she'd last worn it, her hair had been much shorter, and now her head looked lumpy. She adjusted the ball cap to a wider width and put that on. It looked ridiculous. She tossed the cap to the side and jammed on a khaki sun hat. Better. She added the sunglasses. It would work. It had better.

She kept on the wig and put the hat and sunglasses in a bag. Everything else went into a big packing box, which she stuffed in the back of the 4Runner.

Jeans and sneakers worked to finish her outfit. Into the jeans she stuck a fresh pack of cigarettes and a lighter. She'd need those later.

She thought about Roux's building. Contingency planning. She added a hammer, a paint scraper, and a hacksaw to the box in the Toyota. If she needed more than that, she'd improvise.

She turned off her phone, then gave Dexter a big hug before she left. "I'll be back," she told the dog. "I promise."

AT THE HOME DEPOT, she circled the lot, which was filling up with the typical flock of mid-morning contractors. The sky was clear, the day warm but not overly so. A perfect day for a trip to the city. She parked near one of those places where customers leave their carts and stole a beat-up orange platform truck, basically a length of heavy metal with four wheels and a tall handle. It was difficult to get it into the 4Runner, even with the rear seats folded down, but she managed, and the few customers who saw her hoist the cart into the vehicle looked away. Act like you know what you're doing, and people will let you get away with anything.

Inside, she bought two big plants with the largest containers she could find, a two-gallon red gas container, two cans of paint thinner, a first aid kid marketed as being for kids, and a black and red tool bag. She used cash, but would that really help hide her purchases if someone cared to look? Probably not.

She heaved the two plants into the front passenger seat, not caring if she got dirt in the Toyota or scratched the interior plastic. Not her vehicle. The rest of the stuff she put in the back, then she headed to a gas station up the street, where she filled the gas can. The 4Runner had been topped off when it was delivered.

She needed a staging area with some privacy, and she found a Taco Bell that was shuttered for renovations and parked where she was hidden from the street.

First, she hauled the plants out of the Toyota, laid them on their side, and scooped the dirt out onto the pavement. She filled the two empty bottles with gasoline, wrapped each bottle in a trash bag, and stuck the bagged bottles into the plant containers, shoveling dirt back into them so the bottles were hidden. She lugged the plants back into the 4Runner. Good enough.

Into the tool bag, she put all the tools and the paint thinner. She stuck the gum into her jeans. Then she put on all three sweatshirts, the largest one the last one, and stood, looking at her reflection in the 4Runner's window. She looked quite heavyset. She straightened the wig, then put on the sunglasses and the sun hat. Unless someone knew her intimately, she'd pass.

She opened the first aid kit she'd bought, pulled out a cartoonishly pink adhesive bandage, and stuck that to her cheek. Anyone's eyes would be drawn there first, and that's what they'd remember about her — she was wearing a pink bandage on her face.

She then slipped the freshly lettered shirt over the sweatshirts. She'd never have fit in it if she hadn't taken off the sleeves and widened the armholes to make it look like a vest.

She kicked the dirt remaining on the pavement until it didn't resemble a pile, then checked around her and in the Toyota. Everything seemed to be in place.

It was 11:40, a little earlier than she'd hoped it would be at this stage of the plan, but she could slow down once she reached the city. Wasting time in Boston traffic was a given.

Shortly before one, she pulled up outside of Roux's building, slid into the bike lane that had replaced much-needed on-street parking — screw the bicyclists — and put on her flashers. She trotted around the building to the parking area and didn't see Roux's car. He was either on the way to Worcester or somewhere else. As long as he wasn't here.

Back at the Toyota, she raised the rear hatch and dragged out the platform truck, then put the two plants on it, along with the tool bag. She stuck two pieces of gum in her mouth, closed the rear hatch, and locked the SUV, keeping the hazards on. Then she dragged the cart into the building through the front door and over to the security desk, walking slow and bent over like her extra weight was getting to her.

"Hiya, toots," she said to the female guard while snapping her gum. She pointed to the plants. "Gotta bring this up."

"Who are you?" the guard asked, focusing on the bandage, from behind the desk.

Jane pointed at her vest. "Like it says — Plant Lady. I'm here to deliver plants."

"Who sent you?"

"Fuck all I know. I got a message to deliver plants, I deliver plants. Third floor."

"You got paperwork?"

"Lady," Jane said, indicating the truck, "I got plants."

"Okay then," the guard said. She nodded to the SUV outside. "Is that yours out there? That's a no-parking zone."

"Whaddaya gonna do," Jane said, shrugging. "This city, pretty soon there'll be no parking anywhere. Bike lanes suck. I'll be just a minute."

"Make it quick," the guard said, then pointed. "Elevator's over there."

"Don't I know it," Jane replied, snapping her gum. "Don't I know it."

She shuffled to the elevator, pulling the cart behind her, and took the elevator to the fifth floor. No one in sight, but she had to be on a dozen cameras by now. Nothing she could do about that.

At Roux's office door, she tried the knob. Locked, of course. She opened the tool bag and took out the paint spatula, jammed the end into the crack near the lock, and whaled on the end with the hammer until something popped and the knob could turn. She dropped the tools into the bag and stepped into Roux's office, leaving the lights off. The hacksaw would not be needed.

She dug through the plant dirt until she found each

wrapped bottle. She kicked the plants over and onto the rug only because it felt good. She took out the cloth strips and jammed them into each bottle. Two Molotov cocktails, ready for action.

She surveyed the room. She recognized some of the computer stuff but not all of it. She took out her cigarettes and lighter and placed them on a desk, then texted Ryan: *One hundred dollars for ten seconds of work and telling no one about this. Interested?*

He texted back a thumbs-up emoji right away. Kids and their hieroglyphic way of communicating.

She took several pictures of Roux's computer stuff, then texted the photos to Ryan, along with: *Is any of this storage or backup?*

Ryan texted back a minute later, having circled a few black boxes. She sent back a thumbs-up emoji — hieroglyphics were stupid, but more efficient — then got to work.

She used the screwdriver to open the paint thinner cans, unplugged all the computer equipment she could easily get to, then poured the paint thinner over the storage drives, the computers, the monitors, the audio equipment, and all of Roux's folders and files. Satisfied that she'd got everything, she opened the cigarette pack, then lit cigarettes and placed the tips near the computer stuff, with the lit end facing away to give her some time. She then lit the ends of the cloth strips hanging out of the bottles.

The room was eerie, too quiet with all the computer stuff off, and now too smoky with all the cigarettes burning. She wheeled the cart, now carrying only the tool bag, out of the office, shut the door, and headed for the elevator.

In the lobby, she waved goodbye to the guard. "See ya, toots!" She was loading the cart back into the 4Runner when the alarms sounded. She gazed up to the fifth floor. No smoke coming from the windows. Yet.

ROUX CALLED her shortly after three, a few minutes after she arrived back home. "Where are you?"

"Sorry, Mr. Roux. Car trouble. For some weird reason, I need four new tires. I'll have to reschedule."

He harrumphed. "I don't know what your play is, Jane. Why have me drive all the way out here?"

"Like I said, car trouble. Dang thing has no giddy-up with flat tires. It'd take me forever to get to Worcester. And now I'm behind on my research. Better get going."

She hung up, then took Dexter out. So Roux *had* gone to Worcester. He wouldn't get back to Boston for well over an hour, given commuter traffic. Would the building ops people call him? She hadn't seen any security cameras in his office, although she assumed she'd been recorded entering and leaving the office. She'd discarded the wig, the sweatshirts, and the vest, along with the tool bag and gas can, in a rest-stop dumpster, and she'd returned the cart to the Home Depot. Better to borrow than to steal.

On a TV crime drama, where the entire case started and ended in 42 minutes, the good guys would immediately scour all security footage at remarkable speed; they'd have found her already. In real life, would the Boston police really look through every Home Depot's footage? Would they be able to tell that the overweight, black-haired, shuffling Plant Lady was in disguise, and that it was her? Unlikely.

More importantly, what would Roux tell the police, if anything? She already knew the answer. He'd stay silent. When one hangs, we both hang.

She put a hundred dollars in cash in an envelope for Ryan, put the tools away, and snuggled with the dog until Roux called back, as she knew he would.

"You fucking bitch!" he yelled when she answered. "You fucking destroyed my fucking studio!"

"My, the language, Mr. Roux. What studio?"

"My recording studio. The building manager showed me a still from the video footage. It was you. You're going to swing, you're going to burn in hell, you're—"

"Mr. Roux! I won't tolerate this violent talk. Please settle down."

"Jane," he started, then a long stretch of silence, then, "I know what you did. You ruined everything. My equipment. My recordings. It'll take … forget that. I'm going to kill you."

"First, Mr. Roux, I don't know what you mean by destroying your studio. You know as well as I that my car needs … attention. You must agree that there is no way I can drive that car anywhere, especially to Boston. I don't even have it back. Second, you're threatening to kill me. I won't overlook that. Neither will the police. You're on speaker; I'm recording this." She wasn't. "And third … you know where I live. So come and get me. Better yet, leave me alone."

She ended the call, then blocked his number. There was nothing to be gained from talking to him again, she knew. It was his move, and it would be his final move. No more games. She considered what he might do next. He could go to the police, but she didn't think he'd do that. He had too much to lose. Plus he didn't want to see her go to jail for torching his studio. He wanted her to go to jail for murder.

She knew he was the new killer, or at least had his hands in it, but there was still a vagueness about the whole thing that she didn't like. He had circumstantial evidence, but she'd written enough mystery books, attended enough court proceedings for research, to know that technicalities would free her, if it came to that. If all those police departments over the years hadn't tied any evidence to her, how could he? He had a wild theory, is all. Of course, it was the correct theory, but only she knew that.

She knew what he'd do next. He'd come for her.

Her phone buzzed. A text from an unknown number, a different unknown number than all the other unknown numbers. How many unknown numbers were there?

Two words: *Oh, Jane...*

A new photo. In it, she was disguised, leaving the motel room where she'd killed Flounder. She zoomed in. You could tell it was the same person as in the previous photo she'd received, but you still couldn't tell that it was her.

Someone had taken more than one picture of her that night. Someone with a lot of phone numbers. They were trickling the photos to her.

This soon after disconnecting the call with Roux? That couldn't be coincidence. Although the world was full of coincidences, even if she didn't believe in them.

Maybe think about this as causation versus correlation. Correlation: she talked to Roux, hung up, then immediately received this photo. If there was causality, then the photo resulted from that text somehow — she wouldn't have gotten the photo if she hadn't talked to Roux, or if the call had gone differently somehow. But the two events might not be related. Roux had never said anything about her going to a motel room. His actions to date indicated that he'd brag about knowing that — it would be stronger proof that she was up to something than anything else he'd mentioned. Plus he'd never brought up the photos.

The two things could be related — or they could not.

If they weren't, then there were two games being played. The bad thing about that: she had two foes. The good thing: each of her foes knew or suspected something, but maybe didn't know what the other knew.

She texted the unknown number back: *Perez?* She got an immediate reply that her text could not go through. The number was now useless to her.

Roux would be coming for her. Deal with him first. Whoever was sending her the photos? That was a game for later.

Day 13 (Friday)

IN THE MORNING, Perez texted Jane and said she was coming over. She didn't give a reason why. She wouldn't give notice if she was coming over to arrest her, so it couldn't be that. Maybe she was bringing more cake. Jane replied: *Give me an hour.*

Jane then texted Ryan and said she'd bring the cash over to him later that day. Another thumbs-up emoji as a response. It might be easy, she thought, to write books for his generation. A novel might be only 500 actual words, with the rest emojis.

Her nesting instincts kicked in. More like her protect the nest instincts. She showered quickly, then tested out the security cameras, the notifications, the window and door locks, the threads. All good.

She made sure that she could easily pull out the three screwdrivers masquerading as coat hangers. She checked the knives she'd hidden around the house, then put the stun gun under a couch cushion.

Upstairs, she unlocked the gun safe and draped a sweater over it to make it look like just another messy pile in the bedroom of someone who lived alone and had stopped keeping up appearances. It was unlikely that an invited guest would enter her bedroom. If for some reason she needed to get at the weapon quickly, she could.

Preparation like this helped her focus. Control what you can control.

She was upstairs washing her face when the doorbell rang. Her phone buzzed — the security camera notifications worked. She peered at the footage. Perez, alone, holding two takeout coffee cups.

Downstairs, she let the detective in. "Morning," she said, then indicated the coffees. "Hope one of those is for me."

Perez chuckled as she handed one to Jane. "Ms. Hawkins. I'm off today, but I thought I'd swing by, see how you're doing." Perez was dressed like she was on duty, except she'd shed the jacket. Her hair hung loose, and she wasn't wearing her badge or her gun.

"Let's sit at the table," Jane said, keeping the detective in the kitchen.

When they'd settled, Perez said, "First, your car being stolen. I looked over the security footage at the beach. Didn't see anyone steal your car. Mostly because I didn't see your car there. Can you tell me again where you parked?"

Security cameras at the beach? They really were everywhere. "I parked at the back. There are some trails back there that loop around to the beach."

"And there were no unaccounted-for cars in the lot. So whoever stole your car had to have walked there, or gotten dropped off. Maybe took a bike, although we didn't find any bikes."

"Maybe he was sick of walking around all the time, so that's why he took the car."

"Only to drive it a mile down the road and flatten all four tires, then walk away."

"Thief's remorse? It's not a great car."

"Look," Perez started.

Jane cut her off. "Detective, I don't know what else to tell you. Maybe the person got startled. Maybe they're destructive. Maybe they hate old Accords."

Perez leaned back. "Something doesn't add up, Jane."

Jane didn't reply. For someone just "swinging by to see how she was doing," Perez's tone … it wasn't accusatory, but she sure sounded official.

Jane shook her head. "I agree, Detective. Someone must have followed me there. Maybe the same person who sent me those videos."

Perez looked confused. "But we know who sent those. It was Harley Hawley, and he's dead."

"Oh, right," Jane said. "This is all too much. I've never had a week like this one. So not him, obviously." She tapped her chin as if deep in thought.

"What about that podcaster?" Perez asked.

"It could be him, but how would he have known I'd be there? Did you find anything else in the car that could be a clue?"

Perez shook her head. "The Scarborough police looked it over pretty thoroughly. The smashed window, the tires, the ignition, that was the obvious damage. They did search the car and didn't find anything."

"That is such a relief," Jane said. "It's just a car. It could have been much worse."

"It certainly could have been. Then the break-in. Someone forced their way into your house, dumped out your underwear, made a mess, but didn't take anything."

She said it like a statement, not a question, just like after the carjacking. "Yes."

"It doesn't make sense. They didn't hurt your dog, didn't steal anything, just came in, got frisky with your things, and left."

"I don't understand people," Jane said. "But you'll be glad to know that I did finish setting up those security cameras. See?" Jane showed her the footage of Perez arriving earlier. She pocketed the phone after the video ended. The footage of Roux giving the cameras the bird was still on there.

"Jane," Perez said, "you seem remarkably calm after all this. And I get the feeling that you aren't telling me everything." She leaned back, like she was expecting an answer.

Jane shrugged. "I've been through a lot over the years, Detective. I want to get back to my quiet life of writing while I still can. I'm not a frantic woman. I appreciate your checking in on me, however. And for pointing me to Trigger City. I feel safer now. Hopefully all the drama is in the past."

They finished their coffees in silence, then Perez left, adding that she'd check in on Jane again over the weekend and promising to let her know if they got any leads on the car theft. She didn't sound optimistic. Jane felt a little guilty that Perez and the police would be putting time and energy into solving cases that Jane already knew the answer to. But guilt is nothing but a tap on the shoulder, a reminder to apologize for something, and Jane had nothing she wished to apologize for.

At about ten, she got a text: *Visitor pass at the front desk. See you soon!*

What? She checked her calendar. Crap. She'd forgotten. A few weeks ago, an elementary school teacher had volunteered at the senior center along with Jane, and she'd asked if Jane would talk to the fourth graders at their assembly about life as an author for twenty minutes. She was due at the school in forty minutes.

"Dexter, you're going with me." She didn't know if dogs were allowed in the school, but who could turn away a sweet old boy like Dexter? Besides, he was now part of her writing process.

She busied herself getting ready, then got out her purse. Hmm. Nothing would happen in the school, but what if Roux really was driving down here and cornered her? She dropped in the stun gun. She'd leave it in the car — schools were no place for weapons — just in case.

At the school, she got buzzed in five minutes early, then the secretaries oohed and aahed over the dog. The fourth graders were assembled in the gym, sitting on the floor. Once there, Dexter hammed it up, wagging furiously as the kids all came over to pat him. When everyone was back in place, she began.

"Writing is the best job in the world," she told the kids. "I get to create fun characters, then let them loose and see what happens. It's really fun."

After she described her writing process and what it was like to write books, they asked questions as good or better than the folks at the book launch had. And they were direct. What's the longest word you know? How tall is Beachcomber Belle? Have you met J.K. Rowling? Does Beachcomber Belle have a PlayStation? Do you have a PlayStation? How old is Dexter? What does Dexter eat? Do you have any kids?

She faked a smile as she answered that one. "I have a daughter."

At the end, the kids all clapped, then crowded around Dexter for a group picture. Good idea to bring him — any event is better with dogs. She signed books for the teachers, then signed out and left the school. At her car, she checked her phone after getting Dexter inside. Two notifications from the security camera app: one, the camera outside of her house had caught movement, and two, there was no video of the movement because the app had lost contact with the cameras soon after due to the wifi being out at her house.

She took a deep breath, held it, let it out slowly, then dropped the stun gun into her purse.

Think. Think, think, think.

No wifi at the house. She texted Ellen: *Is your wifi up?*

Ellen texted back: *Yes!*

So internet service wasn't out on the street. She pulled up the website for the power company and checked the outage map. Zooming in, she couldn't see any issues in her neighborhood.

Power on, just her internet out.

Her insides felt jellied. Butterflies. Although her butter-flies were both excited and vicious, and they all carried tiny stun guns and syringes. Butterflies prepping for a battle.

If Roux had cut her internet … why? Maybe to disable the security cameras. He obviously knew about them, as he'd given them the finger. Maybe to mess with her head. If he was there, he'd know she wasn't home. Question was, if it was him, where was he now?

She checked her purse again. She had the stun gun. She had a multi-tool. But that thing took too long to open and select the right weapon.

Dexter did that dog thing that's part sigh, part groan. *This is boring. Get going.*

"I need to think," she told the dog as she remained idling in the school parking lot.

She should have stored some weapons in the rental car. In the house, no problem — there were weapons all over the place. Outside the house … not so much. Rocks, maybe. She could use the car to run Roux over, although that was pretty public and he most likely wouldn't be standing in her driveway, unable or unwilling to move.

Funny. Nearly everyone else, if they thought there was a killer in their house, would call the police and stay away from the house. Not her. If Roux was there? No police, no staying away.

She made a plan, a sparse one with too many variables, but one that had to be made quickly because a sparse plan was better than no plan.

Maybe torching his studio had been overkill, figuratively speaking. She could have controlled her rage better. Maybe. But the past had shown her that when she gave into the rage, let it control her, she came out on top, because her rage also guided her. Plus, she admitted, it had been fun dressing up as Plant Lady and conning her way into the building. Sometimes, it was so easy to play people. Act honest, they think you're honest. Act like you belong, they usher you in with few questions.

That's how it had worked with most of the previous ten, hadn't it? Either she'd snuck up on them, or she'd acted friendly, until she'd acted like a killer.

This, however, this was different. Roux was there. She knew it. And he knew she knew, she supposed. More importantly, if Roux was there, he'd violated her home, her privacy. Thank goodness Dexter was with her. Roux may not have touched the dog before, if he even realized the dog was in the house, but if this was their final meeting — and she was feeling, in her gut, in her head, that it had to be — he'd take no prisoners, human or dog.

She still had so many unanswered questions. Was Roux really behind the murders? Was he a killer? How had he connected her previous kills? Why? And who was texting her photos, and why?

That was the biggest question: the why. In her Beach-comber Belle books, the "why" always came out. Found documents, admissions from the guilty, bedside confessions, everything wrapped up neat, everything explained and never mentioned in subsequent books. Real life was messy, and sometimes questions were never answered. Sometimes survival was the only answer.

She called Kate, but her daughter didn't pick up. Not that she had a reason to pick up. She had many reasons to not pick up. When Jane was sure that the call would go to voicemail, she went to end the call, then reconsidered and left a voicemail: *It's Jane. I just wanted ... to say hi. I got a dog. I hope you are well.*

She ended the call. She had thousands of words to say to Kate, but she also had none. Being a parent, even with a non-existent relationship, was terribly complicated.

She pulled out the multi-tool, opened the sharpest of the blades, then dug into her purse, cutting a three-inch line into the end. She then cut four more lines, two from each end of the original cut, one angled up, one angled down. She put the tool away and shoved the end of the stun gun through. The opening was wide enough.

She drummed her fingers on the steering wheel, sighing. What would it have been like to be ... normal? To wake up each day and worry about normal-people problems? To have ways of solving problems that didn't involve secrecy and funerals? To have a daughter and raise a daughter and love a daughter and be your daughter's best friend until she inevitably ran from you, then ran back to you?

What would it be like to talk to fourth graders about being a writer and not know that the next thing you had to do was fight for your life?

SHE WENT over the plan as she drove, but really, it wasn't a plan, it was more of a decision as to what to do first. And not even first, because if Roux was there, she'd get one move, just one, before chaos took over and any plans went out the window.

Honking from behind her. She saw that she was driving 15 in a 40 zone. Maybe that's what happened with all those seniors she'd driven behind, the ones who appeared to live in slow motion. Maybe they were thinking about their pasts and futures. She couldn't blame them.

She pulled into her driveway and parked at the end, not wanting to get close to the house. She hadn't seen Roux's car, although there were a few parked along the road. If he'd changed cars or rented something, she'd never know which was his.

She shut off the car, then stayed seated, slowing her breathing. She felt oddly calm, although her sweating hands betrayed her. Dexter had his nose up against the closed window and was sniffing deeply. He wanted out.

What she felt more than calm right now was lonely. Everyone in town knew her, but no one really knew her. She had a daughter, but their relationship was limited to a name on a birth certificate. Her closest friend was a dog she'd adopted four days ago.

Might as well sink lower. Look at the people she'd helped this week or so, with "helped" being in quotes. She met a nice guy at AA, Scott the reclamation project, and basically urged him to not try every day, which had cast him back to drinking because he'd followed her advice. Her next-door neighbor Ryan, she'd plied him with cash to do her bidding and alcohol to get him to talk. She'd gotten Perez to start smoking again. Bettina at the senior center, all she'd wanted was someone to listen to her. What did she get instead? A dead husband, with someone else's husband the prime suspect.

She'd lied to everyone this week, yes, but she'd also done more, and now she was paying the price. A possible murderer was possibly camped out in her house, an unknown cyber stalker was texting her pictures of her in disguise as she'd murdered Flounder, she'd killed Yip Yothers for no other reason than she wanted to, and she'd killed a man in self-defense ten days ago — saving your own life was an exception, but still, she'd stabbed the guy when he was pretty much dead because it had felt so, so good.

Nice legacy. If she were her daughter, she'd have run away, too, and stayed far, far away.

Maybe it was time for a change. But change wouldn't come if she didn't get through the next few minutes.

She closed her eyes. She believed in God, always had. Her church days were long behind her, what with the murdering and all, but she believed that there was a higher power, just one who didn't take weekly attendance. Why that higher power had set her in motion, that was a mystery, one she'd need to think about more in the future.

Speaking of future, it was time to meet hers.

She opened the car door, grabbing Dexter's leash as soon as she'd reached in, and that was a good thing, because the dog leaped out of the car, barking his head off as he strained to get to the house.

Roux was here.

Jane tugged to keep Dexter from getting free. For a dog with too many rough years behind him, he was surprisingly strong.

As she strained, she caught a glimpse of the black cable company wire that ran to her house from the street, then down the side of the house to the junction box. The cable was cut, with no attempt to hide it.

She lugged Dexter closer. The commotion brought attention, not from inside her house, where she saw no curtains move, and not from Leaf Guy, but from the Blighs. Ryan darted out of his house and jogged over.

"Everything okay?" he asked. Dexter was still yapping. "I heard the barking."

"Don't touch him," Jane replied. "He saw or smelled something. I don't know."

Ryan being here gave her an idea. Plan refined. "Say, Ryan," she said calmly, "would you take him for a walk? I'm tired, and he's obviously not. He needs to be."

"I guess I could." He didn't look particularly eager.

"How about this: walk him into town, take a while, I'll give you cash for the walk, and you can buy yourself lunch."

He looked a bit more eager. He took the leash, and Jane withdrew three twenties from her purse. "I really appreciate it, Ryan. In fact, I'll walk with you the first few minutes to make sure he's calm."

She left her car door open, hoping it would signal to Roux, if he looked out, that she wasn't really going anywhere. She directed Ryan and Dexter down the street, not where she'd already driven, to see if she could spot Roux's car. And she did. His Acura was parked around the corner, half on the street, half on a small strip of grass along someone's tall hedges.

Once she'd passed the car, she bent down and hugged Dexter, who was still chuffing about what he'd smelled, then to her surprise, she hugged Ryan, who flinched.

"Sorry. Just, you know, thank you. For everything."

"It's no problem, Ms. Hawkins," he said slowly, given her a furrowed brow.

And then they were off.

Jane gave them a cheerful wave, although they didn't turn around to see it, then she headed back to her house. Once they'd turned the corner, she put her hands on her knees and gagged, spitting, too many nerves for her slow breathing exercises to take hold.

Gotta keep moving, she told herself as she walked. Gotta keep moving.

At her car, she took out her purse, trying to look carefree.

Her right hand was her dominant hand, so, as she walked to her door, she put her keys in her left hand. She put the purse over her right shoulder and stuck her hand in, finding the on switch for the stun gun.

When she'd open the door, it would swing inside to the left. Unlock it, bang it open, thrust forward with the stun gun. She figured he had two options — hide, or blitz, and hide would give her more of a chance to disrupt his plans. She'd blitz, if she were him. She'd stand to the right of the door as she was looking at it from the outside. There was about four feet of inside wall between the door and the window. She'd crouch, although he was bigger and he might stand and use his strength to pull her in.

The biggest question — actually, the only question — was if he suspected that she'd blitz as well. To her, that was a toss-up. He'd see her walking to the house, he'd hear the keys hit the lock. But would he think she saw it coming, or not?

Two seconds away from the door. Her mouth went dry. Hopefully, her palms weren't too sweaty to pull this off.

She wasn't used to using the keys with her left hand, so she had to stand a little more to the right so that her left hand was directly in front of the lock.

She put the key in, then turned the lock, and felt and heard the click.

Here goes.

She kneed the door open, then crouched and launched herself inside the house, slamming the door shut behind her before putting an arm over her head. Immediately, a dark shape lunged at her from her right, and she jammed the gun through the opening of the purse and against Roux's thigh and pulled the trigger just as Roux shoved a stun gun against the arm over her head and—

Bees, wasps, a hive full of angry insects and ice, ice cold as the prongs of his stun gun bit into her, and she was flung to the floor. Her mind darkened, and her legs felt like they were a mile away. Roux crashed on top of her legs, gurgling, or maybe that was her. She gave instructions to her arm — move! pull! — but the arm refused, and her heart tugged, and she thought about her last physical, when the doctor had said give up your "occasional" smoking, he'd actually used air quotes, which she laughed at because they'd known each other for so long, and exercise more. She was getting exercise now. Or wanted to, but her stupid arm wasn't obeying.

Things started to clear, and she dragged herself away from Roux, who was moaning behind her. She rolled onto her back to get a better view, surprised that she actually accomplished something, although both her arms were more dangling than partners. No need to look for her stun gun — she was still clenching it like it had become a part of her.

She kicked at Roux, but a toddler could have fended off those blows. He rolled onto his back, clutching his leg.

"Get the fuck out of here!" she yelled, although it sounded nothing like that. She knew what she meant. Hopefully he did, too.

If he did, he ignored it. He swung an arm over and down, the hand with the stun gun, and fired a second time, only he shocked the floor, and Jane had a silly, very brief thought that she'd have to replace the floor again after twenty years.

She crab-walked backward, shuffling away from Roux, who was shakily getting to his feet. Her legs were moving better, but her body still felt off, because it *was* off. It had been stunned, idiot.

Roux lunged at her, and she kicked out at him weakly, but high enough to catch him between the legs, and he moaned again and stumbled. Jane got to her feet, shakily, and stumbled to the door, pulling out one of the hidden hanger screwdrivers, then dropped it because the hand without the stun gun was useless, the bastard.

Roux flashed a knife. Where had he gotten that? "You leave me no choice," he growled. She'd hoped stunning someone would have a more lasting effect, and that she'd be somehow immune to the effects.

"Eat shit," she said, reaching up and behind her to grab another screwdriver as she braced against the wall.

He slashed, and as he did, she brought the screwdriver down onto his wrist. The blade nicked her across the pelvis and her hand went numb as Roux dove forward, his head smashing into her thigh.

Both of them screamed, and her stun gun clattered to the floor. Would neighbors come? No, the windows were all closed. Fuck the neighbors. The knife wound flamed in pain.

She kneed Roux's head out of the way and stumbled across the kitchen toward the living room and the stairs. She turned the corner to take the stairs and felt him punch at her foot, causing her to slide against the wall. She kicked backwards, her foot landing on some part of him, and scrabbled on the stairs. He yanked on her foot, causing her to slide down a step and smash her nose on the tread. The pain blinded her, but she couldn't wait for it to clear, so she climbed the stairs like Dexter, feeling Roux behind her. She was yelling, although she didn't know what she was yelling, and at this point, it didn't matter.

She was still carrying her purse over her shoulder. Why? Did she think he was going to rob her? A part of her deep inside laughed at that thought. She got to the top of the stairs, then launched the purse down at him. Sure, a woman's purse can be heavy, but hers sailed over his head and thunked to the landing below. But it was enough for him to duck for a second to avoid the projectile.

She dove for her bedroom, then slammed the door shut. There was no lock on that door. Who needed a lock on their door when they lived alone?

Alone. No time to think about being alone, about living a life of loneliness. Stop. Protect your life first. Wallow in self-pity later.

She lay down on the floor, pulling the sweater off the gun safe, and felt around for the Ruger as Roux shouldered the door open.

"Stop!" she yelled, the gun in a textbook grip, the shakiness not textbook at all. Roux froze.

"You're not going to—"

She pulled the trigger, and Roux flew backward and out into the hall, landing on his chest. She could see only his legs, and they weren't moving. She couldn't hear, and could barely see, as the room went cloudy and smelled like the Fourth of July.

"Roux!" she yelled, but it came out funny. A broken nose will do that to a person.

His legs moved, and she could see him turn to his side.

She'd winged him, or nicked him, or whatever Boss would call it.

She crawled toward the door. Roux went to brace himself with his right arm, but it flopped back, then he fell face-down to the floor.

Again, she thought about the neighbors. Surely, they'd come. But how many times had she heard something that could have been a gunshot but most likely wasn't, so she'd done nothing about it? Weekly? The world was full of loud sounds that everyone ignored.

A dark puddle spread from Roux's shoulder. He tried lifting himself off of his chest but failed.

Jane clambered over, then sat on his ass, pinning him. She pressed the short barrel of the Ruger to the back of his neck. "I'm not a killer, Roux," she said.

He burbled out a laugh. "Right, Jane. I know you are. I'm just surprised that you use a gun now. Nice upgrade."

She thought about him shooting arrows at her at Scusset, about the protagonist and antagonist having a heart-to-heart talk. She didn't want that talk, but she did want answers. Time to go all Beachcomber Belle.

"How did you know?" she asked. A weight lifted. This was her confessional, it seemed.

"The patterns," he said. "The data. The connections. I…" He groaned. "I was almost there. But I knew all along."

"But why copy my kills?"

"I didn't. I orchestrated it. But I've never taken a life. I did watch. I loved it. Probably as much as you did." He coughed as she wiped a surprising amount of blood off of her face. "How about this?" he continued. "Draw. Call this a draw. I leave you alone, you leave me alone. Just like you wanted."

She did want that. Wait — he orchestrated this? He

didn't actually kill anyone? She felt he was telling the truth. There was no reason for him to lie now. So: who?

"Who?" she asked him.

"Who who?" he groaned.

"Who, meaning you orchestrated the kills but didn't kill anyone. Someone did. So who was it?"

"No way. That's for me to reveal. But I promise: you leave me alone, I'll leave you alone."

Who? The same person who'd been texting her the photos? And how did Roux make those connections?

He tried to buck her off. She scooted lower on his legs, then drove her left elbow onto his ass. "Ah, shit, Jane, stop that," he said, but he stopped his bucking.

He wasn't going to tell her who the other person was. He wasn't going to tell her how he'd made those connections. And she knew that he wasn't going to leave her alone. It was too big of a story.

"I have something to confess to you," she said to him.

He stopped moving. "What?"

"I'm not a monster." Then she shot him in the neck.

The sound was catastrophically loud, and the report, even with the little mouse gun, drove her backward, off of the body and into her bedroom, where she lay, the gun flung from her hands, the blood pouring from her nose, the cut on her pelvis on fire, reminding her in a strange way of the one time she'd given birth.

That pain? Now that had been glorious.

WHAT SHE WANTED to do was go to sleep. The floor was very comfortable. Maybe she'd give up her bed. Although Dexter had already gotten used to the bed. You know what? He could have it.

Wait. Dexter. Ryan and Dexter would be back. Probably not for another thirty minutes. But soon.

She still had enough time.

She got to her feet, then braced against the doorframe. All in all, she wasn't in bad shape, although her hearing sucked and the room smelled and there was a dead Roux on the floor. Another rug to be replaced.

Did she really have enough time? No time to question. Just do it.

She put the gun on the rug next to the safe. She used the sweater to wipe the blood from her face. Hopefully her nose would stop bleeding for ten minutes.

She skirted around Roux's body and tottered downstairs in slow motion, then grabbed the bagged kill binder from her hiding place. Right, the stun gun. Where was it? Would Perez even care? She knew that when the police came, Perez would be leading the charge. Perez had pointed her to Trigger City. The detective probably had her own arsenal. Keep yourself safe, Perez had said. She decided to not worry about the stun gun. The police would find it, and Roux's.

She put on a pair of surgical gloves, then brought the binder upstairs. She flexed Roux's right hand, his dominant hand, she'd observed, and put his fingers all over the plastic sheets of the binder, then all over the cover. She put the binder back in the bag and placed it on the floor.

She put on the hoodie, the one she wore when she did yard work. That yardwork day, the day she'd turned sixty, before all this happened, felt like a year ago. She pulled the hood down low to obscure her face.

Keys. She felt around in Roux's pants until she found his key fob, then withdrew it.

She stuffed the binder into a paper bag, palmed the fob, then went outside and walked as naturally as she could muster to Roux's car. She looked straight ahead, as if out for a lovely stroll. If anyone saw her, well, she'd have to think of something, but it was a quiet Friday on her quiet street.

She unlocked Roux's car, then took the binder out of the bag, stuck the binder under the front seat, and locked the car. Then she hurried back to the house, went back upstairs, stuck the key fob in Roux's pocket, then stripped off the gloves and hid them in the hidey hole.

Almost done.

She was hurt, but not too hurt.

She needed to have fought for her life.

She went back downstairs and hunted around until she found Roux's knife on the floor. She made sure all the doors were unlocked, then went back upstairs to the bedroom.

Where? Not where she'd made that ballpoint pen dot so many years ago. She didn't want to die. Not after winning. But she did want to come close.

The human anatomy, she thought, is weird. Stab yourself here, you die. Stab yourself a millimeter away, you don't hit anything of value. Was there anything of value left inside of her?

She placed the tip of the knife along her side. More than a flesh wound, but she didn't want to nick an intestine. Or a kidney. Or were those in the back?

Enough time wasting. She lay on her back, put the tip of the knife a centimeter or so away from her side, and pushed, and the pain was like a volcano, but it was also freeing, and someone laughed, and then she heard a dog bark, and she dropped the knife, and yelled, "Up here!" but she could have been imagining the dog bark, and her hand felt hot and wet, and then she said, "Kate," and then her world narrowed to a pinprick.

Day 36 (Sunday)

LATE MAY on Cape Cod is glorious, weather-wise, and today was no exception. Jane soaked up the sun as she sat in a new baby blue Adirondack chair, one of a set of four gifted to her by the volunteers at the senior center.

Bettina had brought the chairs over last week, once she and other volunteers were assured that Jane was well enough to sit outside and use them. No sense having the chairs mock her through the window. Real New Englanders were practical like that. Don't give someone a gift if it wasn't practical.

Bettina had looked well. Jane had heard that Yip's funeral had been a somber affair but that Bettina had gotten pretty drunk at the post-service family gathering and had lashed out at Yip's blood relatives for pretending that the man had been a saint. Jane hadn't seen Bettina since she'd killed Yip. She'd meant to, but then the whole Roux thing, the hospital thing, had knocked all her plans awry.

The husband of Yip's whore, as Bettina had termed the woman, had an alibi. Jane had already known that but acted surprised. Detective Perez had stopped by to see Jane, first in the hospital and then at home, every Sunday since she'd killed Roux. On the surface, Perez's visits were to check on Jane. Friendly. But something was brewing beneath the detective's surface. Maybe it would surface today, since it was Sunday and Perez would be here soon.

Ryan was out with Dexter, a walk to town and back. Ray and Rae from Knead were keeping Jane constantly supplied with muffins, cupcakes, and coffee. Roux's unmasking as a serial killer had shocked Port Fletcher and the surrounding towns. Boss from Trigger City had stopped by to clean her Ruger and replenish her ammo, even though she'd fired only two shots. Even John of John's Barber Shop had offered to visit and cut Jane's hair for free. She'd politely declined, wanting to look good once she was able to leave the house.

People were usually quite willing to give their time and money and support even on normal days, but once they'd learned that a monstrous serial killer had been wreaking havoc on the Cape for decades, they came out in droves to help. Jane never asked for help, but they gave it anyway. Don't let the facts get in the way of a good story. Especially when those facts would result in Jane getting the needle.

She closed her eyes to soak up the sun, reflexively putting a hand to her side, which still ached. She'd driven the knife in deeper than she'd wanted, the wound not deep enough to kill her, the doctors had said, but it had been a good thing that Ryan and Dexter arrived when they did or else the town would need a new famous or almost famous person to point to when people asked what Port Fletcher was known for.

Her phone rang. Her agent, Margo. Again. Jane let it go to voicemail, this being a Sunday and all, plus she was in no mood to hear Margo's continuing ecstatic updates about how Jane's book sales were through the roof once word of a cozy mystery author slaying a serial killer got out. There was even talk, Margo said, of Jane selling her story to a production company, something that Jane was sure Margo was pushing for. The woman wanted out of Manhattan in the worst way and had dreams of living in Belize. Jane was her ticket out of the city. She'd told Margo to turn down the hype and let her get back to what she wanted to do, which was write, not see herself on TV or on the big screen.

She'd been so grateful for Dexter, who was of little help around the house except for looking cute despite his rough appearance. He'd clung to her since she'd gotten back home from the hospital.

Ellen Bligh from next door had gone on a few dates with Bill Ramsford. Good for her, and good for him, although would Jane want a Port Fletcher detective possibly living next door to her?

Maybe it wouldn't matter. She'd resolved to put killing behind her once and for all. Jane of the Past had only resurfaced to protect that past, and now that past was dead and buried, thanks to Roux.

She looked up when she heard a car door slam shut out front. Probably Perez. The woman refused to knock, not wanting to force Jane up just to open a door she was perfectly capable of opening herself. Sweet. Although there was still that brewing something below the surface.

"Back yard!" Jane yelled.

Perez walked around the side of the house, greeting Jane and taking a seat next to her.

She handed Jane a coffee, keeping the other for herself. "Ray and Rae say hi."

"Thank you," Jane said. "They've given me so much free caffeine that I won't sleep for a month."

"Tell me how you're feeling." Enough chitchat, apparently.

"Fine. Sore. The carpet guys finally came, so the upstairs is back to normal." The cleaning crew had done a good enough job getting the blood out of the carpet and fixing the bullet holes that had gone through Roux's shoulder and neck. She hadn't minded seeing the now very clean shadow on the rug of where Roux and his blood had been. It was a good reminder. Survive or die.

"They tell me that you'll be ready to drive soon," Perez said. Jane wondered who "they" were, like always, but she'd come to realize that Perez had her fingers in a lot of pies. Maybe too many pies.

"Yup." Her car was back to normal as well. Perez had been really helpful, actually, flashing her badge when folks needed to move faster.

Her nose had healed, the black eyes gone. Besides the pain and the scar, it was like it never had happened.

"Figure since I'm here, I'll give you the weekly update," Perez said, looking at the yard instead of Jane. She'd been doing that a lot. Not making eye contact. Maybe it was nothing.

"Still trying to contact a few folks, but most of the items in Roux's binder have been tied to specific victims of those earlier murders. Still think it's weird that he carried it around in his car."

"The man was a mystery," Jane replied. "I've been thinking about him a lot. He would have been, what, barely twenty when he killed all those people, including Donald? What a wasted life."

"Mmm." After thirty seconds, Perez added, "Forgot if I told you this already. We found out his real name. Esmir Roux was born Jeffrey Parker. He changed it years ago."

Jane willed herself to say nothing, having known that

fact for weeks. But Perez was looking at her like she expected a response, so she gave her one. "Esmir Roux sounds more exotic than Jeffrey Parker. Maybe he had a mid-life crisis."

"Mmm."

Again with the verbalized thinking sounds. Perez was being oddly spare with her words, even for Perez. Shut up more, talk less. Guess that credo applied to both of them.

Perez fished out a pack of cigarettes. "You mind if I smoke?"

"Not at all."

"You want one?"

"Trying to quit." She wasn't.

Perez lit up. "This is all thanks to you," she said. "You're quite the bad influence."

"Ha." It wasn't funny. It was true.

Perez smoked in silence for a bit, then said eventually, "Glad your car is back. I talked to the rental agency, just to make sure those rentals of yours got paid for. Looks like you put on quite a few miles while you had them."

"You know how it is. Errands around town really pile up."

"Mmm."

Okay, a third "mmm." This was getting annoying, and slightly passive aggressive. Was Perez trying to bait her? Jane took another slug of her coffee. If Perez had something to say, she'd eventually say it.

"What I don't understand," Perez said, "is why he killed those ten people in the first place. The State Police are still digging, we've talked to his family, friends, anyone who knew him. Weird thing is, he was in college at the start of those killings. Lafayette. Long way to drive, kill, drive back, for no apparent reason."

"People are a mystery," Jane said. "Bad wiring, maybe."

"Bad wiring." Perez said it like she was chewing on it. "Wish I had answers for you. About why your husband, of course, and the others."

Jane waved the comment away. "Nothing's going to bring him back. And as I've told you, Donald treated me horribly for many years. Maybe he did the same to Roux as well."

Perez said, "Still digging into what Roux's fixation was with you. He didn't have to come after you. What do *you* think?"

Perez wanted her opinion? There was the real reason, and the public reason. "Maybe I said something to him at the book launch that set him off. He really wanted me as a guest on his podcast. I didn't want that. He was certainly quick to anger."

"Mmm." Jane had never heard Perez say "mmm" before today, and now she'd said it four times. "Shame about his studio going up in flames. So many potential answers, and now we'll never know."

Perez, Jane realized, was never going to let this go. She'd stamp all the folders "Closed" or whatever detectives did, but she'd never really close this case. Or the carjacker. Or the murders of Harley "Flounder" Hawley and Yip Yothers. Perez would not forget.

Jane had decided to shut up but was saved when Ryan and Dexter came bounding around the house.

"Dexter!" Perez said, crushing out her cigarette as the dog wagged its ass off.

"Got your muffins," Ryan said, handing Jane a bag from Knead. "They wouldn't let me pay, since it was for you."

"I'm going to put Ray and Rae out of business if they keep treating me," Jane said.

Ryan had changed. He'd told his mom that he was transferring to a new school, just didn't know which one yet. He needed to get off the Cape and find his place. He'd also, he'd said, blushing, asked out Cease, who said she'd think about it.

"Which is totally cool," he'd told Jane last week. "She's really private. She wants no drama."

"You think she's worth it?" Jane had asked.

More blushing. "Umm, I guess so. Yeah." That was high praise, coming from a twenty-year-old boy.

The three of them talked about non-Roux stuff — would it be a good tourist season, would the town raise taxes for that proposed new school, how about this weather. Normal stuff. Jane thought they didn't want to upset her, that she wanted to put everything behind her and focus on how great everything had turned out.

It had turned out good, if not great. She could relax again, she hoped. She'd finished the Beachcomber Belle book with that Chechen candy store owner — spoiler: he really had been a Chechen war lord, and Belle exposed him — and had started a new book, this one about Belle digging into a cyberspace crime where an unknown someone was texting risqué videos to townspeople. Art imitates life.

Margo had sent Jane some links to some conferences where she was sure Jane would be accepted as a keynote speaker. Jane wasn't sure about that. She liked routine, didn't like flying, and didn't like crowds. What she really wanted was for everything to go back to the way it had been right before her book launch at Seaside Books. Back when the past was in the past and the future held nothing except living and writing. She'd still been lying about who she really was, of course, but that, she knew, would go on forever.

Another car door slammed, and it sounded to Jane like it was in her driveway. The only two people she opened up to even a little — a college kid and a doubting detective — were already here. Maybe Leaf Guy had visitors.

The doorbell rang.

"I'll get it," Ryan said. He went into the house, and Jane could hear some low chatter. Dexter's ears perked up, as much as a basset hound's ears can perk.

The door opened, and Ryan re-appeared, followed by … Kate.

"Do you know her?" Perez asked protectively, her hand going to her side reflexively, even though she was off-duty and without a weapon.

Jane's insides jelled as she stood, and she felt icy and also like she was going to vomit. "I do."

She hadn't seen Kate in so long, had barely talked to her, had left messages for her without response. Kate looked amazing in that way that your kid always looks amazing. She was what now, almost 31? Shoulder-length brown hair, high cheekbones, dark brown eyes, tall and trim like Jane. Jeans and sandals and a Boston Bruins long-sleeved shirt, the sleeves rolled up.

And she was visibly pregnant.

Kate stopped behind Ryan, who walked, oblivious, back to his chair before realizing he wasn't being followed.

"Mom," Kate said softly. She'd called Jane that only a few times before. Usually it was "Jane" or "you." Or, more than a few times, "fuck you."

Jane ran to her, Kate ran to Jane, and they met halfway and hugged, and Jane didn't want to let go, because Kate felt like love, smelled like love, and her heart nearly burst because the first, last, and only time Jane had felt like this was when she'd first held Kate before she gave her up.

"Kate," Jane said, finding it hard to talk with the lump in her throat. "I wasn't … I didn't think…"

Kate released her, took a step back, and put her hands on Jane's shoulders. "I was in the area, wanted to see how you were doing. I heard about what happened. Saw it online." Jane didn't take that as a dig. She would have told Kate everything if she'd picked up the phone or returned a text, but she wasn't mad about it. Kate had no reason to care about what happened to her.

"Well, I'm glad that you came. Come. Sit. I have muffins." She instantly regretted saying something stupid like that, but Kate smiled.

"Oh, let me introduce you." Jane walked Kate over. "Sophia Perez, this is my daughter Kate. Kate, this is Detective Sophia Perez. She's also my friend." Perez started, but Jane had meant it when she called the detective a friend. Also: keep your friends close.

"And this is Ryan Bligh. He lives next door. Another friend. He's helped me out so much. Ryan, this is Kate."

Ryan grinned and stuck out a hand to shake. Kate accepted, then patted his arm.

"Thank you both so much for helping my … for helping Jane out."

Perez raised an eyebrow, maybe thinking, if you have a daughter, why wasn't she here helping out herself? "Of course," Perez said. "We were just leaving. Ryan, I'll walk you home."

"Why?" Ryan asked before he caught himself. "Oh, sure, right, yes, I'll see you later, Ms. Hawkins." He and Perez left for Ryan's house.

"And this is Dexter," Jane said. The dog had rolled onto his back, his tongue hanging out.

"He's really … he's adorable, Jane. Look at that ear. Bet he has some stories to tell."

Don't we all. "He's a new addition. Come inside."

Jane grabbed her coffee and led them inside. Kate used the bathroom while Jane put on a kettle and leaned against the kitchen counter.

Funny, she thought, how family changes everything. If she'd passed stranger Kate on the street, she wouldn't give her a second look or thought. But knowing that Kate was part of her, down to the cell level? One minute you care about only yourself, and the next, you'd kill for that person.

They took their seats at the table, facing one another.

"I don't know where to start," Kate started. Jane wanted to reach out, take her hand, to feel her, but they didn't have that type of relationship, and she had no desire to fake her way through that. Lying and pretending, those came easy to her. True connections … new territory.

"Start wherever you like." The kettle whistled. "Tea okay?"

"Oh. Sure."

Jane bustled, then put a mug down in front of Kate and sat down again.

"So, this is weird," Kate said, laughing, although the laugh sounded sad.

"It is not how I expected today to go. But I'm glad you're here." Kate had been to Jane's house only a few times.

"After I read about what happened to you … I don't know where to start," Kate repeated. "I mean, I want to hear everything. I want to know how you are. But that isn't why I came."

"We can get to all that. It's a long story. I'm okay, though. The past is the past." That last sentence had about a hundred different meanings, and one of them was that the past never, ever was in the past. The past slapped you in the face every day, kicked you in the stomach, and tapped you on the shoulder so you wouldn't forget about it. The past was her constant companion.

Dexter thumped his tail as he sprawled under the table at Kate's feet.

"Oh, Jane. Mom." Kate put her hands to her face, took a deep breath, released it, then put her hands on the table, palms down. "I'm married, you know."

"I know." She did.

"And obviously," Kate said, reaching down to pat her stomach, "this."

"I saw. I'm thrilled for you." She was. "How far along?"

"Seven months. It's good, I mean it's great, and I want this, I really do." She paused, and Jane waited until she started up again.

"So there's this" — she patted her stomach again — "and there's this."

She tugged on her left sleeve, freeing her arm and shoulder. Bruises. Lots of them. The size of a man's fingers.

Kate teared up. "Sebastian, he's a … he was a … a good man. But…"

The blue curtain of rage hit Jane like a cyclone. Images, pictures, came at her hard, fast, in a blur. Donald hitting her. Cigarette burns. Syringes. Knives. The Ruger. She smelled bleach.

Jane gulped to keep down the bile. "Oh, Kate."

"I just don't know … I have no place to go. I have no right to be here, to ask you for anything."

Jane made to protest. *Of course you have a right. I brought you into this world. And I was shitty about. I let a man who isn't*

*your real father talk me out of keeping you because I was weak. You
deserved the world, and I gave you nothing.*

Kate cut her off. "No. I don't have a right. You've tried
to keep in touch. I have not. But like you said, the past is
the past. I need help."

Pride. That's what Jane was feeling. Pride. She hadn't
felt proud in years. Decades. Ever?

Her daughter, if only by blood, was doing what Jane
had never done. Ask for help. And she would get it.

"Whatever you need."

Kate sniffled. "I packed my car with all the shit I
thought I needed."

Dexter wagged.

"Of course," Jane said. "Of course."

Kate reached across the table and took Jane's hand.
Kate's hand trembled. Jane's did, too. But it also felt right.

Jane's phone, on the table next to them, vibrated.

Kate broke the handholding and laughed, releasing
some tension. "Go ahead and check that."

"It can wait."

Kate rolled her eyes like a teen. "Seriously. Check it. It's
fine. I'll drink my tea. And I have to pee every ten seconds
now anyway." She got up and headed to the bathroom.

It would be good to have some eye rolling in this house.
It'd feel like a normal house.

"Fine," Jane muttered, but she was also smiling.

She picked up the phone. A text, from an unknown
number.

A photo of Jane, the night of Flounder's murder.

This photo was different, because in this photo, it was
unmistakably Jane.

Along with the photo, the sender had added two words.
Oh, Jane...

"Oh, shit."

About the Author

Dave Pasquantonio Weird, sarcastic, and thrilling — the first two words describe Dave, and all three describe his fiction.

Dave is a freelance editor who's helped over a hundred authors get their work out into the world. As a freelance writer, he's written hundreds of newspaper features, columns, and articles. He also works behind the scenes at Sterling & Stone to help get our stories ready for publication.

When he has time to write, he loves twisty mysteries, serial killers, quirky speculative tales, and forcing his characters to triumph with wordplay instead of swordplay.

He lives just south of Boston, Massachusetts, where he grudgingly puts up with winter while listening to 80s music and dreaming up bizarre situations to drop his characters in. (Yes, you **can** end a sentence with a preposition!)